COLLISION COURSE

COLLISION COURSE

DAVID CRAWFORD

 NEW AMERICAN LIBRARY

NEW AMERICAN LIBRARY
Published by New American Library, a division of
Penguin Group (USA) Inc., 375 Hudson Street,
New York, New York 10014, USA
Penguin Group (Canada), 90 Eglinton Avenue East, Suite 700, Toronto,
Ontario M4P 2Y3, Canada (a division of Pearson Penguin Canada Inc.)
Penguin Books Ltd., 80 Strand, London WC2R 0RL, England
Penguin Ireland, 25 St. Stephen's Green, Dublin 2,
Ireland (a division of Penguin Books Ltd.)
Penguin Group (Australia), 250 Camberwell Road, Camberwell, Victoria 3124,
Australia (a division of Pearson Australia Group Pty. Ltd.)
Penguin Books India Pvt. Ltd., 11 Community Centre, Panchsheel Park,
New Delhi - 110 017, India
Penguin Group (NZ), 67 Apollo Drive, Rosedale, Auckland 0632,
New Zealand (a division of Pearson New Zealand Ltd.)
Penguin Books (South Africa) (Pty.) Ltd., 24 Sturdee Avenue,
Rosebank, Johannesburg 2196, South Africa

Penguin Books Ltd., Registered Offices:
80 Strand, London WC2R 0RL, England

First published by New American Library,
a division of Penguin Group (USA) Inc.

First Printing, November 2012
10 9 8 7 6 5 4 3 2 1

REGISTERED TRADEMARK—MARCA REGISTRADA

LIBRARY OF CONGRESS CATALOGING-IN-PUBLICATION DATA:

Set in Charter ITC Std
Designed by Alissa Amell

Printed in the United States of America

PUBLISHER'S NOTE
This is a work of fiction. Names, characters, places, and incidents either are the product
of the author's imagination or are used fictitiously, and any resemblance to actual
persons, living or dead, business establishments, events, or locales is entirely coinci-
dental.
    The publisher does not have any control over and does not assume any responsibility
for author or third-party Web sites or their content.

To my father, Jim, who taught me right from wrong,
my most valuable survival skill

ACKNOWLEDGMENTS

There is no way to thank everyone who helped, encouraged, motivated, and even chided me to write this book. Without all of the motivation, *Collision Course* would have never been finished. Thank you all so much.

I do need to mention a few people by name. My team, Norman Comparini and Elaine Scott Culbertson. Becky Cole for finding me and bringing me to the Penguin family. My awesome editor, Mark Chait, and his wonderful assistant, Talia Platz. Eric Melbardis for always having my back. And finally, my family, Rosemary, Danny, and Samantha, for putting up with me. Words cannot do justice to the debt I owe you all.

COLLISION COURSE

CHAPTER 1

DJ Frost was a likable guy. Most thought him a little on the eccentric side, but they couldn't help being pulled in by his happy-go-lucky personality and brilliant smile. DJ, they would say, could have sold ice to Eskimos. Many wondered why he wasn't in sales instead of security. But DJ liked working security. People respected him, and he enjoyed helping strangers, like Valerie. DJ had turned the corner just as three guys pulled her into a van. He'd chased them down and shot out their tires. Then he had single-handedly apprehended two of them. The police caught the other a few days later. DJ earned the Employee of the Year Award, and he and Val started to date. It didn't last long, but it had been good for a while, and they were still friends.

The uniform did seem to have an effect on women. DJ was no Robert Redford in the looks department, but he wasn't an ogre, either. He worked out regularly and groomed himself meticulously. That, coupled with the uniform and his disarming smile, gave him more than his share of attention from the babes.

The other thing he liked about his job was being able to carry a firearm. Weapons were DJ's passion, second only to women. He had a nice collection and shot them often. Sometimes he was able to combine his two favorite pastimes by taking a woman to the range with him. Most were hesitant at first, but once they fired a few rounds, they were usually hooked. That always put a big smile on his face.

DJ wasn't smiling now, though. In fact, he had a scowl on his face. Things were not good. He'd always told people this could happen. Most of them had laughed at him. Some to his face, but the majority had done it behind his back. They would politely listen as he talked about preparedness, but he knew they were rolling their eyes the minute they turned their backs. He wondered how those people were doing now. Hopefully at least some of them had taken what he had said to heart. Maybe some would make it through unscathed. If the phones were working, he would have called to check on the ones he knew best, but that wasn't possible now.

He sat in his town house apartment, listening to the radio and eating a bowl of SpaghettiOs he'd heated up on his backpacking stove. The news was getting worse. Many people were running out of food, and the governments, both local and national, were losing control. DJ had heard shots down the street just last night. It was probably time to get the hell out of Dodge, he thought, as he listened to the droning reports. He decided that he'd start loading up and head to his bug-out location. He would have left earlier, but once before it had looked as if things were going south and he'd bugged out prematurely. The economy had turned around before anything bad happened, and when he got back, he found that he'd lost his job. He really liked the job he had now and didn't want to lose it, so he had waited. By the time it had become obvious that this was the real deal, the arteries out of the city were clogged. Then martial law had been declared. It would be a risk to leave, but not as big a gamble as staying in the city once the authorities lost complete control over the situation.

There were many theories on what had caused "the Smash." It seemed as if there were new experts on the news every day, and each had his own pet hypothesis. That was before the electricity had gone out yesterday. Some of the authorities had said it was fuel prices; others blamed the shrinking value of the dollar. The bursting of the housing bubble had some proponents, and a few even thought the government had done it deliberately. Three or four had less popular theories, but all the so-called experts agreed that this was the worst thing to happen to America since the stock market crash of '29.

Most people were shocked that things could get so bad in such a short time. It had even surprised DJ to some extent. Of course, the buildup had spanned many years, but the end came astonishingly fast. It really didn't matter to DJ what the real cause was or how fast it had happened. He'd been preparing for this for years, and had tried to get others to do the same. He had succeeded in a few instances, but most people didn't want to be bothered by DJ's gospel. He figured the reason most didn't listen was that they'd have to admit something bad could happen, and most people just couldn't bring themselves to believe that.

When he finished his dinner, he put the dishes in the sink and turned the faucet on. Water came out, but the pressure was low. He knew it was only a matter of time before there would be no running water at all. He had plenty stored for when that happened, but he planned to be long gone by then. The loss of electricity had caused the crime rate to double overnight. At least that's what the radio had said. DJ suspected it was actually much worse, and he knew that the loss of water would push even the law-abiding over the edge.

He finished the dishes and put them away. It seemed foolish to do such mundane things when the world was falling apart, but DJ knew routines should be followed whenever possible. It helped one deal with the bizarre to do the ordinary.

He grabbed a flashlight and headed downstairs to his garage. His trusty old Toyota pickup sat in the bay closest to the stairs, but it wouldn't be the vehicle he'd use to leave the city. The news had covered the mass exodus when the unprepared hordes had tried to leave. The lucky few who departed early had hardly any problems, but the ones who left only a few hours later had damned themselves from the start. As more and more people saw the handwriting on the wall and tried to get out of the city, highways that weren't designed for so many cars became death traps. As the routes filled to numerous times their optimum capacity, travel slowed to a crawl. Cars ran out of gas. Emergency vehicles were unable to reach the scene of wrecks to clear them and help the injured. Fights broke out, first at gas stations along the routes and then on the actual roads themselves.

Finally the criminal element moved in on the helpless motorists like spiders on insects caught in their webs. Many people—at least the lucky ones—had been forced to walk back to their homes, leaving behind most of the possessions they'd packed. The unlucky were still on the highways, silent as their useless vehicles. The governor had had no choice but to call out the National Guard and restrict travel. Heavy military trucks had been fitted with snowplow blades and had cleared lanes on the impacted roads, but now Guardsmen sat in machine-gun-topped Humvees with orders to stop anyone who tried to use those roads without authorization.

DJ walked around the truck and used his flashlight to find the propane lantern on the shelves loaded with his survival equipment. He hung the lantern on a hook and pulled a lighter from his pocket. A second later, the garage was bathed in a yellow glow. He turned and looked at his ultimate escape vehicle. It was a Polaris Sportsman 800. The ATV was the biggest and baddest ever built. It had a top speed in excess of seventy miles per hour and a huge payload and towing capacity. Attached to the back was an off road trailer that would haul a thousand pounds of cargo. DJ had done some modifications to it so that, between the trailer and the racks on the quad, he could easily carry all the gear he needed for his trek.

The bike had less than five hundred miles on it. He and his girlfriend had bought two smaller quads a couple of years ago. When they broke up last year, DJ traded the older pair in for this new machine. He reached down and turned the key. The twin-cylinder motor fired almost immediately. However, instead of the roar that the stock exhaust system would have made, the quad made a *putt-putt* sound that was barely audible over the hissing of the lantern. DJ had installed a second muffler that quieted the four-wheeled beast to a level even a librarian wouldn't find offensive. Hunters most often used the aftermarket exhaust system so they wouldn't spook game animals. It cut the performance of the big bike a little, but the trade-off in power was well worth the stealth it afforded. That wasn't the only modification he'd made to the big bike, either. DJ smugly turned the machine off. He checked the oil and water levels. They were fine. Then he twisted off the fuel cap and topped off the tank. Next he examined the tires. They were all overinflated, but that was on purpose. The higher air pressure made the bike quieter and easier to handle on pavement. When he got off the pavement, he could easily let some of the air out.

The tires checked, he began packing the trailer. He'd practiced this over and over, developing a meticulous system for where everything went. It took less than ten minutes to load the trailer. He finished off by placing four five-gallon jerry cans on the custom mounts that ran down the sides of the trailer. These, combined with the four gallons in the tank, would give DJ over four hundred miles of range, more than enough to get to where he was going.

Next he grabbed a big plastic box that mounted to the rear rack of his Polaris. It took only a few seconds to lock it down, and then he began loading it, mostly with food and cooking gear. When it was almost half-full, he closed the lid. The front rack had a built-in waterproof storage space under it. He quickly filled it, and then a medium-sized duffel bag was bungeed down on the top. He opened the door to his truck and removed several items from inside. One was a small satchel of maps. He looped the strap over his neck to take upstairs with him. Next was a military-type day pack that had enough of everything he would need, except for guns and ammo, to live for three days. That went into the plastic box. Finally he removed his GPS from the mount in the Toyota and placed it in the one on his quad's handlebars. He re-checked everything and was almost done. All that was left was to get his firearms and clothes, but he would load those right before he left. He turned off the lantern and headed back upstairs. Halfway up, he stopped and slapped his forehead. With the aid of the flashlight, he found a roll of duct tape, pulled off two pieces, and placed them over the taillights on the four-wheeler. A little slipup like having a red light showing could ruin his day, he thought.

Back upstairs, he packed a small duffel with a week's worth of clothes and toiletries and laid out what he'd wear in the morning. Then he went to the spare bedroom, opened his large gun safe, and pulled out the weapons he would take. If he'd been able to use his truck, he would have brought all his guns. But since he just had the quad and trailer, he'd take only what he absolutely had to have: three rifles, a shotgun with an extra barrel, and four handguns. They were all cased except for one rifle and one handgun. He placed the handgun in a drop-leg holster that he'd wear. The rifle would go into a custom scabbard that gave DJ access to the rifle while he was moving. It had taken a lot of work to get the scabbard right, but DJ was very proud of it. It was not far from what the cowboys had used a hundred years ago, although his steed and his rifle were unlike anything someone from that era had ever seen.

DJ pulled an odd-shaped container and a .30-caliber ammo can from one of the shelves in the safe. The ammo can was heavy. It had a small wad of cash in it, not that cash was worth much these days. What made it heavy was the assortment of old silver coins and the few gold coins that it held. The coins would ensure him more than just a meager existence when he got to his destination. DJ closed the safe with the hope that he could one day come back here, if for nothing else than to get the rest of his gun collection.

Finally he opened a metal cabinet that sat next to the safe and pulled out loaded magazines for the two guns that weren't cased. Extra ammo was already loaded, some on the quad and quite a bit in the trailer. He put the magazines in a vest that had pockets set up just to carry them and a few other essentials. He carried all of the stuff to his room and placed it at the foot of his bed.

He looked at his watch. It was almost nine. He found his map satchel and pulled out an atlas of his state. He turned to the back where there was a map of the city. He already knew the route he would take, but he traced it with his finger anyway. Examining all of his backup routes, he searched for any other means to get out of the city he might previously have missed. After thirty minutes of scouring the map, he yawned. He stretched and looked around the apartment. On the desk in the corner of the living room sat his now useless computer.

Talk on his favorite Internet survival forums had increased ten- or twentyfold before the Web had gone down. Most of the traffic on those survival and preparedness Web sites was from newbies who were coming face-to-face with the new reality. DJ tried to help them as much as he could, but he knew most of them were screwed. He wondered how the regulars on the sites were doing. Many were more prepared than he was. They lived out in the country and already had gardens and livestock. Others were more or less in the same boat as he was. They had places to go, but would they be able to get there? He hoped so, even for the ones who normally disagreed with him.

He had continually preached that everyone who intended to bug out should have a plan other than automobiles and interstates. Some had listened and taken what he had said to heart.

Many had bought dirt bikes or quads like his. Some were not so far that they couldn't walk to their retreats in a few days. DJ even had a plan for going on foot if it came down to it, although he didn't relish the thought of a three-hundred-fifty-mile hike. He wished his retreat was closer, but when his group had formed, that was the closest they could find acreage that was in their price range. Other than distance, the place was perfect. The soil was fertile, there were plenty of hardwoods for firewood, and it was far enough from a big city that if a mass exodus took place, the hordes would be thinned out before they got that far.

DJ yawned again. Better get some sleep, he thought. He set the alarm on his wristwatch for three thirty a.m. He figured most of the troublemakers would be in bed by four. If he left then, it would give him at least a couple of hours to get well out of town before dawn. Invisibility would ensure his safety, so his plan was geared toward moving in the darkness and sleeping during the day. The most danger would come in the first twenty miles of his escape route. After that, it would fall off as he got farther and farther from town. DJ had played out this scenario over and over in his mind. Now that he was going to have to put his plan into action, he was filled with excitement and a little trepidation.

He took a shower. Even though the water was cold, he enjoyed it. It might be the last one he'd get for a while. He hit the sack and tried to sleep, but his mind kept racing over his escape plan. Would he make it out of the city without incident? What would happen to those who stayed in town? Would this all blow over in a few days as the government was promising? DJ was pretty sure he knew the answer to that one. He turned over and tried to make his mind slow down. Distant gunshots could be heard occasionally, which didn't help, but he finally drifted off into a fitful sleep.

Gabe twisted the top off the bottle and poured the amber liquid into a glass. He stared at the drink blankly for a second and then threw it back. It burned going down and boiled once it hit his stomach. He absently poured again, staring at this second glass for a moment. He hated the alcohol. He hated what it did to him. He hated what it had done to them. Basically, he hated everyone and everything.

CHAPTER 2

When the alarm beeped on DJ's watch, it jarred him into alertness. A few minutes later, he was up and dressed. Normally he would've made the bed, but he was in a hurry. Besides, he thought, what would be the point? He quickly fixed some breakfast and ate. He thought about leaving the dirty dishes, but he didn't want to have a vermin problem if he ever came back, so he hurriedly rinsed them off and put them in the dish strainer.

It took three trips to carry his guns and other gear down to the garage. He placed all of the carefully selected equipment next to his quad. With the aid of his flashlight, he went back up to the apartment and walked through one more time, checking to make sure everything was squared away. He opened his safe and looked lovingly at the firearms he was leaving behind. He would have liked to take them, but there was only so much room. If fortune smiled upon him, he could make a trip back for them. Hopefully, the massive gun safe would protect them until that time. DJ had done his homework, and this was the best safe that would fit through the door of his apartment. Not only did it have the best locking system, but it was also fireproof. DJ had bolted it down to the floor, even though it was against the apartment complex's rules. It would be almost impossible for someone to open it as long as it sat in the apartment, and it would take a tow truck to remove it from its position.

He closed the door and spun the dial. He finished his last inspection and, satisfied that everything was good to go, locked the kitchen door behind him. He packed most of the items he'd brought down that morning in their carefully prepicked positions and then checked his load once again to make sure he had everything and that it was properly secured. This was it, he thought. This was what he'd been planning for. He shivered slightly as he turned the key on his ATV. The machine fired immediately and purred perfectly. DJ really appreciated the electronic fuel injection on this bike. Not only did it increase the fuel economy, but it also didn't have to be choked and warmed up before it ran smoothly the way his old carbureted quads had.

There were five items left on the floor. DJ bent over and picked up the black rifle. He put a loaded magazine in it and chambered a round. After checking that the safety was on, he put it in the special homebuilt scabbard. Next he threaded the drop-leg holster that held his custom pistol onto his belt and cinched up the leg straps. Then he donned his bulletproof vest. He'd bought it used over the Internet. It was rated to stop up to a .30-caliber non-armor-piercing rifle bullet. DJ hoped he never had to find out if that was true. On top of the body armor, DJ put on a load-bearing vest containing several magazines for his rifle, a few for his pistol, and some other important survival equipment. If, God forbid, he was to lose the rest of his gear, he could scrape by for several days with just what was in the vest. The last item was the oddly shaped case he'd removed from the safe last night. He picked it up, opened it, and pulled out the night-vision goggles. Next to his four wheeler, they were the most expensive piece of equipment he had and, in many ways, the most important. He opened the storage box on the back of his quad and put them in the case. He removed the Kevlar helmet from the box and closed the lid. The NV goggles attached to the helmet. He turned off his flashlight, hit the power on the goggles, and put the light in its place on his vest. DJ was almost giddy at the excitement. He'd planned this exodus for years, but he had obviously not been able to actually rehearse it. He had, though, run through the parts he could and had thoroughly thought out the others.

He peeled back the heavy curtain over one of the windows and looked out. No one was to be seen. He lifted up the garage door and then slowly pulled his quad and trailer out onto the driveway. A few seconds later, the garage door was shut and locked and DJ was whizzing down the street.

It was still warm outside, but the wind from his thirty-mile-per-hour speed made it seem almost cool. Two blocks down the street, he saw three guys trying to break into a car in a driveway. DJ watched them closely. When he was half a block away, they heard his tires on the pavement. They began to look around to see what was coming, but he was past them before they could spot him. DJ smiled.

A mile down the road, he came to his first major street crossing. DJ brought the big quad to a stop where he could see both ways but still stay well back of the stop sign. He saw a police car coming down the road shining its spotlight at the front of the businesses that lined the street. He slipped the transmission into reverse and slowly backed up behind some cars parked on the street. It seemed to take forever for the police to pass, but when they finally did, they never even shined the light in his direction, and DJ's tensed gluteus muscles relaxed.

He pulled back up to the intersection. Through the night-vision goggles, he could see he wasn't the only one who hid from the cops. Two blocks up, a couple of people were working on a business's door with what looked like a crowbar. DJ gave his machine some gas and crossed the six lanes with no one the wiser. He was happy so far. Everything was going according to plan.

Five minutes later, the scenery changed. The middle-class neighborhoods he'd been driving through gave way to one of the poorer sections of town. DJ tightened his grip on the handlebars. More people were out and about in this area. Some were sitting in front of their houses with rifles or shotguns across their laps, and others were visiting on street corners. DJ wondered if they were just talking or if there was some kind of drug deal going down. A few were sneaking around houses that were dark and quiet. DJ hoped that there was no one in those houses.

Occasionally people would hear his tires and start looking for him, though dark as it was, they'd almost never spot him until he passed them. DJ increased his speed slightly. His tires would make a little more noise, but the faster he put distance between himself and them, the better.

As the area got worse and worse, a shiver went up DJ's spine. He looked hard for the eyes he could only feel. It was said that even the cops wouldn't come to this neighborhood without sufficient backup, and now DJ understood why. He'd driven through here in his truck during the daylight hours, and, other than the run-down houses and gang graffiti, it didn't seem too bad. But here in the pitch-black night without two tons of steel around him, it gave him the willies. He imagined he could hear screams coming from inside the dilapidated old buildings. Every bush or tree seemed to hold some unseen goblin. Every dark shadow was a demon wanting his soul. He found himself leaning on the throttle until his speed was almost fifty.

He knew he had only a couple of miles before he hit the railroad tracks. They would offer him a safer route out of the city, but first he had to get there. He tried to focus on the street, though he couldn't help noticing more and more people lurking about. When he'd planned his escape, it had seemed less risky to take the short route, even if it was through the shady part of town. Now he found himself questioning his logic.

Suddenly the streets appeared to be empty. DJ relaxed some, but he kept his speed up. Two more minutes, he thought, as he approached a slight curve in the street. The moment he could see around the bend, his heart jumped into his throat. There was a line of cars parked side by side blocking the street.

DJ yanked the brake lever as he cursed himself. He knew there was a possibility of running into a roadblock, and he had practiced turning around quickly, but not at the fifty miles per hour he'd been going. Hopefully they hadn't heard him, or better yet, maybe the automotive barricade was unmanned.

DJ's hopes were dashed when a set of headlights shined right on him. The night-vision goggles automatically shut down at the sudden blaze of light, and DJ pushed them onto his helmet. Two more cars turned their headlights on, and he squinted through the blinding beams. He felt the back brakes lock, and the heavy trailer pushed the bike to the right. Just then, he saw a muzzle flash and heard the report of a rifle over the top of the barricade. A fraction of a second later he heard the angry buzzing of a bullet passing him. He immediately slid off the seat to the left, holding on with just his hands and his right leg, which was hooked over the top of the bike. His left knee was on the floorboard on that side and his body hung below the top of the quad. This stance would help shield him from the gunfire and keep the bike from turning over.

DJ looked to his left and saw an empty driveway. He released the brake, and the bike began to change directions as the wheels started to roll. He turned the handlebars toward the driveway and pushed the throttle a little. The big bike dashed into the drive. He thought he could hear another bullet scream by as he continued turning around in the front yard of the old house. DJ mashed the throttle more and sped across three or four yards until one filled with junk forced him back onto the road. He pulled himself back up on the seat and looked over his shoulder as he rounded the bend in the street. He prayed they wouldn't follow him. He was quick, and off road, no full-sized vehicle would be able to keep up with him, but on the pavement he'd be no match for a car.

He flipped on his headlights and continued to accelerate away from the roadblock. Three blocks down, he turned right, went a block, and then turned right again. He slowed and turned off his headlight. A second later, he heard a car scream past. He placed his night-vision goggles back over his face and looked around. He couldn't see anyone. At the next corner, he turned left and resumed his practiced speed of thirty miles per hour. He noticed that his heart was pounding hard, and his whole body seemed to be shaking. He tried to force himself to calm down by taking some slow, deep breaths. It didn't work.

A minute later, he turned back to the right. This put him back on his original heading, even if he was eight or nine blocks to the south of his original course. DJ began to pay attention to where he was, and this seemed to have a small calming influence. He checked the GPS and saw that he only had a few more blocks until he turned onto Davidson Drive. This was part of his primary escape route. Davidson went through an older, industrialized section of town and crossed the railroad tracks that would take him out of town. He would be on it for an extra half mile now, but it should be fairly deserted. He made the right turn and was thankful that nothing appeared amiss.

Three minutes later, DJ turned onto the dirt road that ran along the tracks. This was railroad company property, but he didn't expect they'd mind, given the circumstances, even if they did see him. In fact, DJ was sure that there wouldn't be anyone along this route. He'd used the Internet and a site with satellite pictures of the earth to examine every foot of this course. It only passed through industrial areas and became more and more rural each mile he went.

DJ looked at his watch. It had been fifty minutes since he left his apartment. He'd made better time than he had allowed, even with his unexpected detour. DJ thought about the mistake he'd made by traveling faster than the speed at which he could easily control the bike. He vowed not to vary from his carefully crafted plan again. After about a mile, he stopped his bike and inspected it for damage. Thankfully, there was none, so he continued on.

The next hour passed quickly and quietly. DJ had to climb onto the tracks to cross a few creeks on the bridges, but he'd expected that. He was always careful to look for trains before he put the quad between the rails. Once, on a longer bridge, he even turned off the bike and put his ear to the rail to make sure no trains were coming. He suspected the trains weren't running, but he didn't want to find out differently at a precarious point.

DJ finally reached his first waypoint. It was an area along a creek where the trees grew thick and he could camp for the day with little danger of being seen or bothered. When the bike was in the middle of the small wooded area, he turned the four-wheeler off. He pitched his tent, ate a quick snack, and covered the quad and trailer with some surplus camouflage netting. He climbed into the tent just as the horizon was turning pink. With the adrenaline worn off and his rifle by his side, he fell almost immediately to sleep.

Gabe heard the car door slam. He was almost asleep in the chair, but not quite. He jumped at the noise, even in his drunken state. He struggled out of the chair and staggered to the window. That damn boy! What the hell did he want? Gabe stumbled to the door of the trailer and opened it, almost falling out onto the small landing.

"This ain't your day," he slurred. "What the hell do you want?"

"Mr. Horne, my mom and I came by to make sure you knew what was happening."

"Oh yeah? And what would that be?"

"Things are getting really bad, Mr. Horne. It's like the world is ending or something. The government has de—"

"Do I look like I give a shit?"

The boy's eyes got big at the interruption.

"Well, do I?" Gabe shouted.

The young teenager said nothing.

"Now, you get the fuck out of here and leave me alone. It's not your day." Gabe took a wobbly step back into his house, forgetting to close the door. He wasn't able to see the boy climb back over the gate and into the old pickup, but he heard the engine start as they drove away.

Why would I give a shit anymore if the world ended?

He poured himself another shot of whiskey.

CHAPTER 3

D J woke up and looked at his watch. It was just past noon, and the air in his tent was warming up. He pulled his boots on and stepped outside, his rifle in hand. Nothing looked as if it had been disturbed, but he carefully walked around the perimeter just to make sure all was as it should be in this small wooded area. Content that nothing was amiss, DJ looked out beyond the trees. Fields surrounded his camp, except for the creek, the tracks, and one lone farmhouse, which looked to be a mile or more away.

He would wait for dark to continue his trek. That gave him about eight hours to kill. He fixed himself a nice meal, taking his time. Once he'd eaten, he strung up a net hammock between two trees and pulled out a book. As he read, cottonlike clouds began to move in on the breeze. They covered the sun and dropped the temperature a few degrees. The breeze, cloud cover, and large meal were just the right formula for a nap. DJ didn't even notice the book slip from his hand.

A faint rhythmical thumping woke him up. He didn't know what it was, but he knew it wasn't right. He dumped himself out of the hammock and clutched his rifle. At first, he thought that a piece of farm equipment might have been causing the sound, but a quick look around revealed no machinery in any of the fields. When he listened closer, he realized it was coming from down the tracks. It didn't sound like a locomotive, at least not one of the big ones. Maybe it was a small engine used for track maintenance. DJ checked to make sure nothing in his campsite would give him away without a thorough search of the woods. The white pages of the book lying on the ground could be visible through the trees. He quickly picked it up and stuck it under the cover on his ATV. Satisfied that his hide was now as secure as it could be, given the situation, he peered down the tracks to get a better look.

DJ almost laughed when the old Cadillac rounded the bend. One side's tires were inside the tracks and the other's were on the outside, but still on the wooden ties. As the car neared, DJ could see that the whole thing was shaking. The suspension was unable to absorb the bumping the evenly spaced ties caused.

The Detroit dinosaur was only advancing at twenty or twenty-five miles per hour. As it crept toward DJ's woods, he moved behind a tree where he could conceal himself but still see. As the car finally passed, DJ could only make out a driver. The old man appeared to be in his seventies or early eighties. He looked straight ahead as he passed with a grip on the steering wheel that had turned his knuckles white.

When the fins on the old car disappeared around the next bend, DJ glanced at his watch. It was almost four p.m. He returned to his hammock and book and read for about an hour and a half. He fixed another meal and ate. Then he pulled out his maps again and scoured his route for the night. He'd have ten hours of darkness, and he planned to make a good distance tonight. His next hideout was about a hundred and fifty miles away. He'd stay on the tracks for about two-thirds of that distance. A section of gravel county roads was after that, and then he would head down a power line easement. He hadn't been down the easement before, but he'd gone down every road that intersected it and had marked it both on his map and in his GPS. Happy with the plan, he put the maps up and tried to get a little more sleep before he left.

He dozed, fitfully, his previous nap having taken the edge off his tiredness. Finally it started getting dark, so he broke camp and loaded everything up. It wasn't completely dark when he left, but it was close enough.

The first few miles went just as he planned, but the road beside the tracks became gradually rougher the farther he went. This wouldn't normally have been a problem. The quad and trailer were made for much rougher conditions than these, but his night-vision goggles severely hindered his depth perception. Many of the potholes and bumps he was hitting just looked like flat ground, and a few times, he almost got pitched off the big bike. He was still making good time, but it wasn't as fast as he'd planned. He could take off the night-vision goggles and use his headlight, but that would make him more vulnerable if someone was waiting along the tracks. He decided the best thing to do was to continue at a cautious pace.

DJ also found that he had to climb up onto the tracks more often than he'd anticipated, and not just for the creeks. He knew where all of those were. He was also forced to avoid many downed trees, which had fallen over the access road. DJ figured this section of the road must not have been used in quite some time. In many places, the grass had grown up quite tall, and he had to be especially careful of uneven ground in those spots. Between creeping through the grass and navigating around the trees every few miles, he finally decided that riding on the tracks like the old man in the Cadillac would be faster, but would it be safe?

No trains had traveled down this track in the eighteen hours he'd been next to it, but that didn't guarantee there wouldn't be one. DJ wondered if he should risk it. He'd be able to see a train coming toward him, and although he was worried about the possibility of a train sneaking up from behind, he figured he'd probably be able to hear it approaching. He decided it was worth the risk. He wished he had a rearview mirror on his bike, but he never thought he'd need one. Oh well, he couldn't think of everything.

DJ wondered how old the satellite pictures he'd used to plan his route were. He wouldn't have thought the railroad would let their access road get so overgrown, but they obviously had.

The trailer was equipped with taillights, but he'd left them unconnected. He decided to hook them up. They would hopefully be visible to a train if it approached and perhaps the engineer would blow his horn if he got too close. *Besides,* DJ thought, *I really don't have to be that concerned about anything but a train from behind me, so the taillights are okay.*

The tracks proved to be a lot better than the road had been, and DJ was able to pick up his speed. He had to deal with the unevenness of the ties and the gravel between them, but that was minor, and the bike easily soaked up the bumps as long as he kept a reasonable pace. He made sure to check behind him every minute or so.

At midnight he began to get hungry. He pulled the four-wheeler off the tracks and found a nice little open spot. Opening the storage box on the back of the Polaris, DJ removed and opened an MRE with the aid of his red LED headlamp. He activated the chemical heater with a little water and slid the main course into the heater pouch. While he waited for his chicken and noodles to warm up, he snacked on the crackers and cheese spread. MREs weren't DJ's favorite food, but they were easy and filling.

When he had finished the meal, he stuck the trash into a large Ziploc bag. He'd burn it when he got somewhere safe enough to build a fire. He started the quad up and put his night-vision goggles on. Back on the tracks, he continued making decent time, happy that things were working out almost as well as he'd expected.

A little while later, DJ was rounding a long, slow bend in the tracks. As he finally got to where the tracks straightened out and he could see for quite a ways, he hit the brakes on the quad. At the moderate speed he was going, the big bike stopped almost instantly. There was something on the tracks about half a mile in front of him. It was hard to judge distance with the goggles, so he removed them, but all he could see with his naked eyes was blackness. He put the goggles back on and slowly pulled the bike down into the tall grass beside the tracks. He was careful to keep the engine rpm as low as possible in order to remain discreet.

He shut the bike off and dismounted, deciding it would be best to go check it out on foot. He removed the black rifle from the scabbard and set it down next to him. Then he draped the camo netting he'd packed over both the quad and the trailer. Picking up his rifle, he checked the chamber to make sure it was loaded and slowly started to make his way toward whatever was on the tracks.

DJ moved carefully through the tall grass. Every fifty steps, he crept up closer to the tracks until he could get a look at the obstruction. He was very cautious to only stick his head up just enough to see. This would present whoever or whatever was down there the smallest target possible if they were watching for someone.

He'd covered almost half the distance when he finally recognized the Cadillac that had passed his camp that afternoon. DJ watched the car for several minutes but could perceive no movement around or in it. He wondered what had happened. Had someone jumped the old man? Maybe he'd broken down or simply run out of gas. Or could this be some kind of trap? He slowed his pace even more, using all of his senses to examine his surroundings.

He got closer and closer to the car, but he didn't see or hear anything out of the ordinary. He moved past the car about a hundred yards to make sure no one was set up on the other side. Once he was satisfied it was safe, he sneaked up to the car. Peering inside, he saw the old man lying on the front seat. DJ wondered if he was asleep or dead. The backseat was full of all kinds of stuff; pots and pans, clothing, tools, canned food, and many other goods were stacked from the floor to the top of the seats.

DJ crept around the car looking for any signs of foul play. He didn't see any, but he did identify the reason the Caddy had stopped. One of the ties had rotted, and the front tire of the big car had fallen through and become wedged between the ties.

DJ caught movement from inside the car out of the corner of his eye. His head swiveled around to see the old man sit up behind the wheel. DJ instinctively ducked down behind the car, gripping his weapon a little tighter. Brake lights washed out DJ's view through the goggles. He pulled them off his face as he heard the hum of an electric window.

"Is anyone out there?" the old man called out.

DJ wondered whether to answer or not.

"Is anyone out there?" the old man repeated, a little louder.

What could the old man do to him? "Yeah," DJ answered.

"Do you think you could help me get my car unstuck? I can pay you."

"Do you have any weapons?"

"Just an old shotgun and a revolver," the old man said, "but I need them. I can pay you cash, though."

DJ found the man's answer amusing. He had no need for relics. "I don't want them. I just want to make sure you're not going to shoot me."

"You don't worry about that, sonny. I wouldn't do no one no harm unless they was trying to harm me."

"That's good to know. Do me a favor. Take your foot off the brake pedal."

The brake lights went out.

"Now turn on the interior lights," DJ said. Then he saw the dome light come on. "Please stick your hands out of the window."

"What for?" the old man said.

"Do you want my help or not?"

"Yes."

"Then please do as I ask. Don't worry. I'm not going to hurt you. I just have to make sure it's safe," DJ said with authority in his voice.

"Okay, my hands are out of the window."

DJ stepped out from behind the car and activated his weapon-mounted light. He shined it in the old man's eyes as he continued to move clockwise. "Now use the outside door handle and open your door."

The man did as he was told.

"Step out and put your hands on top of your head and interlace your fingers, please."

Again the man complied. His back was toward DJ, who shined his light up and down, looking for a weapon. Nothing was visible.

"Now turn around and face me."

When the man was facing him, DJ again looked for a weapon and sized him up. The old man was average height but very thin. The look on his face said he wasn't dangerous, but DJ knew looks could be deceiving.

"Where are your weapons?"

"The shotgun is in the trunk, and my handgun is in the glove box."

"Good. We're almost done here," DJ assured the man. "Turn back around, and I'm just going to pat you down a little."

The man turned, and thirty seconds later, DJ was convinced he wasn't a threat. He turned off his weapon light.

"Sorry about all of that," DJ said, "but you can't be too careful, you know?"

"I guess that's right," the man said thoughtfully. He stuck out his hand. "My name is Jacob Kessler."

DJ grabbed the hand firmly. "DJ, DJ Frost. Where are you headed, Mr. Kessler?"

"Please call me Jacob. Everybody does. I'm going to my son's place. At least I was until I got stuck. He lives about twenty miles from here, I think."

"I see. Aren't you afraid a train might come along?"

"No. I live beside the tracks just outside of town. Some days, there are eight or ten trains that go down these tracks. Four's about the fewest there ever is, but there hasn't been a single one since the electricity went out. I guess they need power to track where the trains are and run the switches and stuff."

DJ hadn't thought of that, but it made sense. He looked at his watch. It was pushing three in the morning. Obviously he wouldn't be making anywhere near the distance he'd planned. He would help the old man out and then try to find a good spot to hole up for the daylight hours. He'd packed plenty of extra food just in case he got delayed a day or two.

"Where did you come from?" Jacob asked.

"I came from town, just like you."

"Where's your car?"

"I don't have one," DJ said.

"You're not walking, are you?"

"No, I have a four-wheeler about half a mile down the tracks. I just walked up here to make sure this wasn't a trap."

"That's a good idea," Jacob said. "Both the four-wheeler and checking for a trap, that is."

"Well, let's see if we can't get you unstuck." DJ pulled a small flashlight out of the cargo pocket of his trousers and shined it on the problem wheel.

"I can't get her to budge frontward or backward."

"Do you have a jack?"

"Yes, but I already tried that. It's one of those scissor jacks and the place you have to put it is too close to the tracks to get it under the car."

"Let me see it," DJ said.

The old man opened his car's passenger door and retrieved the jack from the floorboard. DJ tried to get the jack behind the stuck wheel, but there wasn't quite enough room. He looked in front of the tire, but there was no place where the jack could mate up. It was made to only attach to the vehicle at the four jack points. Probably some lawyer design, DJ thought. If only he'd been able to bring his truck, he would have had his high-lift jack. But there was no use dwelling on that—he'd just have to make do with what he had.

He examined the back of the car and saw that it was slightly farther away from the tracks than the front. Probably a result of the old man spinning the tires as he struggled to get out, he thought. DJ tried the jack in front of the back tire, and it slipped into place with almost no room to spare. It would fit here and might raise the whole side of the car up enough; they'd just have to see.

DJ attached the handle and began to crank. What the little jack lacked in versatility, it made up for in lift. As the car began to rise, DJ watched the front tire. It remained stuck between the ties until the jack was almost as high as it would go. Then it popped out.

"All right!" Jacob said as the tire finally came free.

DJ smiled and finished cranking the jack up the last inch or so. "Now we just need to find a board or something to bridge the broken tie," he said.

"What if we just fill the hole with gravel?"

"Why not?"

The two men took positions on each side of the wheel and used their hands to pack as much gravel as they could in the hole. When they were satisfied, DJ let the jack down. The tire was almost level with the others. Jacob started the car and easily pulled forward. He got out of the car with a huge smile on his face.

"Thank you so much, DJ." He pulled his wallet out and retrieved a hundred-dollar bill. DJ could see that there wasn't a lot of cash in the leather case. "Here you go."

DJ almost waved the old guy off. After all, the money was probably not worth much, but he realized it might come in handy.

"Thank you, Jacob," he said as he stuffed the bill down in his pocket.

"Is there anything else I can do for you? Would you like a ride to my son's place? It's not much, but you could get a decent meal."

"Thanks, Jacob, but I just better be on my way. Good luck to you."

"Same to you, DJ. You stay safe," Jacob said.

"You might want to keep that revolver where you can get to it quickly. No telling in these times what you might run into."

"So noted," the old man said. "Thanks again. If you change your mind about coming by my son's place, it's about five miles north of the tracks on Route Eighty-seven. Just look for the big-mouth bass mailbox that says Kessler."

"Thanks," DJ said with a single nod of his head.

Jacob climbed back in the Cadillac and started down the tracks. DJ walked back toward his quad, thinking about how he hadn't even made a third of the distance he had planned. When he reached the vehicle, he noticed that there were enough trees and other cover right there to hide him well enough until tomorrow evening. He pitched his tent and hit the sack.

Gabe woke up. He smacked his lips and made a face. His mouth was dry and gummy, and it tasted as if mice had nested in it. He got out of bed and trudged to the bathroom. The face in the mirror looked like crap. Bloodshot eyes, four days' worth of beard—coming off a three-day bender could do that to a man. Of course, a genuine hatred for one's self didn't help any. The face stared back with the same abhorrence that everyone held for Gabe. Well, almost everyone. He put some toothpaste on the brush and began the long process of making himself half human again. Next came a shower and then a shave.

As he combed his hair in the dresser mirror, he almost recognized himself. He was thinner, and his face was haggard, but he still looked a little like the Gabe from before. This thought pulled his eyes to the picture of the three of them. He only let himself look for a second, though. Any longer would send him back to the whiskey.

After dressing, Gabe walked into the living room and surveyed the single-wide mobile home. Nothing looked damaged or too out of place, indicating that he'd just drunk until he passed out this time. The front door was open, and he wondered why.

Had someone come to see him? He couldn't remember for sure, but it seemed that someone had. He closed the door and then hurriedly straightened up the rest of the house.

Hunger gnawed at his stomach. Had he eaten in the past three days? The single plate in the sink said yes, but he couldn't remember when or what. He fixed some bacon, eggs, and biscuits and sat down at the table. He ate quickly, as his hunger really manifested itself after the first bite. When he was finished with breakfast, he quickly grabbed his hat and headed for the door. There was dirty work that needed to be done, and he was just callous enough to do it.

CHAPTER 4

D J slept soundly until about ten. He probably would've slept
longer, but the sound of voices jarred him awake. A little dis-
oriented at first, he needed a minute to remember where he was
and why. When it came back to him, he began to wonder if he'd
been dreaming. The answer came when he heard them again. He
quickly and quietly dressed and stepped out of the tent, rifle in
hand.

He stood outside the door and listened. A moment later, he
saw movement, and he squashed his instinct to hit the dirt. Even
though he was more exposed than he'd like, it was safer to be
still. He tracked the movement with his eyes, and a second later
he identified two people on bicycles. A young man and a young
woman were heading the same way he was going. They both had
their mountain bikes loaded with gear, and the man had a trailer
attached to his bike. It was one designed to carry children. DJ
didn't know if it held its intended cargo or just more gear, but he
thought it was a good plan. Not as good as his, but without night-
vision equipment and a quad, it would be hard to improve on.

Of course, they shouldn't be talking, and he didn't see anything for self-defense, but it was still a good plan. They were moving quickly, the bikes were quiet, and they were able to carry a good bit of gear. Fortunately they passed without even knowing DJ was there. He relaxed and was thankful they were moving quickly because in daylight he realized the woods he'd set up camp in weren't as thick as they'd seemed in the dark. His tent stood out the most, so he took it down and packed it. He moved the quad into a better spot and covered it again. Satisfied that things were as good as he could get them, he decided to fix some breakfast.

As he ate, he realized he had to be more careful about where he set up camp. If the bicyclists hadn't been talking to each other, he probably wouldn't have woken up. He wondered if anyone had passed when he was asleep. He doubted it, but it was possible. He might have to start using some precautions just in case someone did stumble onto his camp.

Later in the day, DJ was playing solitaire when he heard voices again. They were coming from down the tracks, and he guessed they were at least fifty yards away. It seemed as if the tracks were turning into a main thoroughfare.

I've got to get off these tracks as soon as I can.

He carefully moved to where he could see down the tracks. A small group of four or five was walking between the rails in a tight cluster. They were moving too fast to be watching for ambushes but too slow to cover much ground. The one in the lead had a shotgun, but DJ couldn't tell about the others, and the group was making no effort to be quiet or conceal themselves. DJ wondered how they'd made it this far with their lack of noise discipline. He could take them out easily if he had the notion. It was a good thing for them he was one of the good guys, he thought.

He was thankful for their leisurely pace, though. It gave him time to examine his camp once again. The four-wheeler was still not hidden as well as he would have liked, but the camouflage cover helped. If these people were looking for threats as they should have been, it might have been a problem, but DJ was sure they would pass right by just as the bicyclists had.

He found a spot where he could watch them as they walked by, but they wouldn't be able to see him. He lay down on his stomach with his rifle in front of him. His heart was beating at an increased pace, and he concentrated on his breathing to bring it back down to a normal level. The walkers were getting closer, and he was able to make out some of the words.

"... tired ... when ... stop ... ," a distinctly female voice said. The response by a male voice was too muddled to discern.

"... sucks!"

DJ snickered quietly. After a few more minutes, the travelers came into view of DJ's hide. There were four of them, a family from the look of things. The father was in the lead carrying a huge backpack. He also had a hunting-type shotgun in his hands. His overlapping belly almost balanced out the backpack. A woman was behind him, presumably his wife. She wasn't as fat as her husband, but she was close. She had a large purse draped across one shoulder and a small duffel-type bag over the other. A teenage girl followed next, trailed by a preteen boy. The kids both had day packs, probably the ones they used for their schoolbooks. They were both in decent shape, especially compared to their parents. Mom and Dad were sucking wind, but the kids didn't seem to be too overworked.

"Can we at least stop and rest for a few minutes?" the mom

asked. It was the same whiny voice DJ had heard before. He held his breath—he didn't need them resting this close to him.

"Look, Linda, we can't stop every five minutes if we want to make it to your sister's before we run out of food," the father said. "It'll be dinnertime before too long, and we'll take a nice rest then, okay?"

The woman said nothing.

DJ breathed a sigh of relief. He wondered how far the family was going. Probably not too far at the pace they were going. As they got even with his camp, he noticed that the girl, while not beautiful, had a cute face and a superb body.

She might have been sixteen or seventeen, he thought. She began to look side to side as if she knew someone was watching her. DJ realized that he was staring at her and he quickly averted his eyes. He had heard that people could feel when they were being watched. It seemed like too much of a coincidence that the girl had just started looking around.

"Hey, Dad, what's that?" she asked.

DJ realized she was pointing right at his four-wheeler.

"I don't know," the dad answered. "It looks like stacks of boxes that somebody covered up. I'll take a closer look." He dropped his pack. The woman dropped her two bags as well and plopped down on the duffel.

The man was stepping over the track as DJ positioned his rifle. He didn't intend to shoot the man, but DJ had to cover him just in case. The man was only twenty-five or thirty yards away, and his shotgun could make mincemeat out of DJ at that range.

"Hold it where you are," DJ barked. The man froze, his grip on the shotgun tightening. Slowly he began to turn toward DJ.

"Please don't move," DJ said. "I have a rifle on you, and I'll have to use it if you point that shotgun at me."

"Don't worry," the man said nervously. "It's not loaded."

What a moron, DJ thought. He wondered if the man was a bigger idiot for carrying an empty gun or for admitting that it wasn't loaded. Of course the man could have been lying, but DJ had a strong suspicion that he was telling the truth. DJ thought about how easy it would be for someone to kill the man, woman, and boy and take the girl.

Lucky for them I'm not that kind of guy.

"Well, there's no way for me to know that for sure, so how about you just set it down?"

The man complied. His eyes moved back and forth searching for whoever was talking to him.

"The stuff you see is mine, and I'd just as soon you didn't mess with it," DJ said.

The man's head turned toward DJ. His eyes were still looking, but his ears had at least narrowed down the search field. "I understand. We'll just be on our way." He started to bend over and reach for his weapon.

"Don't do that!"

The man stopped at midbend. "I can't leave my gun here."

"I don't expect you to. Let's just get your daughter to pick it up and carry it until you get out of sight."

"Whatever you say, mister. I don't want any trouble." He backed up to his pack. "Tammy, go pick up my gun."

Tammy looked back and forth as though her dad was talking to another person and she was trying to figure out to whom. DJ was amused by the girl's reaction. He decided to have some fun.

"Yes, you, Tammy," he said. "Walk over to your daddy's shot-gun."

The girl obeyed.

"Now put your hands up and turn around so I can make sure you don't have any weapons."

The girl did as she was instructed, and DJ watched, but not for weapons. He smiled. "Even better than I thought," he said to himself.

"Okay, now pick up the gun and make sure the muzzle is pointed straight up. You can give it back to your dad once you round the next bend."

Tammy just nodded and continued to follow instructions. DJ wondered if they would make it to where they were going. The way they were traveling, making noise, and walking down the middle of the tracks in broad daylight, their odds weren't good. He could have helped them, but he was already behind schedule, and slowing to walking speed would only throw him further behind. He couldn't afford that, especially now that more people seemed to be using the tracks. He would just give the man some advice.

"Listen, buddy, when Tammy gives you the gun back, I'd suggest you load it and stop making so much noise. Anybody could have killed you before you even knew they were there if they wanted to. I heard you four or five minutes before you even got here. If you're smart, you'll get off the tracks and walk in the brush. Quietly."

"Okay, mister. Thanks for your help."

DJ watched them walk out of sight and wondered if they would take his suggestions to heart.

The rest of the day passed uneventfully. Finally it was time to leave. DJ packed up what little he needed to and pulled a fuel can off the trailer to fill up his bike. It took a little more gas than he'd expected, probably because he'd needed to slow down to avoid obstacles. It was all right, though. He had brought extra gas just in case. He examined the tracks to make sure they were clear. Then he mounted his machine. Pulling up between the tracks, he was glad to be on his way.

Walking down the steps of his trailer, Gabe looked up at the sun. He didn't need a watch to know it was three thirty. That was another indication he'd really tied one on. He saw that weeds were trying once again to take over his garden, pulled a hoe out of the shed and fought back the undesirable flora. Sweat from the heat and the work poured out of his body. He could smell the toxins he'd poisoned himself with over the past weekend. His muscles protested at the work, not because they weren't used to the physical demand but because Gabe's single meal in three days had already been burned. Gabe pressed on, ignoring his body's pleadings.

When the weeding was done, Gabe grabbed a big bucket and started picking vegetables that had ripened over the weekend. There were so many that the harvest spilled over into a second and then a third bucket. He took the bounty into the kitchen and washed the produce, piece by piece. The tomatoes, most of them softball-sized, were Gabe's specialty. They used to be Hannah's, but he'd inherited them when she'd left. He sold them at the farmers' market on Wednesdays. Well, the woman down the road and her son did. No one in town would have bought anything from Gabe. They all hated him. He was the town drunk, after all. Just as that Otis fellow on the *Andy Griffith Show* had been. Only he didn't just walk into the sheriff's office and lock himself up. The sheriff's deputies had done that—more than once, too.

Gabe began to separate the vegetables into two piles, one he'd sell and one he'd eat. He found a tomato that was a little odd-shaped. Although there was nothing really wrong with it, he knew it wouldn't sell. The city slickers who shopped the market wouldn't buy anything that didn't have a typical shape and color. He looked at the odd tomato for a moment and then bit into it as if it were an apple. The sweet fruit filled his mouth with a flavor little would match. If only this could obscure the memories the way the bourbon did, he thought.

CHAPTER 5

DJ was pleased with the progress he was making. According to his GPS, he had eight more miles to go before he got off the tracks. Then it was just a short jaunt down a county road to the power line. Once he got to the campsite he had intended to reach last night, he could decide whether to go on or not.

The bridge over the river was the last big obstacle before he turned off the tracks. He couldn't wait to get on a smooth road. The constant thumping of his tires over the ties was starting to drive him crazy. It would take some time to cross the bridge, but DJ knew his plan would work.

His quad's tires weren't big enough to span the gap between the ties on the bridge. This would have made it impossible to cross if he hadn't been prepared. He figured he could let some air out of his tires on one side and let the wheels run directly on the track on that edge. On the other side, he'd use the two-by-eights he'd stashed next to the bridge. They were both twelve feet long, and he could lay them across the ties. He'd have to leapfrog the boards all the way across the bridge, but if what Jacob had said was true and the trains weren't running, he'd have plenty of time.

DJ had figured long ago that any bridge over the river was a natural choke point. Not only did it have the probability of snarling traffic, but it was an obvious place for an ambush. When he was first planning his bug-out route, he'd figured that the railroad bridges were much more likely to be open and safe than a bridge built for cars. In fact, that was how he'd come up with using the railroad in the first place. The only problem was how to cross when there was nothing between the ties. Conjuring the idea to use boards had been easy. The problem was how to carry them to the bridge. Since they'd have hung way over the back of the trailer and taken up valuable space, DJ had decided that the best thing to do was to preposition the boards. That, too, seemed simple enough, but how could he get them there? He'd gone over many possibilities until he settled on renting a small boat and motor and using the river to get to the bridge. Once he was there, it had simply been a matter of burying the boards and motoring back to the boat ramp.

The boards were treated, and he'd carefully wrapped them in heavy plastic and sealed them with duct tape. It would only take a few minutes to uncover them and pull them up onto the tracks. *Not much farther now,* DJ thought.

He rounded the last curve before the bridge and blinked a couple of times to make sure what he saw was really there. A train sat motionless on the tracks. DJ squeezed the brakes on his ride and came to a stop, staring at the train as if it were a ghost. He hoped it had stopped before it got onto the bridge, but he knew that was unlikely—unless it was a very short train. It looked to be one of the trains that hauled coal to the power plant on the outskirts of town. He'd seen them before, and they were usually very long.

Other questions flashed through his mind. Had it just stopped temporarily? Why would it stop on the bridge? Could he get someone to move it? If it were abandoned, could he move it himself? Could he squeeze his four-wheeler past it? This was a situation he'd never considered, and he didn't know the answers. He would just have to check it out.

He pulled the quad down into some tall weeds and covered it. Then, taking his rifle with him, he slowly approached the train. As he got closer, he was able to tell two things. First, the train was empty. This made sense because it was headed away from the power plant. Second, and most important, the train had started to make its way across the bridge. DJ's heart sank—he knew his carefully mapped route had most likely been ruined by this unforeseen event.

He slowly walked up to the bridge, carefully watching for anyone lurking. When he got closer, he realized there was no way to squeeze his quad between the train and the side of the bridge. His body could barely fit into the limited space. He walked across, cautiously and deliberately centering his feet on the ties. Once across, he walked the considerable distance to the locomotives. There were five of them, sleeping giants with no regard for his Lilliputian plans. They had stopped, ironically, at the road he had planned to take, most likely for a truck to pick up the crew.

He climbed up on the lead engine, opened the door, and stepped in. He turned off his night vision and fished his flashlight out of a pocket on his vest. Looking over the controls, he thought they seemed rudimentary, but after fumbling with a few buttons, DJ had to admit that he had no idea what he was doing. He thought about how in the movies the hero always found the keys on top of the visor. Unfortunately, there was no visor, and this was no movie. Disappointed, he hiked back to his quad.

Once there, he pulled out his maps and started searching for a way around the bridge. Unfortunately, the last road he had crossed bigger than a goat trail was almost halfway back to where he'd started that night. He groaned as he saw how far out of the way he'd have to travel taking that route. It looked to be at least an extra twenty or thirty miles, not to mention the forty or so miles he would have to backtrack, and who knew if the bridge over the river going that way would be traversable? He searched for another way, but he realized he didn't have any other options.

He checked his gas tank and saw that it was over half-empty. Going back would use at least another half a tank. That was close to five gallons wasted. He refigured how much he would need to complete his trip and realized he'd be short. He plopped down sideways on the seat of the quad and put his head in his hands. For almost fifteen minutes, he didn't move. Finally he pulled his head up and shook it.

"I have to figure out what to do," he said out loud. He briefly considered leaving the quad and going the rest of the way on foot. He'd known that there was always the contingency that the quad might become disabled and he had gear in case he had to resort to plan B. It would be hard to carry enough food to walk the rest of the way, but he knew he could do it. But the quad and the items he'd have to leave behind were just too valuable to abandon if there was an alternative.

Perhaps he could find a little more gas. He looked at the map again. It wasn't likely he'd find an open gas station on the back roads he'd selected. He could go to a more populated area and try to find a station, but would it even be open or have any gas? DJ knew that gas would soon be worth its weight in gold.

He looked at the map again. Jacob had said that his son didn't live too far.

Maybe I could find him and trade the hundred dollars for some gas.

That seemed like the best idea. Even if he didn't find the old man, maybe he'd stumble on a farmer who would sell him some gas. If he had to, he could even steal some. He didn't like that option, but it wouldn't be the first time he was guilty of some petty thieving. He would just have to do what he had to do.

DJ climbed back on the quad, feeling a little better about his options. He pulled up onto the tracks and began the trip back. Just before dawn, he found a good camping spot not too far from the turnoff. He set up camp, making sure it would be hidden enough in the daylight, and went to sleep.

Gabe wondered why the woman hadn't shown up. He paced back and forth from the door to the table where he had all the produce ready to go. It wasn't like her to be late. In fact, he couldn't remember her ever being late. If he had had a phone, he would have called her. Maybe her truck had broken down, he thought. Maybe she or her son was sick. No matter what the reason was, Gabe didn't like altering his routine. He decided to get in his truck and go see what the problem was.

The half-ton Chevy groaned as he let out on the clutch. Gabe turned onto the road when he got to the end of his gravel drive and urged the almost-thirty-year-old truck forward with a slight mash of the accelerator. The truck was in nice shape for its age. Gabe was able to keep it in good repair since it was easy to work on. It didn't have all the fancy things a new truck had like power steering or air-conditioning, but the straight-six engine ran well and didn't use much gas. Of course, Gabe only went to town once a month for groceries, so gas mileage was really not a factor for him. Many months, he used more gas in his Rototiller than he did in the truck.

Three and a half miles down the road, he came to the mailbox with a chicken painted on the side. The name painted beside it said J. WALKER. Gabe turned into the woman's drive and drove up to the house. It was modest but well kept, and the small yard in front was manicured. Gabe could hear the chickens clucking in back when he turned his truck off. As he opened the truck door, the woman opened her front door.

"What do you want?" she asked. The look in her eyes held the disdain Gabe was used to. It was, however, the first time he could recall seeing it from her. He was much more comfortable with this look, though. In fact, it was the first time he could remember being comfortable enough to look her in the eye for more than a second.

"I just came to see why you didn't come pick up the vegetables."

The woman ignored Gabe's question. She took a step toward him and lowered her voice. "Robby told me what you said to him the other day. If you want to be mean and nasty to everybody else, fine, but you don't ever talk like that to my boy. You understand?"

Gabe blinked. He didn't remember talking to the boy. *Wait,* he thought. *It seems like someone did come over the other day.* Maybe it had been the boy. There was no telling what Gabe might have said. Obviously it must have been pretty bad to make his mother this mad.

"Is that why you aren't going to the market today?" he said.

Now the woman looked taken aback. She stared at him for a moment, and then the look that Gabe didn't like started coming back. "You don't know, do you?"

"Know what?" he asked, looking down at the grass.

"Don't you listen to the news?"

"No."

"You better come in. Let me fix you a glass of tea."

"No, that's all right. I'm fine. Just tell me."

"Well, to start with, they're not having the farmers' market this week," she said. "To be honest, I don't know when they'll have it again. Things are bad, Mr. Horne."

He hated the way she said his name.

"The economy has tanked, and there are riots in the cities. The president has declared martial law. Hopefully things will settle down soon. That's what they keep saying on the news—but so far things seem to be getting worse. They say the power's off in the city, and they don't know how much longer our power will stay up."

Gabe stood silent as the news slowly sank in. He had often wished that the world would end, but he had never considered the possibility that it could. "What happened?" he finally said, his eyes not their usual slits.

"No one seems to know for sure, or they aren't saying. Most of the experts say it's a combination of oil prices and the national debt. They're calling it 'the Smash.' I'm afraid it might not be long before some of the rioters come out here. Supposedly they're causing lots of trouble in the suburbs."

Gabe stood silent for a minute. "Well, okay, then." He turned and stepped back toward his truck.

"Wait, Mr. Horne."

Gabe's face scrunched. "Yes?" he said without turning around.

"Please take some eggs. I've got so many I don't know what to do with them all."

"No, thanks. I'm fine."

"I insist," she said. "You wait right there."

Gabe heard the screen door slam. He stepped to the truck and reached for the door handle. Before he could push the button, he heard the door's hinges creak.

"Here you go."

Gabe reached behind the cab of his pickup and grabbed the big bucket of tomatoes.

"You take these." He turned and pushed the bucket toward the woman. She walked to him, and they handed each other their signature produce.

"Thank you, Mr. Horne."

"Tell that boy I'm sorry about the other night." He climbed into his truck and tried his best not to see how she was looking at him. Pulling out of the driveway, he thought about the last time he had said he was sorry. It was that night, so long ago, when they had left.

Back in his house, he turned on the old hi-fi and put on a George Jones album. Then he opened a bottle and poured. It was two days earlier than usual, but he didn't care. Now time held no meaning for the rest of the world, either.

CHAPTER 6

DJ finally gave up trying to sleep and got up. He'd tossed and turned all morning, worrying about his fuel situation. *Damn train*, he thought. He filled the quad and then checked to see how much fuel he had left. Including what was in the quad, he had thirteen gallons. Looking at his map, he saw he had two hundred and eighty miles left if he didn't have to make any more detours. He had expected to get twenty miles per gallon, but he was actually only getting seventeen so far. Even if he got the mileage back up, it was only enough fuel to go two hundred and sixty miles.

The good news was that this route took him right by where Jacob's son lived. Hopefully, he could get some fuel from the old man. DJ figured if he could get five or six gallons, he'd have plenty, even if he had to take a few small detours. Confident in his plan and now more relaxed, he lay back down to get some quality shut-eye.

The heat of the afternoon woke him up about four. He fixed a meal and spent some time reading again. A group of seven walked by him on the tracks. They never saw him, and if he'd been asleep, he doubted he would have noticed them. They moved quietly and were all armed. Even the kids, who looked to be around ten and sixteen, had rifles. The little one only had a .22, but that was a lot better than nothing. DJ was glad he'd made sure this camp was well camouflaged.

At dusk, he broke camp and was ready to roll by the time it got dark. He was only four miles from Route 87. When he pulled onto the paved highway, the smoothness of the road was an instant reward. Able to travel at thirty-five miles per hour, DJ felt as if he were flying. There were quite a few houses along this route. Most were dark, but a few had pale lights shining out of the windows. DJ thought it was less than smart to have any light showing. It was an open invitation to troublemakers.

As he approached the five-mile mark, he slowed a little and started looking for the old Caddy. It seemed like no time before he saw the Kessler place. It was just an old trailer on a small lot, and Jacob's car was parked in front. The mailbox was shaped like a fish and said JAMES KESSLER. DJ only noticed the first name because the "J" in DJ stood for James. He pulled into the dirt drive and stopped his machine. No lights were showing in the trailer.

"Jacob," DJ called out, but not too loudly. "It's DJ, the guy who helped you the other night."

No one answered. He called out again, a little louder this time. Still there was no answer. He dismounted and climbed the rickety wooden stairs up to the front door. He knocked softly and waited for a response. None came. He walked around to the back of the trailer. There was no one there, either, but he noticed that the back door stood ajar, so he walked up to it and stuck his head in the door.

"Hello. Is anyone home?"

It was as quiet as a tomb. DJ took a step into the home and, with the aid of his night-vision goggles, saw a man slumped over on the couch. He looked as if he had passed out drunk.

"Hey!" DJ said as loud as he dared.

The man didn't move. DJ stepped toward the man to try to wake him, but something wasn't right. There was something unnatural about the way he was lying on the couch. DJ turned off his goggles and turned on his flashlight. The first thing he noticed was that this man looked almost exactly like Jacob. The only difference was that he was younger and heavier. Suddenly DJ snatched his pistol out of his drop-leg holster and doused the light. The man had a hole in his chest. DJ turned his goggles back on and began to clear the house. He found Jacob behind the counter in the kitchen. He was lying on the floor in a pool of blood. DJ knelt down beside him and felt for a pulse. There was none.

DJ could hear his heart pounding in his ears. His throat had a burning bile taste as he tried to choke back the urge to hurl. He focused on the task at hand, and slowly and carefully cleared the rest of the house. As he went from room to room, he could see that things were missing from the home. The TV and VCR were gone. The stand and the loose cable wires, along with dust outlines, gave their former presence away. Dresser drawers in the bedrooms were opened and clothes were strewn about the room. He finished searching the house having found no one—at least no one who was still alive.

He sat on the bed in the last room he cleared, turned the night-vision goggles off, and stared into the darkness. Thoughts of how Jacob had died for nothing but a few material possessions flooded his mind. He felt a single tear roll down his cheek. It could have been the first of a torrent, but DJ held back his emotions. He couldn't lose it now. It was too dangerous in here. The perps who'd killed Jacob and his son might come back.

DJ stood back up and went outside to move his quad around to the back. There was nothing he could do for Jacob, so he'd get the gas he needed and get as far away from here as he could. The first thing he needed was a siphon hose. There was a garden hose hooked up to the spigot next to the back porch. DJ pulled out his knife and cut a six-foot piece off. He removed the two empty gas cans from his trailer and went around front to the Cadillac. Opening the gas cap, he stuffed the hose in until he heard a dull thud. The tank sounded as if it was completely empty, but that didn't make any sense. Even if Jacob had barely had enough gas to get here, there still should have been enough gas to cover the bottom of the tank. DJ put his lips to the siphon hose and blew. He hoped to hear bubbles, but all he heard was the sound of air rushing through the hose. He looked under the car with the aid of his flashlight and saw that someone had punched a hole in the tank to drain it.

DJ felt his face screw up with anger. Not only had these ruffians murdered his friend, but they'd also endangered him by stealing Jacob's gas. He wished he'd been here when they had arrived. He knew the story would have ended differently. He also knew that he'd only just met Jacob, but since he was the other half of DJ's only "normal" conversation in the past week, and likely the only one for a while, DJ figured the word "friend" was a fitting description.

Again, he made himself focus on what he needed to do. He returned to his quad in the back and noticed a small storage shed in the far corner of the property. Inside it he found a lawn mower and some other tools. A lawn mower would mean gas, and DJ searched the shed until he found a two-gallon can of the liquid gold. It was only half-full, but that was better than nothing. He also noticed a chain saw case sitting on a shelf with a small gas can and some bar oil. He reached for the case and was happy it had something in it. Opening it, he saw that the saw was of good quality. He decided to take it with him, along with the gas and oil. He didn't need it, but Jacob's son didn't have a use for it anymore, either. He might be able to trade it for some gas. There was nothing else of interest in the shed, so he closed the door and made his way back to his quad. Strapping down the chain saw, he wondered if there might be anything else in the house that would make good barter items. He poured the lawn mower gas into one of his cans and threw James's can under the back porch.

DJ quickly swept through the house, but it looked as if the killers had done a good job of swiping anything of value. All of the kitchen cabinets were empty, as well. All he found were a couple of cheap pocketknives and a Chinese-made multitool in the kitchen junk drawer.

He looked down at Jacob and wished he could do something. It was so undignified the way the old man was sprawled on the floor. DJ briefly thought about wrapping him and his son in some sheets and putting them on one of the beds, but that would take time he didn't have. Besides, that wouldn't bring them back.

Back on the Polaris, he resumed his new course, determined to come up with another plan to get more gas. He thought about how senseless Jacob's and James's deaths were and wondered what kind of people could have killed them for so little. He knew things could get this bad—he'd often told people such on the Internet forums he frequented. Most didn't like his blunt and brusque approach, and he'd been banned on many of the sites, but they couldn't say he hadn't warned them. He smiled as a small wave of vindication washed over him.

When Gabe woke up to total darkness, he realized something wasn't right. Even if all the lights in the house were off, some illumination from the security light out front should have filtered through the window blinds. He got out of the chair and felt his way to the kitchen. He felt the floor change from carpet to vinyl, and then he felt the crunch of glass under his shoes. He wondered what he'd broken this time. He tried to step carefully, not wanting to slip and cut himself on whatever was broken on the floor. If anyone had been able to see through the darkness, they might have thought him a high-wire artist practicing his craft. Gabe knew he was drunker than he should have been, but he still wasn't as drunk as he'd like to be. He'd have to take care of that.

When he finally reached the back door, he flipped the light switch up, but nothing happened. The back landing light switch was right next to the one for the kitchen, but it, too, produced no light when he turned it on. He flicked it up and down several times, as if that might produce the desired result, but it was in vain.

Cursing at the electricity, he turned and stumbled to the drawer that held his flashlight. He forcefully rooted around until he found it. When he pushed the button, the light came on dimly.

He knew he had new batteries and used the flashlight to find them. Changing them in the dark proved to be more difficult than he'd expected. His motor skills, degraded by the alcohol, were no match for the fine threads and spring tension of the back cap of the flashlight. He dropped the cap twice and had to feel around to find it, cutting his hand on the broken glass. The slippery nature of the blood on his hand added to the difficulty of screwing the cap on, but he finally succeeded. Hitting the switch again produced a very bright beam that almost illuminated the whole kitchen. He saw several broken glasses on the floor, kicking a large chunk out of the way and stepping around some others on his way back to his chair. He set the flashlight on the coffee table so that it pointed at the ceiling. The beam reflected off the white surface and bathed the room with just enough light to see

Gabe poured four fingers' worth of whiskey and sat back in his chair. He gulped the whole glass in one motion. The way the flashlight was balanced on the table reminded him of the time he and the boy had placed the light on the kitchen floor in the same way, pretending to be pirates as they swigged apple juice straight from the bottle. It was one of the good times, well before the alcohol had taken over his life, before that uncaring bastard had taken them away from him. Gabe felt his throat closing and his eyes tearing up as the memories flooded back. He clumsily grabbed the light and threw it. He heard a crash as the light went out. He needed another drink. He grabbed for the bottle and filled his glass. That was something he was good at, even in the dark.

CHAPTER 7

DJ wasn't happy about being forced to take this detour, but he was thankful to be off the tracks. He hadn't realized how much the constant bumping and noise of the railroad ties had worn on him. Now he was flying. The miles zoomed past with an ease that let him think more clearly and relax his tense muscles. His biggest priority—besides not getting killed—was gasoline. If he was lucky, he might find an abandoned car that had some left, but that was a long shot. His best bet was finding someone to sell him some, but how would he locate a person he could trust?

A set of headlights on the horizon pulled him out of his thoughts. DJ drove down into the ditch along the road and waited for the vehicle to pass. It seemed to take forever, but the pickup finally passed him. There was no sign that anyone in the truck had noticed him. DJ waited for the taillights to disappear. Then he resumed his course.

At about two a.m., he began to get hungry. He found a place to pull off the road and opened an MRE. While he was eating, he took out his atlas and studied. There was a small town named Greendale ahead, and he could make it there before dawn if he hurried. Perhaps that would be a good place to look for some gas. He quickly finished his meal and hit the road.

It was forty-five minutes until daybreak when he reached the outskirts of the little town. He didn't know where he would hide his quad and trailer for the day, but the answer seemed to provide itself. A bridge crossed a small stream right at a sign:

Greendale
POPULATION 644

DJ was able to take his Polaris about a hundred yards up the stream and hide it in a copse and underbrush. There was no place flat enough to set up his tent, so he strung the hammock up and went to sleep.

He awoke at nine thirty and sneaked down to the bridge to see if he could spot anything going on in the town. With the help of his binoculars, he could see a couple of people milling around. He decided to walk into town, but he couldn't do it in his tactical clothing. He worked his way back to his quad and changed into a pair of jeans and old work boots. He pulled on a plaid button-down over a dingy T-shirt, and put a grease-covered John Deere cap on his head. DJ would have liked to carry his rifle with him, but he knew it would draw more attention than he wanted. He slipped an inside-the-waistband holster next to his right kidney and filled it with a compact pistol. The untucked outer shirt covered it neatly, and the extra magazine in his front left pocket gave him a total of thirty-one rounds at his disposal. Grabbing one of his fuel cans, he headed into town.

Greendale looked like most small towns in rural America.

Older houses were interspersed with mobile homes and the occasional newer house. DJ noticed that the windows were open in almost all of the homes, but only a few people were outside. Those who were about seemed engrossed in their tasks, and if they noticed him, they didn't give any indication that they were interested. He walked up to a small store that had two gas pumps in front. When DJ opened the screened door, a bell attached to the doorframe rang. A man was leaning on the counter next to the cash register.

"Help you?" he asked, looking DJ in the eye.

"I hope so," DJ said with his best smile. "My vehicle ran out of gas a couple of miles up the road."

"I see," he said. DJ noticed that his eyes shifted to the left. "Sorry, but we've got no gas, and even if we did, the electricity is out, and there's no way to pump it."

"You don't have just a few gallons you could sell me? I can pay top dollar."

The man looked DJ up and down for a minute. "Nope, sorry. We don't have any."

"Do you think anyone in town might have some?"

"I doubt it. Leastways none they'd be willing to part with," the man said as he stood up straight. His hands stayed below the counter. "Is there anything else I can help you with?"

DJ looked around. The shelves of the little store were empty except for a few nonfood items. There was nothing he needed. "Let me look around for a minute."

"Help yourself," the man said. "We don't have a lot left, though."

As DJ walked up and down the aisles, a beat-up old truck

pulled up and stopped in front of the gas pumps. A second later, two young men walked into the store. One of them was carrying something in his hand. DJ's security experience made him watch the hand to make sure it didn't contain a weapon. He couldn't tell for sure what it was, but it wasn't a knife or a gun. The young man started to speak to the proprietor, but the older man tipped his head toward DJ.

From his position in the back of the store, he could see a pump shotgun leaning in the corner behind the counter. No doubt the man had a pistol under the counter as well. DJ noticed the young man who had started to speak had an old revolver stuck in the front of his jeans. The hair on the back of DJ's neck stood up as he saw the way the three men were looking at him. He strode toward the front of the store, trying not to look as though he was in a hurry.

"I don't see anything I need," he said as he passed the counter. "Thanks for your help."

Glancing back over his shoulder, he was thankful that no one followed him as he'd left. He took a few more steps and checked again. It was still clear. He turned around and quietly back-tracked along the side of the store, where he hoped he could hear what was being said inside.

". . . up the road," the store owner said.

"We just came from that direction, and we didn't see any-thing," another voice said.

"Well, that's what he told me."

"Who cares? What'll you give us for the watch?" the third voice said.

"Three."

"Three gallons?" the third voice asked incredulously. "You got to be shitting me! That's a five-thousand-dollar watch!"

"Okay, five, but that's it."

"All right. Let's do it."

"Not now," the store owner said. "I just told that guy in here that I didn't have any. Come back after dark."

"Okay, but you better not screw us," the second voice said threateningly.

"You know you don't have to worry about that. I'll see you about eight thirty."

DJ edged around to the back of the store, where a set of heavy double doors stood open. Screen doors covered the openings. DJ stayed well clear of them. A minute later, he heard the old truck start up and take off. Thankfully, it went in the opposite direction from his camp.

He decided he'd go back and rest and then come back after dark with his night vision. He walked briskly back to the bridge, recognizing again that the people outside were pretending not to notice him. One thing he hadn't realized before was that several people were watching him from inside their houses as he walked by. When he got to the bridge, he checked to make sure no one could see him and then slipped down to the creek and back to his quad.

He changed back into his black clothing and climbed into his hammock, intending to read. But what had happened at the store began to anger him more and more, and he wasn't able to focus on his book. It had been obvious to him that the man behind the counter had lied to him from the very beginning. The two younger men only verified that he had gasoline and was trading it for stolen goods. Perhaps the watch belonged to one of the young men, but DJ doubted it. They'd probably stolen it from someone. Maybe it had even been Jacob's or his son's. He knew it was unlikely, but it was possible. DJ recognized the young men as predators. They would eventually run up on someone who would ruin their day, but until then, there was no telling how much death and destruction would be left in their wake.

As much as DJ hated them, he hated the older man even more. He had to know where the goods he was trading gas for were coming from. That gas should be going to help people like him. Of course, it was worth a lot more than what it had cost before the Smash, but to trade it as if it were worth its weight in gold was only giving the predators more reason to steal. The old man was the root of the problem.

If DJ had known who the sheriff was in this county, he would have contacted the man and turned the three in. But even if he did, the sheriff might have bigger fish to fry now that things had gone bad. Even worse, the sheriff might be corrupt and could even be in on the scheme. Law enforcement in small, rural counties was often on the take from what DJ had heard. If he really wanted to help out the people around here, he could take the three out when they showed up to make their exchange. He wouldn't do it, but it was entertaining to consider. He finally fell asleep thinking about all the fun ways he could punish these punks.

As the sun got low on the western horizon, DJ woke up. He fixed some dinner, ate, and then broke camp and loaded his quad. By ten after eight, it was pitch-black. DJ put on his night-vision goggles. He removed his rifle, turned the holographic gun sight to its night-vision setting, and set out for the store. When he was within fifty yards of it, he leaned up against a large fence post next to the drainage ditch running down the side of the road.

Unless someone stepped on him, he would be almost impossible to see. He was dressed in all black, and his balaclava covered his face with only the smallest openings for his eyes. He got comfortable and waited.

He didn't have to wait long. The pickup pulled up at eight thirty-two. The proprietor of the store came out with a flashlight and said something to the passenger, who got out and followed the older man into the store. The driver exited and pulled a gas can out of the bed of his truck. A moment later, the owner and the other man came out of the store carrying something. DJ watched the three of them walk a few feet toward him and set down their payloads. The owner reached down and removed a cover to his underground tank. He then threaded a long hose into the hole as the driver unscrewed the top of the gas can. A moment later, the old man was turning the handle of a manual pump. DJ picked his rifle up into shooting position and aimed at the old man. He moved the rifle from man to man until he had obtained a good sight picture of each one. He wondered what the men would think if they knew someone had a rifle on them at that moment. How would the other two react if he shot one of them? They would probably crap their pants. DJ's face was almost split in two by the wide grin under his balaclava. He had to bite his lip to keep from laughing out loud.

It didn't take long to fill the can, and when they were through, the three men spoke very briefly and parted ways. When the truck left, it shined its lights right on DJ, but the men didn't notice him. He watched as the store owner carried the pump and hose back inside and then came back out with a shotgun. He secured the door with two padlocks before noisily walking across the gravel parking lot. DJ's heart began to beat louder and louder as the man got closer. He flipped the safety off and gripped his weapon tighter. The man walked within twenty feet of DJ, but he kept his light directly in front of his feet. He crossed the road to a house that sat diagonally from the front of the store. He opened the front door and called in, then sat in a chair on the porch. The vantage point was almost perfect to guard the business.

A minute later, a woman brought out a tray to the storeowner and he began to eat as she went back inside. DJ watched as the man finished his dinner with the aid of the flashlight. He finally set the tray to the side and doused the light. DJ could still see him through the goggles as if it were daytime. He saw the man pick up the shotgun and rest it across his lap. DJ scooted to a more comfortable position and continued watching.

It took a long time, but the man's head began to nod down and then jerk up suddenly. As time passed, his head would stay down longer and longer until finally it nodded down for good. DJ moved his legs slightly as he watched to make sure the store-owner wasn't going to wake up. After half an hour, he carefully stood and walked back to his camp. Once there, he got the two empty gas cans and a small pair of high-quality bolt cutters out of the trailer. With the aid of the night-vision goggles, he was able to get back to the store undetected.

The owner was still slumped over in his chair across the street. It was so dark that DJ doubted the man would be able to see him even if he did wake up. He put the cans down next to the tank cover and walked to the back of the store. These doors were padlocked top and bottom just like the front doors. DJ took the bolt cutters and put them on the top lock. As quietly as he could, he pushed the handles together. With some effort, the lock gave way. It made a metallic snapping noise as it broke.

DJ peeked around the corner. The owner was still sleeping. DJ felt that if he had attacked the locks on the front, the man might have heard. He returned to the back doors and cut the bottom lock off. He entered the store and found the manual pump. It was a little unwieldy for one person, but he was able to get it out to the tank. He removed the cover, stuck the long hose down into the tank, and began to pump the gas into his cans.

When he was changing from the first can to the second, the short hose hit the empty can on the side, sounding like a bass drum. DJ froze and looked across the street. His heart skipped a beat when the man moved, but he only shifted in his chair, never looking up. DJ finished filling the second can. He capped both of them and then carried them behind the store. He returned to get the pump and lugged it back into the building. Walking up to the cash register, he found a pen and a notepad. He scribbled down: "For ten gallons of gas and two padlocks." Then he set the hundred-dollar bill Jacob had given him on the counter and put the note on top. He walked out the back and closed the doors. Picking up the bolt cutters, he made his way back to camp and started his ride.

This was the most dangerous part of his plan. He had to get the bike past the sleeping guard and load the gas without waking the man up. He drove slowly, the engine on his quad at little more than an idle. Watching each house as he passed it, he saw no sign that anyone was aware of his presence, but his heart was beating in trepidation nonetheless. As he got within sight of the man on the porch, he stopped and watched him for a couple of minutes. Satisfied that he was still sleeping soundly, DJ pulled the big bike behind the store and quietly loaded the gas onto his trailer. He now had plenty of gas to make it to his hideaway. He smiled as he climbed back on the quad and pulled onto the road.

The hot sun shined through the window and onto Gabe's face. His eyes blinked open, and he tried to straighten himself in the chair. His hand went to his neck and rubbed the muscles that had tightened up from sleeping slumped over. He realized that his neck hurt worse than his head did. That almost never happened. He looked at the bottle. It wasn't even half-empty. That, too, was rare. He made his way into the bathroom, and when he tried to turn on the light, the events of yesterday came back to him. He grabbed a few aspirin tablets, but when he turned on the faucet, only a dribble of water came out. *Of course*, he thought, *no power for the pump.* He choked down three aspirins without water and then brushed his teeth. He would have climbed into a hot shower to relax his stiff muscles, but that wasn't possible.

He put his hands down on the counter and leaned into the mirror. "Well, Gabe, the world just handed you a big shit sandwich to eat," he said to the reflected face. "But then, what else is new?"

He walked back into the living room, his body telling him to pour another drink. He reached for the whiskey, but the sight of the empty spot on the wall stopped him. He spotted the framed picture lying facedown, glass shards covering the floor all around it. Gabe shook the broken pieces of glass off it. Turning it over, he was comforted to see that the picture itself wasn't damaged.

It was Gabe's favorite picture of them. They'd all three gone to the beach and had a wonderful time. Gabe had taken the photograph himself shortly before Hannah and Michael left. Gabe was no photographer, but it was one of those one-in-a-million shots. The sun was low in the sky, and the light reflected off them like the seraphim. It was the way he remembered them most. They were smiling and happy, a son wrapped in a mother's loving arms.

Gabe's eyes blurred and his lungs wouldn't work. He turned to look at the bottle. *No*, he told himself. He had to clean this mess up first. He knew it would never happen, but he tried to keep the place nice in case they ever came back to him. There would be plenty of time for drinking later. He carefully placed the glassless picture frame on the table and got to work. After he'd disposed of the larger pieces of glass in a bucket, he went to the closet to get the vacuum cleaner. As his grip tightened around the handle, he realized it wouldn't work without electricity. His shoulders slumped even more as he returned to his bucket and picked up the rest of the broken pieces.

CHAPTER 8

D J woke and looked at his watch. It was midafternoon. He hadn't slept this long since he'd left home. Now that he had gas, his mind was at ease. He'd only been able to drive for a little over an hour after getting the gas the previous night. The thought of the store owner finding the hundred-dollar bill and the note DJ had left brought a smile to his face. He imagined the man stomping around, fuming at how his gas had been taken right from under his nose.

Although he hadn't gone far before daylight threatened to creep up on him, DJ had found a good hiding place in an old deserted barn. He'd easily make it to the bridge tonight, and, once across the river, he'd reach his hideout in just a couple of days. He fixed himself a large celebratory lunch and tore ravenously through the food. Somehow it tasted better than it had before.

He pulled out his maps and identified his location. It was only twelve miles or so to the bridge. Given the two-lane road it took across the river, DJ figured the bridge probably was on the small side, but as long as it wasn't jammed with some monumental wreck, it should get him across.

DJ paced from one end of the barn to the other. He looked outside each time he got to the doors. The sky was gray this afternoon, and it looked as if it might rain. He hoped the weather would hold up, but if it was going to rain, he wanted it to happen soon so that it would pass by nightfall. He thought about stringing his hammock up between a couple of the large beams that supported the barn, but he didn't think he could be still long enough to get any rest. Excitement coursed through his body. He did some push-ups and sit-ups, but they did little to calm him. He returned to his pacing, staring out at the darkening sky on each loop and willing himself not to look at his watch.

Gabe had thrown the broken glass into the trash, vowing to pick up a new frame next time he went into town. He returned to the picture to check again that it was okay. Hannah's happy face briefly brought a smile to his lips. She was the love of his life. Ten years younger than Gabe, she had swept him off his feet. Her family didn't like him, especially now. They'd tried to talk Hannah out of marrying the older man, but she had assured them that the love she felt was forever. After Michael was born, things seemed to get better with her family. God, how he missed them. Gabe was just about to pour another glass of whiskey when he heard a truck door slam.

He looked out the window and spotted Jane Walker coming toward his trailer. He wondered what she wanted now. A second later, he heard the knock. Gabe set the bottle down and opened the door.

There she stood. He said nothing.

Her nose scrunched up. "Have you been drinking?" she asked.

"Some," he mumbled.

"Are you drunk?"

Gabe shook his head. "No, not really. Why?"

"Because Robby and I need to go to town and get a few things. The way things are, I thought it would be safer if a man went with us. I figured you could probably use some things, too," she said.

"You don't want me."

"It's not about want. It's about need. Now, go change your clothes and put on some cologne or something. I don't want my boy smelling alcohol on you."

Gabe hung his head and trudged into his bedroom. He didn't know why, but somehow he was compelled to do as the woman said. He gargled some mouthwash, applied a generous portion of Aqua Velva to his body, and put on clean clothes. When he walked back into the living room, he found Jane looking at the picture.

When she saw him, she put the picture back down where she'd found it. The old look, the one Gabe hated, was back in her eyes. He gazed down at the floor. She walked up to him, a little closer than he was comfortable with. He heard her sniff.

"That's better," she said. "Let's go."

Gabe followed her out the door, locking it behind him. He climbed into the passenger seat as the teenage boy scooted into the middle. The young teen's eyes held the hatred and disgust to which Gabe had grown accustomed. No one said a word as Jane drove them into town.

When they pulled into the parking lot of the small local grocer, Gabe was surprised at how full the lot was. Jane found an empty space on the far edge of the lot and parked. The trio got out of the truck and walked toward the store. A long line extended from the entry door around to the side of the store. In front of the exit door was a table with two men and a sheriff's deputy standing beside it. It seemed to be the checkout station. A young couple was first in that line. One of the men was taking their items out of the basket and calling off prices to the other man, who had a calculator in his hand. The deputy was watching intently, and every once in a while, he'd look nervously around the parking lot. A second deputy was pushing an empty cart out of the lot and toward the entry door.

There were two hand-painted signs posted on the front of the store, close to the entryway. The one with the biggest lettering said $50 LIMIT PER HOUSEHOLD. CASH ONLY. As they got closer, Gabe could read the other. It said ALL FOOD IS FIRST COME, FIRST SERVED. NO FIGHTING. ANYONE CAUSING ANY PROBLEM WILL BE ASKED TO LEAVE WITHOUT ANYTHING. NO EXCEPTIONS.

"Do you see the sign, Mom? You think people are fighting over the food?" Robby asked.

"I don't know, son. What do you think, Mr. Horne?"

Gabe just shrugged. Her face looked disappointed when he didn't speak. "Maybe," he said quietly. "People fight over stupid stuff all the time."

"That's true," the boy said as he turned and looked at his mother. Gabe saw the look on the young man's face and wondered if he was referring to some of the fights Gabe had had when he was drunk. Gabe was infamous for some of the brawls he'd caused in this sleepy little town.

The three got into line and waited. Jane kept trying to make small talk, but Gabe kept his answers to one or two words. Finally when she asked him what he planned to buy, he'd had enough.

"Look, I agreed to come with you, but I don't want to play twenty questions," he said rudely. The hurt and disappointment returned to her face. She turned to the front of the line with her back to him. Gabe was thankful for the reprieve.

Over the next half hour, he overheard others in line discussing the state of things. One man was talking about the gas station rationing fuel. He said that just like the fifty-dollar limit here at the grocery, the station was only allowing ten gallons per vehicle and wasn't letting anyone put gas in fuel cans. A woman mentioned that her husband went to the gun store to buy her a shotgun for self-defense, but that the shop wasn't selling any guns. Others talked of crimes and shortages, but most of it sounded like rumor to Gabe.

Finally they rounded the corner of the store and they were only ten or twelve people from the door. As they were nearing the entrance, one of the deputies came over to the line. "When they give you a basket and a flashlight, you can go in. We have men inside, so no fighting. If you start any trouble, you'll be escorted out of the store without your food. Understand?"

The deputy looked up and down the line as people nodded. When he saw Gabe, he stared at him for a minute. Gabe wasn't sure if he knew who he was, or if he was trying to figure it out. The deputy continued. "The store is expecting a delivery in a couple of days, so if they're out of something you need, you can come back next week. Remember, you can only buy fifty dollars' worth, and they are only taking cash."

The deputy gave Gabe one last look and walked back over to the checkout table. Very shortly thereafter, Mrs. Walker and her son went into the store. Two minutes later, Gabe was given a basket and a flashlight. He entered the store and looked around. There was enough light from the windows in the front to see down the aisles, but not enough to make out exactly what was on the shelves. Gabe pushed his cart down an aisle and shined his flashlight onto the items. He saw that the store had gotten out their old pricing guns and marked everything. Bar codes and scanners were of no use without electricity.

He had all the vegetables he could eat at home, so he passed on everything in the canned fruits and vegetables row except for some peaches. He grabbed some sugar and flour because it seemed as if he should. There wasn't any salt left, though he did find some pepper. The dried goods were almost all gone. All the large bags of rice were gone, but he did get two small bags. The only pasta left was angel hair, and he bought three one-pound packages. He found some jars of pasta sauce. They weren't his favorite, but he bought three anyway. There wasn't any bread, milk, or fresh meat. The canned meat was well picked over, too. He was almost sad to see there was no Spam left. He found some off-brand soup and put twenty cans in his basket. He looked for batteries, but they were out. The only candles he could find were the expensive, aroma type, so he passed on them. There were a few cans of grape juice on a shelf, and he got them. He looked for cheese, but to no avail. Figuring that there wasn't much else he needed, he pushed his basket into the checkout line.

When the lady in front of him started to check out, she asked the clerk if they had any diapers. The man said they expected some on the next truck, but that they'd go fast. He suggested that if she needed any baby products, she should come early on Monday. He called out her prices, and before her basket was empty, the calculator man stopped the price caller.

"That's already fifty-two eighty-six," the man said.

"You'll have to stop here," the other man said.

"Oh, okay. I really need the rest of the stuff in the basket. Can you add it in, and then let me take some other things out?"

The calculator man rolled his eyes. "Look, lady, we've got a lot of people to check out. The world doesn't revolve around you, you know?"

The woman shrank. Her face looked as if she had been unexpectedly punched in the gut.

"It'll just take a minute, Joe," the price caller reasoned. "Besides, it's not like we haven't done it for others."

"All right," the younger man said, with exasperation in his voice.

Gabe saw the lady mouth the words "thank you" to the price caller, who had MIKE printed on his name tag. He hurriedly called out the last items, and Joe declared the total at just over fifty-nine dollars. The woman started picking items off the table, and Joe deducted them until she was under fifty dollars. She paid him, and he made her change out of a cigar box. The second deputy pushed the cart to her car.

Gabe started unloading his basket, and Mike began calling prices. It didn't take long for him to finish, and Joe called out his total.

"Forty-two sixty-one. Mister, you're the first one today who didn't go over or right to the fifty-dollar mark," he said. "I'd like to shake your hand."

Gabe waved his hand at the man as if it was nothing. He paid, got his change, and then one of the deputies grabbed his cart.

"That's okay, Deputy, I can take it," Gabe said. He wondered if he'd ever met this deputy before.

"All right, but I have to bring the cart back anyway," the peace officer said as he fell in step next to Gabe. As they made their way to the truck, the deputy lowered his voice and spoke. "You're Gabriel Horne, right?"

Gabe nodded.

"I'm just a reserve deputy, so I don't know what the deal is, but Jack Harris over there, he's a regular deputy—doesn't seem to like you much. He told me that if you caused any trouble, he'd run you in. You don't want to go to jail right now, Mr. Horne. It's just about standing room only. We're starting to get some troublemakers out of the city, and you know how small the jail is. We can usually barely fit the local boys."

"Thanks for the warning," Gabe said quietly.

When they reached the truck, Gabe put his bags in the bed and gave the cart to the reserve deputy. He stood beside the truck and watched as the lawman pushed the basket back to the entrance of the store. A few minutes later, Mrs. Walker came out of the store and got into the checkout line. The same deputy grabbed her cart and started pushing it toward the truck.

When they had almost reached the truck, a ruckus broke out on the other side of the parking lot. The deputy turned and dashed over to the trouble. Gabe saw someone moving up behind Mrs. Walker and Robby from between some cars. The man, whom Gabe recognized as a fellow lowlife, pushed the woman away from the cart and grabbed the handle. Robby tried to catch his mother, and, while he probably broke her fall, the two of them ended up in a heap. The thief was pushing the cart for all he was worth toward Gabe and looking over his shoulder to see if the lawmen had noticed. As he got closer, Gabe stepped out from between the truck and the car next to it. He extended his arm at ninety degrees from his body and the basket-jacker turned his head just in time to see the clothesline catch him in the throat.

The man's eyes got wide as his feet flew out from under him. The basket was still traveling on its own as the man crashed down onto the asphalt. The impact knocked the wind out of him, and he looked like a goldfish that had jumped out of its fishbowl.

Jane and Robby picked themselves up and ran over to Gabe. "Are you all right?" she asked.

"Fine," Gabe said. "You?"

"Just a little scraped up. Thanks for saving our groceries."

"No problem."

Robby ran after the basket and was pushing it back when Deputy Harris came running up. He grabbed Gabe's arm and swung him onto the trunk of a car. Twisting the arm behind its owner, he reached for the handcuff case on his belt.

"Deputy, you have the wrong man," Jane said. "The man who tried to steal our groceries is lying right there." She pointed at the man on the ground, who had a dazed look on his face and was trying pathetically to get up. "Mr. Horne here just stopped him."

The deputy turned and looked at her without relinquishing his grip on Gabe. "Are you sure?"

"Yes, sir," she said. "Mr. Horne's with us. He's our friend."

*   *   *

The rain started around four. Light at first, it increased until it became a steady, monotonous shower. DJ had strung up his hammock and tried to read, though he was unable to focus on the book. His mind kept obsessing over how long the rain would last and how much further behind schedule it would throw him. The constant sound of the rain on the tin roof, a sound he normally liked, only served to taunt him. He felt as if the rain were sucking the energy out of his body. After what seemed an eon of tossing and turning, he fell into a fitful sleep.

When he woke up, it was almost dark. The rain was still coming down, not quite as hard as before, but steadily. DJ fixed some dinner and poked at the meal. When would this damn rain stop? He spent some time going over his quad, though he knew it was fine. He recalculated his fuel range and now had plenty, even if he had to take another major detour. Looking over his new route on the map, he determined that it was still his best option. After an hour or so of piddling around, he decided to get some more sleep.

He awoke with a start. What was that? He looked around, but it was pitch-black. He listened but didn't hear anything. Then he smiled. The rain had stopped. That's what had wakened him. He walked to the door and looked out. The sky was clearing, and he could see the stars. Looking at his watch, he saw that it was two thirty. He might not make a lot of distance, but at least he'd get over the river. He felt well rested, and he was excited to get going. He hurriedly packed his stuff and readied himself for the ride.

Climbing onto the big four-wheeler, he pulled out of the barn and traversed the muddy field to the road. It was cooler than he'd expected, but it felt good. Once he got on the road that would take him over the river, he pulled out a jacket and put it on. He increased his speed some and soon could see the bridge ahead. There were a few cars stopped on it, but he could easily zigzag around them. He smiled.

As he approached, he slowed slightly so he could weave through the cars. He twisted the handlebars from side to side with a big grin. It was fun snaking through the stalled vehicles, and he applied a little more throttle to test his prowess on the big bike. The tires produced a small screech as the weight shifted from side to side. About halfway across, it occurred to DJ that the cars were more evenly spaced than would have seemed natural. It appeared as if someone might have strategically placed the vehicles where a car or truck could pass, but only at a reduced speed. The quad was able to move through them more quickly, but he wondered if it would be quick enough. Was this a trap? He stopped the four-wheeler to try to ascertain just that.

The answer came a split second later when he heard an engine crank and saw a truck pull up next to the last car on the bridge. A knot formed in his stomach. He quickly turned to look behind him. If they had a car on each end, he was a sitting duck. Nothing was moving behind him. He breathed a small sigh of relief.

The engine on the truck shut off, and he heard two doors slam.

"You, on the bridge, we know you're there," a voice called. It was vaguely familiar to DJ. "This is our bridge. You have to pay a toll to cross."

DJ quickly weighed his options. He could turn around and find another way. He had the gas to do it, but what if he ran into the same situation at the next bridge? How much further behind would that put him? The longer he stayed out here on the road, the more dangerous things would get. Turning around might be a good backup plan, but he wanted to cross here if at all possible.

He could fight his way across. There was a chance he might get hurt, but there were probably just two or three guys guarding the bridge. All of a sudden, he knew where he recognized the voice from. It was one of the rednecks from the store—one of the men who had wanted to trade the watch for gasoline. If it was just those two, DJ could take them out easily. After all, he was a security specialist, and they were just a couple of yahoos. Creating a ruckus was the last thing he wanted to do, though, and there was always the chance that they had more guys than he could easily dispatch.

The last option he could think of was just to pay them. Maybe they didn't want much. It seemed foolish not to try this avenue at least, he reasoned, even though it could still be a trap.

"How much to cross?" DJ shouted.

"What have you got?" the redneck called back.

"I've got about twenty bucks," DJ said.

Laughter came from the other side. DJ listened closely and only heard two men. "Buddy, you could have twenty thousand bucks, and it wouldn't be enough. Haven't you been watching the news? Money's worthless unless you need to start a fire or wipe your ass." The man laughed at his joke. "We want something we can use."

"What did you have in mind?" DJ asked.

"Gas is good."

DJ thought for a moment. Other than his firearms and his quad, there was nothing more valuable to him than the gas. Still, if he could get by on two or three gallons, it would be worth it. "I might have a couple of gallons I could spare."

"Two gallons? I don't think so. The least I'd be willing to take is ten."

The irony that these guys wanted the same amount of gas DJ had taken from the store last night wasn't lost on him. It occurred to DJ that if this was a trap, they'd have just agreed to the two gallons and then tried to take whatever they wanted. He relaxed some and tried another tactic.

"How about an ounce of gold?" he called out.

"How about ten?"

Crap, don't these bumpkins know any number besides ten?

DJ decided that bargaining with these hooligans wasn't going to work. He'd go back down the road some and then decide what to do. "I don't think so. I'll just turn around and go back."

"Then we have a problem. You see, you're already on our bridge, so you owe us a toll no matter which way you go."

Now DJ was mad. Who did these idiots think they were? DJ reached down and grabbed the pistol grip on his rifle. He'd show them. As he began to remove the weapon from the scabbard, more rational thoughts took over. They were probably ready for that. Better to do this on his terms. The old truck they were driving didn't look too fast. He could be gone by the time they made it across the bridge.

"Okay, I'll give you the gas," DJ said. He hit the starter on the eight-hundred-cc engine and backed up from the car he'd been using to hide behind. When he had enough clearance, he whipped the bike and trailer around and made his way off the bridge as fast as he could. At the end of the bridge, he realized that, with his night-vision goggles, he was going too fast to see anything in the road in time to stop. He thought about turning on his headlight, but that would give his position away. He'd just come this way, so it should be safe, unless a cow or something had wandered into his path. It was a chance he'd just have to take. Looking down at the speedometer, he saw that he was already over sixty miles per hour. The big quad continued to accelerate. At this speed, it was really cold, but DJ kept his mind on the task at hand.

He would travel at high speed until he could find a side road. Since he'd spent so much time examining the maps, he was pretty sure that the nearest road was about a mile and a half away. He glanced down at the red needle; it was pointing at seventy-five. As he looked at his GPS, it seemed as if his estimation of how far it was to the first turnoff was accurate. It would only take a little over a minute to get there. He glanced over his shoulder. The truck's lights were on, and he could see the beams weaving through the cars on the bridge. If those guys had been smart, they'd have blocked off both ends, he thought.

DJ made out the road coming up on his right. He let off the throttle and prepared to turn. Looking back, he saw the headlights of the old truck—one bright and one dim—way behind him. Would they expect him to turn at the first intersection? If he was one of them, he would. Deciding that he'd better continue past the first road, he hit the throttle again and strained his eyes to see the next turnoff.

Thirty seconds later, he saw a road on the left side, but he was going so fast that he couldn't slow down in time to turn onto it. He looked at the GPS again, but the road didn't show on the screen. It was probably new or not important enough. He glanced over his shoulder. The truck was a little closer now. He had to find a turnoff quickly, or they'd be on him. The GPS showed the next road in a mile.

He finally saw the road sign and squeezed the brake lever hard, bleeding off his speed. He turned hard to the right and accelerated to a comfortable speed. The road was dirt, but that didn't bother the quad. He kept looking over his shoulder, and a few seconds later, the pursuing truck sped past. DJ blew a long breath out and realized that he had a death grip on the handlebars. He took his thumb off the throttle, and the big bike coasted to a stop. DJ shook out his arms.

He wondered what his next move would be. He could turn around and try to go across the bridge before the rednecks gave up on chasing after him, but if there were more than two of them, and some had stayed behind, they'd shoot first this time. No, he'd look for a place to camp and wait until tomorrow night. He'd creep quietly across the bridge and be past them before they knew what was happening. And if he had to shoot at them to keep them from blocking him off, he'd do that, too.

He resumed his course down the road. It seemed to go on forever, running between fields and not intersecting any other roads. The farther he went, the narrower and rougher it became. He wondered if it was going to end up as a cow path. Since it was so uneven, DJ kept his speed down. He scanned back and forth for a good hideout, but there were only fields and pastures. An old barn or any little copse would work for him this far off the beaten path, but he couldn't find anything.

Then he noticed that the white tops of the metal fence posts were flashing in a not-so-rhythmic pattern. Looking back, he saw the cockeyed lights of the pickup closing fast.

CHAPTER 9

DJ hit the throttle on the big quad. His mind raced as he tried to figure out how the rednecks had found him. He pushed his goggles up and turned on his headlight. It would have been impossible to stay on the bike at full speed on a bumpy road like this with the night vision. As the bike passed sixty miles per hour, DJ looked behind him. The rednecks were still closing. He could see by their headlights that the potholes in the dirt road were making the truck bounce violently all over the place. However, the driver seemed to have little regard for the damage it might be causing his vehicle.

Even though DJ had the throttle lever pushed down completely, he found himself putting more pressure on it. The quad was now starting to pull some air on the bigger bumps, and he could feel the trailer's weight acting as an anchor as it returned to the ground after each aerial event. This was an unsafe speed, he knew, but slowing down wasn't an option.

He looked for a way out. The fences on each side were barbed wire. They would cut him to ribbons if he tried to drive through them. He could only try to outrun his pursuers. He wanted to look back, but at over seventy miles per hour, he had to keep his eyes forward. "Come on, baby. Give me just a little more," he urged the Polaris.

Headlights finally engulfed DJ and he realized that he wouldn't be able to outrun the truck. He wondered if they were going to shoot at him. He instinctively flattened his body against the quad. There was nothing else he could do. Then he felt a nudge and heard metal-to-metal contact. A second later, the truck pushed the trailer again, harder this time. DJ's mind raced for solutions, but none came. He could bail off the quad, but if the impact with the ground didn't kill him, getting run over by the truck would. He squeezed the sides of his ride with his knees as a horseman would his mount. "Hold on tight" was all that kept running through his mind.

The truck was making harder and harder contact with the trailer. The impacts would give DJ a push and some space, but it never lasted longer than a few seconds. He felt like a mouse being played with by a cat. Finally the truck hit the trailer hard enough that the bumper climbed on top of it and got stuck. The driver hit his brakes at the unexpected result. DJ felt the bike being pulled down by the weight of the bigger vehicle. *This is it*, he thought. *I'm a goner.*

The hitch coupling gave way under the enormous strain. DJ felt the quad rocket forward like a rodeo bull finally released from the gate. The headlights of the truck started making wider and wider arcs to the sides as the truck skidded wildly down the road. Suddenly, the lights disappeared from DJ's view. He sneaked a quick peek back and saw the truck plowing through the pasture on his right side. He felt the muscles in his face tighten and his vision turned red. "Those assholes are going to pay," he promised himself.

He slammed the brakes on the big quad and slid it to a stop. Grabbing the grip on his rifle, he pulled it out of the scabbard and brought it to his shoulder in one smooth motion. His thumb flicked the safety off as his finger found the trigger. In a split second, his tritium-powered scope was centered on the truck and he was unleashing the .22-caliber projectiles as fast as his finger could twitch.

The truck driver was still fighting for control of his vehicle when several bullets stitched across the windshield. DJ heard the engine rev up on the truck, and it seemed to regain its purpose as it barreled away from the gunfire. Finished with the first thirty round magazine, DJ quickly changed to a fresh one and sent several more rounds of encouragement toward the retreating pickup. The truck went a couple of hundred yards and then ran back through the fence and onto the road. DJ watched until the small circular taillights disappeared from his sight.

For the next several minutes, DJ leaned against the quad's handlebars, his mind in a fog. He could feel his heart pounding like a bass drum, and he had to constantly swallow in order to fight the urge to empty his stomach. His left heel jumped up and down in reaction to all the adrenaline pouring through his bloodstream. He tried to stop the movement, but his foot seemed to belong to someone else. After several more minutes, his heart beat slowed to a mere gallop, and he was able to unclench his fist from around the pistol grip of the rifle. His fingers felt like ice, in spite of his insulated riding gloves. DJ flexed them to try to restore some feeling.

He replaced the partially used magazine in his rifle and then returned it to its scabbard. Removing the flashlight from his pocket, he looked at the back of his quad. Nothing looked damaged or amiss, other than the missing trailer. He motored over to where the truck had gone through the fence the first time. There lay his precious trailer in the shallow ditch that ran beside the road. It looked more like an accordion than a trailer. Parts of it and its cargo were scattered across the ditch. DJ could feel the hot blood returning to his head as the realization of what this meant sank in. His rigid body seemed to melt, as his head hung and his shoulders sagged. How could he carry all of his stuff without the trailer? How would he make it without all of his carefully assembled gear? He sat and pondered those questions for a long time.

Finally he began to collect his stuff. First he looked for his firearms. The rifle case was dirty but undamaged, and he opened it up to find that his rifles were fine. The pistol case was crushed on one corner, but the contents were intact, except for one ruined magazine. His shotgun, however, hadn't fared so well. It had been run over by the truck. Both barrels were noticeably bent, and he wasn't sure if the receiver had any damage or not.

Then he gathered the jerry cans of gasoline. The empty one was only dinged up a little, but two of the full jerry cans had split open on the seam. Now he had only five gallons of fuel, besides what was already in the quad. He'd have to find more somehow. As he fought the urge to just plop down in the middle of the field, he wondered if he'd ever get to his destination.

Almost all his dried goods were trashed, but most of the canned food was still good. The aluminum poles for his tent were bent beyond repair, and his cook stove was totaled. Jacob's son's chain saw had come out of the case on impact; it was packed with dirt and debris and DJ suspected that it would no longer work. DJ threw the unusable gear into one pile and prioritized the rest, strapping items onto the racks of his quad.

The firearms and gas were easy to place, even if they did sit higher than he would have liked. He had to make some choices on ammo. He left the shotgun ammo behind since he no longer had a working scattergun. What he had the most of was the ammo for his carbine, so he decided to take half of it. He took all of the ammo for his bolt-action rifle and the rimfire rifle, but he only took the pistol ammo for his main sidearm. He found a spot for a little of the food that had been on the trailer. He still had five or six days' worth between his emergency pack and the MREs already on the quad. His sleeping bag, tool kit, and gravity-fed water filter took up the rest of the available space. He looked at the things he was going to leave behind and sighed. He could do without them, but he hated the idea of leaving behind things he could use.

Well, I'll be damned if I'm going to leave them here for someone to take, he thought. He looked across the road and saw that the cornfield there wasn't planted all the way to the fence. There was a path wide enough for a tractor to turn around between the crops and the property line. DJ dug out his folding shovel and climbed over the fence. The ground was hard, and the digging was strenuous, but he finally had a deep enough hole to bury the usable items he couldn't take. Carrying them across the fence and covering them only took a fraction of the time it took to dig the hole. DJ packed the dirt in as tightly as he could and camouflaged the mound to the best of his ability. He saved the location in his GPS with the hope that he'd be able to come back one day to retrieve the cache. The pile of worthless gear and the hole in the fence were the only signs of what had happened.

Back on his quad, he returned to the bridge. This time he pulled the quad off the road on the side of the overpass and hid it. Taking his carbine, he crept from car to car, looking and listening at each stop for anyone manning the roadblock. He hoped the rednecks were here. If he found anyone, he wouldn't give them the chance to deter him this time. Retribution would be fast and merciless; he didn't care what the law had to say. DJ had bent a few laws when he was younger, and a couple of them had landed him in some mild trouble, but what he had in mind now would have been unthinkable under normal circumstances. But what was heretofore unthinkable was now necessary. That's just the way things were. The world had turned hard, and he'd just have to be harder.

He finally got to the other side and saw that the bridge was clear. A few minutes later, the river that had caused him so many problems was now in his wake. He hardly noticed, as he was still brooding about his latest shortage of gasoline and the loss of much of his gear.

Gabe woke up and immediately knew something was amiss. His brain raced, trying to figure out what was wrong. It took several seconds for him to realize that he simply wasn't used to waking up this early on a Saturday, and certainly not without a hangover. He couldn't recall why he hadn't had anything to drink last night.

Jane Walker had insisted that he eat dinner with them. He was amazed at how well the woman was dealing with life without electricity. She had oil lamps, running water, and even a wood-stove. She wasn't using it yet, but winter was coming. He'd wondered how she'd come to have these things, but he hadn't asked. In fact, he hadn't said much at all last night. Robby had blathered on and on about how Gabe had stopped the thief and how cool it had been. Jane had said thank you about a million times, but Gabe had kept quiet. He had eaten, expressed his gratitude with a mumbled "thanks," and gone home.

He lay back down for a moment, thinking about the events of yesterday. He was glad Jane had been there. Otherwise, he would have been in jail. Deputy Harris might have reacquainted Gabe with his nightstick, too. Gabe's hands felt up and down his ribs. It had seemed like forever before the purple circles had gone away. Even though it was more than a year ago, Gabe thought he could still feel the slightest tenderness in those spots. He hadn't had a drink in town since, because he certainly didn't want to relive that experience. It had been bad, even in the semiconscious state he'd been in at the time.

Pushing those unpleasant memories out of his mind, he got out of bed and put on his clothes from yesterday. He scrunched up his nose at the strange mixture of alcohol-laced sweat and Aqua Velva. After he pulled on his boots, he grabbed a clean bucket and went outside. The air was heavy, and he noticed some dark clouds on the horizon. He made his way behind his shed, where he had a rainwater collection system that fed into fifty-five-gallon barrels. He normally used it to water his garden between rains. Scooping up a full bucket, he carried it back into the kitchen. It had some small particles floating in it, and he wondered how he could get them out. He knew he could boil the water to purify it, but that wouldn't rid it of the floaters. He saw the coffeepot on the counter, and an idea came to him.

He grabbed a coffee filter out of the cabinet and duct-taped one side of it to the bucket underneath the spout. Then, by tipping the bucket and holding the other side of the filter, he was able to fill a large pan with water while keeping the particles trapped in the filter. He lit the old propane stove with a match and set the pot on a burner. It finally started boiling, and he let it go for five minutes. When he took it off, he poured about half of the water into a large bowl and took the rest into the bathroom. He poured it into the basin. While it was cooling, he got some clean clothes and stripped off the dirty ones. The water was still too hot for him to leave his finger in for more than a second or two.

He thought about how long the water in his barrels would last. He needed water to wash his clothes, cook, bathe, and drink. That was probably more than three barrels would hold between rains. He'd have to figure something out. Finally the water was comfortable enough for him to take a bath. He would have preferred a shower, but he still got clean. Donning fresh clothes, he felt ready to take on the day.

He headed outside and started working on his garden. Before long, it began to rain, and he quickly jumped at the chance to gather more water. He grabbed two five-gallon buckets out of the shed and started dipping water out of the barrels. He carried them into the bathroom and poured them into the tub. When it was full, he started on the tub in the other bathroom. The barrels now close to empty, Gabe focused his efforts on gathering all the buckets he had and putting them on the back porch to fill. Stepping back inside, he noticed how cold the rain had been. He removed his clothes and hung them up to dry. He dried himself off with a towel, vigorously rubbing the goose bumps on his arms. He pulled on an old pair of sweatpants and made his way to the kitchen. The soup he'd bought at the store looked tempting, and he fixed himself a can. Sitting down with some crackers, he ate slowly. The meal warmed him up.

CHAPTER 10

The loss of the trailer and gear left DJ defeated. He hadn't been able to get any sleep worrying about how he was going to make it to his hideout. He gave up at noon and climbed out from under the poncho he'd strung up for a shelter. The rain had cooled things off some, but the air was still humid and thick. The sky was cloudy, and it looked as if it might start raining again at any moment. DJ thought about eating, but he really wasn't hungry.

He decided to try to do something useful to keep his mind occupied. He pulled out his map and started looking for a shorter route or a likely place to find some gas. DJ was staring at the map so hard an onlooker might have thought he was trying to burn a hole in it with his eyes, but his mind wouldn't focus on anything except how unfair it was that he was in this predicament. Now, with only half of his gear and not nearly enough gas, he had to come up with a new plan. One stalled train and two damn rednecks had ruined all his careful plotting and preparations. He felt the back of his neck warm up as he thought about what had happened last night. He wondered if he'd hit the rednecks with his gunfire. He hoped so. They deserved it.

He focused his attention back on the atlas, looking for any possible means to shave a few miles off his journey. There really wasn't any way and he knew it. He'd already scoured the map to the point that it was almost committed to memory. There were a few towns on the map that could have gas, though. Who knew what dangers they might hold? But they were probably his best bet. He had almost three gallons of gas in the quad, and he had one five-gallon can. If he was fortunate, that would take him two-thirds of the way to his bug-out location.

He should have reached his destination already, he thought. He considered what he could have done differently. If he hadn't stopped to help Jacob, it probably would have saved him a day, and he might have missed the rednecks on the bridge. "Like they say," he said to himself, "no good deed goes unpunished."

It started drizzling. He climbed back under the poncho and lay down on his sleeping bag. *What else can go wrong?* he wondered, as he put his hands on his head. The drizzle slowly increased to a steady rain, and he brooded over his predicament. His despair seemed to deepen as the rain fell harder and harder, until finally he dozed off.

He wasn't sure how, but even in his sleep, he could sense that something was wrong. As he slowly came back to full consciousness, he lay still and kept his eyes closed. There it was again. He heard the slightest sound of leaves crunching. A few seconds later, he heard another crunch. This time, he was able to tell that it was coming from his left, on the other side of his quad. It sounded close, but he wasn't sure. It could be a deer, a coyote or another stealthy animal, but DJ doubted it. It was probably a two-legged predator.

He cracked an eyelid the tiniest amount and moved his eyes toward the sound. He couldn't see anything, even though he heard another footstep. It was definitely approaching his quad. He opened his eyes a little more. It was still raining some, but not enough to mask the sound of footsteps. DJ slowly turned his head and looked under the quad.

Two feet in dirty, ragged athletic shoes were pointed in his direction. The quad was still hiding DJ from the intruder, but in a couple more steps, he'd be able to see over it. DJ watched the feet, and in the rustle of the intruder's next step, he unsnapped the holster on his leg. The following step allowed him to draw the big Glock pistol. When the next step came, DJ sprang to his feet as quietly as possible and pointed the pistol at the trespasser. The man, who was very thin and unshaven, was staring down at his own feet. When he looked back up and saw DJ, his eyes widened and his hands shot up over his head.

"I wasn't gonna do nothing," he said quickly. "I was just lookin' for something to eat."

"Is that so?" DJ asked. The man nodded vigorously. DJ couldn't see any weapons. He stepped around the back of the quad to get a better look at the prowler. The man appeared to be in his midthirties, but it was hard to be sure with all the grime that covered him. He had on a pair of ratty blue jeans and an old holey waist-length overcoat. He was soaked to the bone and obviously shivering. DJ figured he was probably telling the truth, but he couldn't be sure. Vagabonds were good liars. DJ was a little surprised to see one this far from the city. However, in a few weeks or months, there would be a lot of people who looked like this scarecrow.

"Do you have a weapon?" DJ demanded.

The man shook his head.

"Unzip your jacket and open it up. No sudden movements, though."

The man did as he was told.

"Now turn around, slowly."

The man hesitated. DJ saw the reluctance in his eyes.

"Do it now!" DJ yelled as he motioned with his pistol.

The man slowly spun in place, and DJ saw the knife wedged between the jeans and the belt. His nose scrunched at the sight of the weapon, and he felt his breath go hot. He closed on the man and removed the weapon from its roost. It was only a cheap kitchen knife, but it was still deadly, just as deadly as a pickup truck.

DJ threw the knife behind him. He grabbed the man by his jacket just below the neck, and the barrel of his pistol crashed down on the back of the man's head. The man crumpled, and DJ came down onto the vagabond's back with his knee. Then he dug the muzzle of his pistol into the back of the man's neck.

"No weapon, huh? Only looking for food, huh? You would have killed me in my sleep, given half a chance, wouldn't you, asshole?" DJ hissed.

"No, no, I was just looking for food! I only use the knife for defense! I wouldn't have hurt you!"

"Yeah, right." DJ grabbed the man by one of his sleeves and yanked up to turn him over. It surprised him that it was so easy. He wasn't sure if it was because the man was so thin and frail, or if he was just so angry. He stuck the big .45 in the man's face. "You would have slid your knife right between my ribs and stolen all of my stuff if you thought you'd get away with it. I ought to kill you right now."

"No, please, please. I just needed some food. I saw your tire tracks cut off of the road and followed them hoping to ask for something to eat."

"Eat this, then!" DJ shouted as he punched the man in the mouth with the pistol. He could feel the teeth break through the metal and polymer handgun. The man must have believed DJ was going to shoot, or the pain of having his teeth knocked out was too much to bear. He passed out.

DJ stood up over the man and laughed. The only thing that would have made this better was if this hobo had been one of the rednecks who had wrecked his trailer. He got a roll of duct tape and bound the man's hands together.

After quickly loading the few items he'd used for a shelter back on to the bike, he climbed on and took off. He didn't want to leave in the daylight, but if one person had found him, others could, too. As he headed back to the road, he looked over his shoulder and saw the man starting to stir. DJ expected that he might feel a little bad for what he'd done, but the feeling was more akin to elation than regret. He pressed the throttle on the big bike and roared down the road, barely noticing the rain.

Gabe was boiling water to drink and wondering what he'd do for water during the dry season. His brow furrowed as the question of how long the Smash might last occurred to him. Many items that people took for granted might be difficult to come by. The good news was that the folks out here in the country seemed able to provide more of what they had to have and get by with fewer luxuries than their city counterpoints. Even if this lasted several years, which he doubted, he could probably grow enough food to feed himself and trade for other things he needed. Of course, no one could grow water, so that was his biggest concern. If he had a generator, he could hook it up to the well and pump water whenever he needed it. He and Hannah had talked about getting one several times. It was on their list, but they'd been saving every penny they could to build the house.

They'd always dreamed of living on land like this. Fifty acres located far enough out of the city so they could really see the stars at night. A place they could grow their own food and have room for their son to roam without having to worry about gang wars and drive-by shootings.

It was when Michael had started school that they realized they had to get out of the city. Even the elementary schools weren't safe. Drug dealers hung around and would sell to any kid with the money. Gabe had been shocked that some of the fifth graders were almost as big as he was. It was no place to raise a child. They found this fifty-acre tract, but it took all the money they had saved plus the proceeds from their house in the city to buy it. They found a used mobile home that only needed minor repairs and moved it onto the property until they could save the money to build a house. Gabe, a computer programmer, had worked out a deal with his boss to work from home all but one day a week. Hannah had started a garden to help defray food costs. They'd often talked late into the night about living self-sufficiently on their own little farm. That dream had died, and, since then, Gabe had been trying to cope with being single again. He'd admit that he wasn't coping well.

Gabe pulled himself out of his memories and returned to the here and now. He wondered what the Walkers were doing for water. Jane hadn't said. He wondered if they had a generator. She seemed calmer about the whole situation than he would have expected a single mother to be. If she had a generator, how was she fixed for gas? How long would it last? Could they get more? Every question made him think of two more.

Gabe noticed that his mind was clearer than it had been in the last few years. This "Smash" situation was obviously not good, and it had the potential to get nasty. His brain raced back to what had happened at the store. The lawlessness he'd left behind in the city was suddenly rearing its ugly head out here in the country, too. One of the deputies had told him they were having problems with the city folk. If things continued to slide, there would be more and more people leaving the cities. Those folks would be desperate and might do anything for food, water, and shelter. Many of them would fall prey to the vile scoundrels society kept at bay most of the time. Others would join the ranks of the wicked just to survive. One thing was sure, with the veneer of civilization gone, these predators would take whatever they wanted, however they wanted. The possibility sent shivers down Gabe's back. He couldn't bear the thought of something happening to Jane or Robby. A mother and son would need protection and he'd do whatever he could to make sure nothing bad befell them.

He walked to his bedroom and opened the closet door. Digging through the dress clothes he no longer wore, he found what he wanted. The lever-action rifle had been a gift from Hannah. He hadn't touched it since she'd left, and it was covered in dust. He opened the bottom drawer of his dresser and fished out a cleaning kit and two and a half boxes of ammunition for the rifle. Gabe contemplated where he could find more ammo.

His revolver was also in the dresser, along with a full box of cartridges. He took both firearms and the cleaning kit to the kitchen. Spreading some old newspaper on the table, he began the process of restoring the weapons to serviceable condition. After he finished with them, he found his dad's old shotgun and both of the .22 rifles. Gabe's father had bought one of the rifles for him when he was ten years old. The other he'd bought for Michael. It was still new in the box. He cleaned his .22 and the shotgun. Michael's gun was still spotless, although it needed a little oil. Then Gabe did a quick ammo check. He had lots of .22 shells, but only a couple of boxes of bird shot for the shotgun. He also found half a box of .357 Magnum ammo for his wheel gun with the shotgun shells.

Gabe found the holster for his revolver and threaded it onto his belt. He stuck the stainless steel gun into the leather holster and looked at himself in the mirror. It struck him how thin he was. The revolver stuck out conspicuously on his narrow frame. He'd previously thought of himself as a Marshal Dillon type, but he had to admit that he looked more like another one of television's legendary lawmen. "Where's your bullet, Barney?" he asked himself in the mirror with a smile. It quickly disappeared as he realized how long it had been since he'd used those facial muscles.

Deciding that the holster looked a little silly, Gabe removed it. There might come a time when he'd need to wear a gun when he left the house, but not yet. He put the gun into a soft, zippered pouch. He could keep that close without looking ridiculous.

He walked back into the kitchen, picked up the lever-action, and loaded the tube magazine. He left the chamber empty for safety's sake and walked out to his truck. He stuck the rifle into the scabbard built into the front of the saddlecloth seat cover. It kept the rifle out of sight, but it was easy to draw the weapon as long as the door was open.

Gabe drove down to the Walker place. As he pulled into the drive, he saw Jane step out through the front door. She had on an apron and was drying her hands on a dish towel. For a split second, she reminded him of Hannah, but he pushed that thought quickly out of his mind.

"Mr. Horne, what a surprise," she said. "I was just starting to cook dinner. Would you care to join us?"

Gabe was a little shocked. He hadn't noticed that it was dinnertime. Or had he? He reached out the window to open the truck door. The inside handle had been broken for some time. "No, thanks," he said, "I wouldn't want to be any trouble. I just came over to check on you and ask a few questions."

The look of pity on her face—that familiar look Gabe couldn't stand— changed almost imperceptibly at his answer. Gabe couldn't tell for sure what this new look meant. Perhaps it was gratitude that he'd thought about them.

"It's no trouble," she said. "Why don't you come in and help me while you ask your questions?"

She turned around without waiting for an answer and walked into the house. Gabe followed her quietly. Once they were in the kitchen, she gave him a knife and some of his own champion tomatoes to slice.

"Where's Robby?"

"He's down at the pond trying to catch some perch for supper."

"That sounds good," Gabe said without thinking.

"You're welcome to join us."

"Ah, no. No, thank you. I have some stuff to do this evening," Gabe said as his face went hot.

"Suit yourself," the woman quipped with the smallest of smirks on her face. "What did you want to ask me?"

"I was mostly wondering what you were doing for water. Do you have a generator?"

"Don't I wish?" she said. "No, we have a thousand-gallon tank that the well pumped full. It's up on the hill behind the house, and it gravity-feeds the water into here. We're being very careful with it because when it's gone, I don't know what we'll do. I guess we'll have to get water out of the pond and filter it or something."

"I see," Gabe said. "How long do you think it'll last?"

"Well, Robby and I are trying to limit ourselves to ten gallons a day, but the chickens have to have water, too. I figure we have about six weeks' worth."

"Hmmm."

"Why? What are you doing?" she asked.

"I caught a bunch of rainwater yesterday. I have gutters on my shed, and they fill some water barrels. Of course, I don't have anywhere near a thousand gallons."

"That's a good idea."

"I was thinking about what else we might need if this thing doesn't get better real soon," Gabe said.

"Like what?"

"Like food and fuel."

"I was thinking about that, too," Jane said, looking him right in the eye. Gabe had never noticed that hers were hazel. He quickly looked back down at the tomatoes he was slicing. A man could lose a fingertip watching those eyes.

"I figure we'll have enough eggs to feed an army," she continued, "and we can butcher some of the chickens to eat, too. Your garden can grow lots of vegetables, and I could can some of them to get us through the winter. I'll need some lids for the jars, but I have everything else. I don't know how long the fish will hold up in the pond, but we can eat fish as long as they do. Do you know much about hunting? My ex-husband used to hunt deer some. At least, he used to go. He almost never got anything. I think it was more of an excuse to go off and be a worthless drunk without me nagging him to get a job."

Gabe's head snapped around at the words "worthless drunk." Jane noticed his reaction, and immediately her face turned crimson. Gabe tried to act as if nothing happened and went back to chopping the carrots she'd set in front of him.

"The deer hunting around here isn't the best," he said. "There are a few, but not too many. If people start to hunt them hard, they could decimate the herd in short order. What we have a lot of are feral hogs, though. I play hell keeping them out of the garden at times. I shot a few when we first moved out here, and if you cook them right, they're as good as venison. We also have lots of rabbits and squirrels. A boy with a .22 rifle could keep the whole neighborhood in meat."

"Well, I guess that's good news."

"Does Robby have a .22?"

"No. He's been asking me for one, but I don't know anything about guns, and I was scared to let him have one without getting some proper training," she said. "Could you teach him how to shoot and be safe? I'd feel a lot better about him having one then."

"I guess I could."

"Thanks. Although it really doesn't matter, I suppose," Jane said. "Even if we could find a place to buy one, Robby's dad hasn't sent any child support in over four months, and with the farmers' market shut down, I spent almost all the money I had at the store the other day."

"Well, maybe the supermarket will buy some of your eggs and my produce," Gabe said. "Why don't we drive into town tomorrow and see? Even if they don't, I have a little cash at my place. We can buy some more staples and some gas if we can get any."

Jane looked at him and smiled. "It's a date."

Gabe dropped the knife as if it were blistering hot. "I have to go," he muttered quickly.

"I'm sorry, Gabriel," Jane said. "I didn't mean it like that."

Only Hannah had called him Gabriel. It was like a second dagger in his heart.

"I know. I just have to go check on some things," Gabe said as he hurried out the door. From his truck, he could see Jane in the doorway, rubbing her hands on a dish towel as if she was debating what to do. Gabe turned the key and pumped the accelerator. It seemed to him he'd cranked the engine forever, but it wouldn't catch. Worried that he might overheat the starter motor, he let go of the key. He saw her take a step toward the truck. His heart jumped into his throat, and he couldn't swallow it back down. He mashed the gas pedal all the way to the floor and bumped the starter again. Thankfully, the truck roared to life. Gabe shoved the shifter into reverse and dumped the clutch. He could see Jane looking at him, and he gave a quick wave as he backed out onto the road.

When he got home, he grabbed for the bottle. It was still where

he left it when she'd made him go to the store with them. He real
ized she'd stopped him from drinking for a few days, and now
she'd driven him right back to the bottle. He poured four fingers
of the amber numbness. Picking up the glass, he rolled it between
his thumb and fingers.

What had scared him? Was it the fact that another human being saw him as more than just a worthless drunk? Or was it more?
Could it be that, for a day or two, he'd actually believed that he
wasn't worthless? Well, there was little doubt that he'd disappoint
whoever believed in him before long. He always had, and he always would.

CHAPTER 11

D J didn't like being out in the daylight like this. There were too many things that could go wrong. Besides that, his quad was leaving visible tracks in the muddy road. That's how the vagabond had found him and probably how the rednecks had followed him, as well. He had to find a place where he could hide for the rest of the day, preferably a place that would also protect him from the rain.

He drove down the road slowly, looking for a place to hole up and keeping a sharp eye out for trouble. Finally he spotted an open pasture with an old lean-to in the corner that might have been used for cattle or horses in the past. It was fenced off from the road, but there was a gate. DJ pulled up to the gate and saw that it was locked with an old rusty chain and padlock. He smiled. He had a way to deal with this situation.

He got his bolt cutters and used them on the chain, opposite the lock. Opening the gate, he pulled his quad into the barn and positioned it so that it wouldn't be visible from the road. Opening the small storage under the front rack, he removed a black zip tie. He walked back to the gate and saw that his quad had left some tracks. The rain would probably wash them out before long, but he couldn't take a chance.

Spotting a small tree growing along the fence line not too far from the gate, DJ broke off a medium-sized branch and used the leaf side to wipe out all the tread marks between the road and the gate. Then he closed the gate and used the zip tie to reattach the chain into its previous position. Unless a person looked hard, even if he was unlocking the gate, he'd never know that the chain had been cut. This was a procedure he'd intended to use as he went down the pipeline easement. DJ smiled at his own ingenuity.

After the gate and lock were returned as closely as possible to the condition in which he'd found them, he picked up the branch and rubbed out all of the tracks leading to the small barn. Some of the ruts were deep, and he used his boots to smooth out the gumbolike mud and then wiped out his tracks with the branch. Once back to the weathered structure, he surveyed his handiwork. It wasn't perfect, but it was very good. The rain would finish up the job in less than an hour with the way it was coming down. DJ tossed the limb beside his quad.

Turning back inside the three-sided barn, DJ busied himself with making an area to rest. The old tin roof was leaking in a few spots, but considering how hard it was raining, it was doing an admirable job of keeping the interior mostly dry. He hung his hammock up between two of the support beams and tied his poncho over the hanging bed to deflect the few drops finding their way inside. He climbed in to get some sleep but found that his excitement wouldn't let him unwind.

He'd dealt with bums like the one who had tried to mug him before. They would often try to find a spot in or around the mall to sleep or eat for free. Some of them were downright disgusting. He didn't know how anyone could live the way they did. Many times, he'd run them off, only to find them later on the other side of the huge shopping complex. He had always wanted to send a real message to the most persistent ones, much as he'd done today. However, the owners of his place of employment were worried about getting sued, so security was only allowed to use force if someone was being attacked. The rules of engagement were clear, and DJ wasn't allowed to do more than escort them off the premises unless they posed a clear and imminent threat to patrons or employees of the large establishment. The bums all knew this, and they'd come back over and over again. It always pissed DJ off.

He found himself laughing out loud. It would be a long time before that guy tried to sneak up on a victim again. DJ, despondent over the loss of his gear just a few hours ago, was almost giddy now. It wasn't that he'd really enjoyed kicking the bum's ass, even if the vagrant had it coming. It was the understanding that he was no longer bound by the rules that had once dictated his actions. He was in charge now. It was his world.

Realizing that it would be a while before he would be able to sleep, he cooked a big lunch. He was about to start eating when he heard the gunshot.

Gabe was fuming. He was mopping the kitchen floor to clean up the bourbon. This was the second time he'd thrown something in the last few days. The glass hadn't broken, but it had left a nice crescent-shaped dent in the refrigerator. That's not why he was mad, though. He didn't really know what was bothering him, but the anger had kept him from drinking, so perhaps it was a good thing.

After the mess was cleaned up, Gabe busied himself with washing his dirty clothes. He filled one side of the sink with hot water and some detergent and started scrubbing the clothes he'd worn the last two days. He began with the whites and worked his way up to his dirtier outerwear. His anger seemed to recede in relation to the dirt that ebbed out of his clothes. When he was finished rinsing the garments, he took them outside to hang on the line. The sky looked like rain, and he hoped it would hold off long enough for his clothes to dry.

His garden needed attention, and he used the last few hours of daylight to weed and harvest. Just before dark, he took the clothes off the line and noted that everything except for his jeans was dry. He hung those over the vinyl-covered chairs in the kitchen and put the rest away. Dinner was simple yet filling, and he went to bed early.

The next morning, Gabe was up with the sun. He planned to go to town, but he didn't know if Jane would still want to go with him after he'd left so quickly yesterday. He wasn't sure why what she had said bothered him so much. He knew it was just an expression and that it didn't mean anything.

He dressed and cooked breakfast. Using the stove made him wonder how much propane there was in the tank. In the summer, he only used it for the stove and the water heater and that only took a minimal amount. However, in the winter, he also heated the trailer with it. The three-hundred-gallon tank would only last a couple of months in the cold. He would check to see how much he had after breakfast.

When he was about to sit down and start eating, he heard a knock on the door. He took caution as he answered it, and was slightly taken aback when he saw Jane standing in front of him.

"Good morning," he said awkwardly.

"Good morning," she replied. She stood there for what seemed a long time.

"You want to come in?" Gabe finally asked.

"Sure," she said, stepping into the house. "That smells good."

"Just some of your eggs I scrambled up. You want some?"

"No. I was talking about the coffee."

"I'll get you a cup," Gabe said, thankful for something to do.

He walked into the kitchen and poured Jane a cup. Turning around, he was surprised to find Jane right behind him.

"Here you go," he said, extending the cup to her. "You sure you don't want some breakfast?"

"No. I already ate, but you go ahead and eat."

Gabe sat down and started to eat. Jane stood for a moment and then pulled out a chair across the table from him and sat down. He felt like a heel for not offering her a seat, but he was thankful Jane didn't say anything. It had been so long since he'd entertained any company that he wondered what else he was forgetting. He kept his eyes on his plate, devouring the eggs as if he hadn't eaten in a week. When he was finished, he pushed the plate away and saw Jane smiling at him. The look on her face made him uncomfortable.

"The coffee's good," Jane said.

"You want some more?"

"Yes, please."

Gabe got up and topped off both of their cups.

"Thanks, Gabe. Are you still planning to go to town?"

"Yeah, I guess. Did you still want to go?" he said as he scratched at an invisible stain on the table.

"Absolutely," she answered with just a little too much enthusiasm for Gabe's liking. "I want to see if I can trade my dad's old pocket watch for a .22 like you were talking about for Robby. Would you help me pick one out?"

Gabe remembered the woman at the store had mentioned that the gun store wasn't selling any firearms. Of course that might not be true, and he really didn't want to get into a long, drawn-out conversation about it with Jane, so he just nodded.

"Did you bring some eggs to sell to the grocer?" he asked.

"Yes. I have almost six gross."

"You want to take your truck or mine?" Gabe asked.

"The eggs are already in mine. Plus, I want to try to get some gas."

"Okay. Just let me grab my buckets, and we can go."

"Need some help?" she asked.

"No. I can get it."

Gabe had to make three trips to get all of the buckets of vegetables he wanted to take to town. Jane stood next to the truck and watched him go back and forth. Once the buckets were in the back of her truck, they started to town. Neither of them said anything for several miles. Gabe was glad for the quiet, not just because he was uncomfortable with making small talk. It allowed him to think about the things he needed.

All of a sudden, he slapped his head.

"What is it?" Jane said with a measure of alarm in her voice.

"Nothing really. I just meant to check and see how much propane I had left."

"Are you getting low?"

Questions like this were why he didn't like to talk to people, Gabe thought, mentally rolling his eyes at the question. He decided to be civil, though. "That's what I wanted to check and see," he said.

"I should probably check mine, too," Jane said. "There are so many things we might need if things don't return to normal. I just don't know where to begin with the limited budget I have."

She paused, and Gabe knew she was waiting for him to say something, but he had no idea how to respond. He could see the disappointment on her face, and they remained quiet the rest of the way to town.

They first stopped at the grocery store. The line was longer than it had been last week. The manager agreed to buy the eggs at one dollar a dozen, and he bought all of Gabe's produce for forty dollars. They knew they could have made a lot more by selling their fare themselves, but they had more pressing business to attend to.

They got into the long grocery line to spend the money they'd just received. Gabe didn't know if they were letting more people into the store at one time or if the whole process was working more smoothly, but it didn't seem to take as long for them to get to the front as it had before. Once they were inside, it was obvious that it wouldn't take long to select their purchases from the limited items available. The store had gotten a shipment, but it must not have been very diverse. There was a plentiful supply of a few items, but most of the shelves were bare. He was able to get some salt this time, and he found some cans of generic Spam. There was still no cheese, and even the expensive candles were gone now. They both moved smoothly through the checkout line, and fortunately, there were no incidents in the parking lot this time.

The next stop was the gun store. It wasn't just a gun store but a pawnshop, as well. It had been many years since Gabe had been in the shop, but the fat slob of an owner looked exactly as Gabe had remembered. He was leaning over the counter looking at a large diamond ring through a jeweler's loupe. Two employees were also behind the counter on opposite sides of the store, and they watched every move Gabe and Jane made. They each had a handgun on their side, and Gabe noticed several shotguns and rifles propped up behind the counter at regular intervals.

"Help you?" the fat man said as he stood up straight and slid the ring into his pocket.

Gabe looked at Jane and saw that she wanted him to do the talking. "Yes," he said. "First, I need some ammunition."

"I don't have much left. What kind of gun do you need it for?"

"A Marlin lever-action," Gabe answered.

"Sorry. I've been out of .30-30 since week before last."

"No, it's .35 caliber."

"I might be able to help you there," the man said as he waddled to a shelf. He returned a minute later with three very dusty boxes of .35 Remington cartridges and set them on the shelf. "Anything else?"

"You got any .357?"

"Nope. But I've got some .38 Special +P left. You want it?"

"Yeah, give me a couple of boxes. How about twelve-gauge buckshot?"

"Sorry. We're all out of twelve-gauge except for some steel-shot duck loads."

"How about .22s?" Gabe asked.

"Pretty much out of it, too, except for some high-dollar match ammo."

"Are you going to get any more?"

"I hope so," the man said, "but God only knows when. If you need some, you better get what I have."

"That's all right. I probably have enough to last awhile. How much is this?"

"Let's see, it's forty bucks a box for the .38s, and I'll let you have the rifle ammo for twenty-five dollars a box. That comes to a hundred and fifty five even."

Gabe raised his eyebrows at the quote. "That's a little high, isn't it?"

"Hey, you don't have to buy it. If you think you can find a better deal somewhere else, then go for it."

"What if we bought a rifle, too?" Jane asked. "Would you discount the bullets then?"

"Lady, I can't sell any guns. The FBI isn't answering the phone, so I can't do the background check."

"I didn't want to buy one. I was hoping to trade for one for my son."

"It don't make no difference, lady." The man sounded exasperated. "What did you want to trade?" he asked a second later with just a hint of curiosity.

"This." Jane reached into her purse and handed the man her father's watch.

The man opened the watch, and Gabe saw his eyes widen with glee for a split second. He quickly regained his signature look of eternal boredom as he examined the relic for another minute.

"I tell you what I can do. I have a .22 that's my personal weapon. I could trade you that and three hundred rounds of .22 for it. I really shouldn't. This thing isn't worth much, but I just happen to like old watches, and I'm in a generous mood today. Let me get the rifle for you to look at."

He disappeared through a door for a moment and returned with a beat-up rifle. He handed it to Jane, who passed it over to Gabe. The name on the rust-pitted barrel said Revelation. He pulled the bolt back and saw it was filthy inside. Gabe knew it was a piece of crap, mostly because it hadn't been given the proper care. He set it back down on the counter.

"Give us a minute, will you?" Gabe asked the man as he pulled Jane back toward the entrance.

"Jane," he whispered, "I don't know what that watch is worth, but it's way more valuable than that piece-of-crap rifle."

"But I really need to get Robby a rifle," she said.

"I know, but you need to get him one that will work. I doubt that thing will even shoot straight."

"I guess I could throw in all the ammo you want, too," the fat man hollered.

"What do you think?" Jane asked in a voice low enough so only Gabe could hear.

"I think that if he's willing to break the law by selling a gun without a background check for that watch, it must be worth a lot more than you know. I won't let you do this. I have a rifle Robby can have, but we're not trading your watch."

Gabe was surprised at himself. He wasn't sure if it was because he was being so assertive or that he'd offered to give away the .22 he had bought for Michael a long time ago.

"Whatever you say, Gabe."

His surprise for himself was overshadowed by the look on Jane's face. It was respect.

CHAPTER 12

Gabe went back to the counter. "We're going to pass on the rifle," he told the man. "I'm only going to take the rifle ammo
and one box of the .38s."

"I have a better rifle you might be interested in," the fat man
said quickly. "It's worth a lot more than this one, but I think I
could still swap you even and throw all the ammo in, too."

"No, thanks," Gabe said as he held his hand out for the watch.
The man reluctantly placed it in Gabe's palm with a longing last
look. Gabe carefully handed it back to Jane, then dug into his pocket
and pulled out a small roll of bills. He peeled off a hundred and fifteen dollars and handed it to the man. Then he picked up the four
boxes of ammo he'd paid for and he and Jane turned to leave.

"I could sweeten the pot some if you change your mind," the
shop owner called out as they walked out the door.

Gabe waved good-bye with his free hand without turning
around. He opened the passenger door on Jane's truck and placed
his ammo on the front seat. By the time he climbed in, Jane had
the engine running, and they backed out onto Main Street.

"Thanks, Gabe," Jane said.

"No problem," he replied. "I hate guys like that. I have no problem with anyone making a profit, but it was obvious he was trying to take advantage of you. That watch must be very valuable."

"No . . . what I meant was, well, thanks for watching out for me, too, but I was thanking you for offering the rifle to Robby."

Gabe was quiet for a long minute. He thought he'd be sorry he had made the offer, but somehow he was excited. He was actually looking forward to seeing Robby's face when he gave it to him and was eager to teach him how to shoot it. He felt, well, he had no words for how he felt. "You're welcome," was all he said.

Jane pulled into the line at the gas station. It wasn't too long, and soon it was their turn. Signs read ONLY TEN GALLONS PER FAMILY. NO GAS CANS. Gabe got out of the truck to pump the gas. Before he could pick up the nozzle, a man rushed toward him.

"I'll do that!" he yelled.

Gabe took a step back to give the younger man room. The man wore a grease-stained, one-piece coverall. HARRY was embroidered on one side and the name of the station on the other. Gabe found it ironic that Harry had a shaved head. There was a gun belt and holster around his waist, which held a ridiculously long-barreled stainless steel revolver.

"Six dollars a gallon, paid in advance," Harry said.

Jane leaned out the window and handed Gabe three twenty-dollar bills that he passed to Harry.

"That's a big hog leg," Gabe said to the attendant.

"Yep," Harry replied, patting the holster that was obviously made for a much smaller gun. "Forty-four Magnum. The most powerful handgun in the world."

Gabe wasn't a gun nut, but he knew that there were more than a few handguns more powerful than the .44 nowadays. There was no point discussing it with Harry, though. The way he said it made it clear that he believed it to his core.

"You fellows having any trouble?" Gabe asked, noticing that the other attendant was also armed. His pistol wasn't as big as Harry's, though.

"Not yet, but we're ready for it," Harry said smugly.

A minute later, he was hanging up the hose. Gabe thanked him and climbed back into the truck.

"He was a little gung ho, wasn't he?" Jane asked.

"Just a little. But they're probably smart being armed. In fact, if it was my station, I'm not so sure that I wouldn't have three or four more guys just standing around with rifles to make a bigger show of force."

"Do you think they're going to get attacked?"

Gabe exhaled a long breath. "It's only a matter of when," he said. "We've been lucky so far, probably because we're so far away from the big city, but as things get worse, and they probably will, the riffraff will make its way out here. We have a pretty good sheriff's department, and they've activated all the reserve deputies, but they can't cover the whole county. If push comes to shove, I don't know if they can even keep the town safe."

Now it was Jane's turn to be quiet for a moment. Gabe saw her knuckles turn white as her grip on the steering wheel tightened.

"How do you know all this?"

"Some from what the deputy at the store told me the other day. Other parts are from looking at human nature."

"What do you mean?"

"Well, if you and Robby lived in the city and there was no food or water, what would you do?"

Her eyes opened a little and she just stared at him for a long moment. Then they narrowed. "So, what do we do?" she asked.

"I don't know for sure, but we need to talk about it."

Jane just nodded. They were both quiet for a long while.

"Gabe?"

"Yes?"

"Can I ask you some questions about your family?"

A second later, another shot rang out. DJ couldn't tell how close it was fired from, but sound didn't carry as far in the rain as it did on a clear day. He grabbed his rifle and started to run in the direction he thought it had come from, but then he stopped. If the shots were that close, it could be some sort of trap.

He went back to his bike and quickly donned his ballistic vest and climbed on the quad. He wasn't about to leave his most valuable possessions behind. Starting up the big machine, he backed it out of the shed and pulled up to the gate. A quick slice of the zip tie with his knife allowed him to open the gate. DJ noticed that the rain was letting up. Looking toward the west, he saw the sky was blue. Jumping back on the quad, he slowly made his way down the road, listening intently and looking for where the shots had been fired. A quarter mile down the road, a dirt driveway intersected the road. There were fresh tire tracks in the mud. Trees grew along both sides of the drive and hid whatever was behind them. He stopped his bike, and his mind raced to figure the best course of action. A minute later, two more shots rang out.

There was no doubt that they were coming from the other side of the trees.

DJ heard a woman's voice. "Okay, okay, we'll come out!"

"Do it!" a man yelled. "Do it slow."

DJ climbed off the bike with his carbine. He approached the opening in the trees in a semicrouch, and spotted a modest house. An old hot rod was parked in front. He lifted his rifle and looked through the scope. Three young men wearing gang colors were pointing weapons at the house. DJ had dealt with their kind, never in the way he had wanted, though. DJ knew what these types were capable of.

The front door on the small frame house opened, and a woman stepped out onto the porch with her hands in the air. A small child was hugging her tightly around the tops of her legs, making it impossible for her to take a normal-sized step.

"Is anyone else in the house?" the thug in the middle demanded.

The woman shook her head. Even at the almost hundred yards that DJ was from the house, he could tell through the scope that she was good looking. The middle guy, who DJ assumed was the leader, waved her toward him with his gun. The woman started moving toward him slowly as the child's grip tightened, making it harder for her to walk.

"Hurry up, bitch!" he screamed.

The woman's pace didn't change, and the impatient leader waved his free hand at his boys. They pounced on the woman like cats on a mouse. One peeled the child away from her, and the other grabbed her arms and held them behind her with one hand and pointed his pistol into her neck with the other. The leader stuck his pistol into the back of his droopy pants and walked up to her. DJ couldn't tell if he was frisking her or feeling her up. The little girl was screaming, and the leader looked at the hoodlum holding her and said something. DJ was scared that he was going to pistol-whip the little girl, but he just shook her until she shut up.

The leader returned to his supposed search of the woman. He quickly found his way to her feminine parts. The woman screamed, "No," and began to twist and thrash around. The leader slapped her and grabbed her blouse, tearing it open. Then he slapped her again, this time so hard that she fell to the ground face-first. She went limp and still. DJ didn't know if the hit had rendered her unconscious, or if she'd hit her head on the ground. The leader rolled her over with his foot. His hands went to his belt buckle and his face split into an evil smile. DJ felt his face go hot. He knew what was next, and he wasn't going to let it happen if he could help it.

His carbine came to his shoulder as if it were part of him. All the hours of dry-firing in his apartment and the time he spent at the range had engrained the movement into his muscles. He leaned the forearm of the rifle against the trunk of the tree to give him the steadiest shot possible. The red chevron reticule of the scope found the middle of the leader's head. DJ flipped the safety, and the pad of his forefinger found the trigger. He squeezed, and the carbine barked.

The back of the leader's head disappeared into a pink mist. DJ felt the scowl on his face turn to a grin. The sight of his highly frangible bullet intersecting with the cranium of the perp was the coolest thing he'd ever seen. The man's body even stood erect for a moment. DJ had heard of this phenomenon, and he'd always wanted to see it. His gleeful reverie was broken a second later, as the other two delinquents began to run. He quickly adjusted his sight picture and fired again, this time at the torso of the man who had held the woman. He fell to the ground. The last punk was running for the car, firing his handgun wildly in DJ's general direction. DJ fired three times before he hit him. The man stumbled but continued to run for the car. DJ sent several more bullets his way before one stopped the man in his tracks.

It was strange. The world had gone silent. DJ wasn't able to define the feeling that saving the woman had given him. It wasn't joy, but it was close. He figured it could only come from the fact that he'd kept the woman and her daughter from being assaulted or worse.

He maintained his position for a moment to make sure there weren't any more tangos that he hadn't seen. The little girl started to cry. He changed magazines and stood up, reexamining his surroundings. The three youths were probably too stupid to have a lookout, but he had to be careful. It only took one well-aimed bullet from an unseen adversary to ruin your day.

DJ cautiously made his way to the house. He could see the little girl lying across her unconscious mother and sobbing so hard that her body shook uncontrollably. When he was about halfway to the house, she saw him and began to scream. DJ lowered the rifle from his shoulder and held out his hand to assure her that everything was okay. The gesture did not have the desired effect, as the girl only screamed more hysterically. DJ didn't need some neighborhood do-gooder thinking he was one of the bad guys and shooting him by mistake.

"It's okay, it's okay," he said in a hushed voice, looking from side to side. "I'm here to help you. I stopped those bad men from hurting you and your mom."

"Are you going to shoot us?" the girl asked in a trembling voice.

"Of course not," DJ reassured her. "I'm here to help. Did you see any more bad guys?"

The girl, who looked to be six or seven, shook her head. DJ was now close enough to see that the woman was unconscious. He knelt down beside her and felt her neck for a pulse. It was strong, and he could see that she was breathing. There was a large lump on her forehead where she'd hit the ground. He turned and looked at the mostly headless attacker and saw the grip of a very large pistol sticking out of the waistband of his jeans. DJ pulled the pistol out to find it was a Desert Eagle in .357 Magnum.

DJ figured he'd better check on the other two hoodlums. The second one he'd shot was dead, and it looked as if the bullet had gone through his heart. DJ could only imagine how badly the thinly jacketed projectile had shredded the organ. When he walked around the car, he found the guy who had run for it was still breathing in ragged gasps. He stared at the young man for a minute. It looked as if the injuries from the three hits, while not immediately fatal, were not survivable without medical treatment.

The man groaned and turned his head. His eyes opened, and he looked up at DJ. He moved his mouth to talk, but no sound came out. His eyes pleaded to the man standing over him as no words could. He was probably only sixteen or seventeen and had most likely not had the advantages of a loving home or anyone who really cared about him. His fate had been sealed from the moment he'd been born.

DJ knew that the phones were probably not working, and even if he could call 911, he didn't want to have to explain this situation to the law. They'd likely see things his way and let him go, but that wasn't a chance he was willing to take. He could load the young man into the car, try to get him to a hospital, and just dump him at the door. They might be able to save him, but save him for what? He'd only return to his evil ways if he survived. It was all he knew, and how many resources and supplies would the hospital have to use that might be used to save a truly deserving person?

It was a dilemma DJ had never considered facing. He held this boy's life in his hands. What should he do? If he took him to a hospital, would he be able to get back to get his quad? That would also use up gas in the car that he really needed. He decided that it was only humane to put the boy out of his misery.

DJ flipped the safety off on his AR-15 and placed the muzzle right in the middle of the young man's forehead. The kid's eyes widened.

"See you in hell, kid."

DJ's finger touched the trigger, but he couldn't pull it. He stared back down into the youth's terrified eyes, going over his options again. Before he came to a conclusion, the eyes closed and the body slumped over.

DJ was thankful he hadn't had to put the coup de grâce into the kid, but he also didn't feel any remorse that he was dead. He wondered briefly if he should. He heard the girl start to cry again, and he walked back around the car.

"It's okay," he said as he knelt down beside the girl and gently patted her shoulder. "What's your name?"

"Nancy."

"Well, Nancy, what do you say we get your mama inside and look after her?"

The little girl nodded. DJ slung his rifle behind his back and slid his arms under the woman. The hours he'd spent in the gym made lifting the small-framed woman easy. Her torn blouse fell open, and he couldn't help noticing what a nice figure she had. He walked toward the door. Nancy ran ahead of him and opened it. He carefully stepped through, making sure he didn't bump the woman's head again on the doorframe. The house was modestly furnished but was clean and neat.

"Is she going to be okay?" Nancy asked as DJ set her mother down on the couch.

"I hope so, Nancy. You don't have any ice, do you?"

Nancy shook her head. DJ pulled out his flashlight and turned it on. He opened one of the woman's eyes with his thumb and shined the light in it. Then he did the same to the other eye. Both pupils contracted, and he knew that was a good sign. He tried to recall the paramedic training he'd taken after the police department had turned down his application. He'd applied to the fire department and had been accepted, but after just a few weeks of EMT school, he found it wasn't for him and dropped out.

"Do you have running water?" he asked the girl.

"No, but Mommy filled up the bathtubs before it quit."

"Good. Would you go get a washcloth and wet it real good for me?"

Nancy nodded once and then disappeared down a hallway. He looked around the room and saw a picture of Nancy with her mother and a man. It was the kind of portrait that only families take. He reached down and pulled the woman's left hand up from her side and saw a simple wedding band.

He wondered where her husband was. If this was his woman,

he wouldn't leave her in this situation. He only had to wonder for a moment, as Nancy came running back into the living room. DJ took the cloth from her, folded it in half, and laid it across the woman's head.

"Nancy, where's your dad?"

"He's driving his truck. Mommy says he should be home any day."

"He drives a big truck?"

The girl nodded.

"I see," DJ said. "Do you have a car?"

"Yes, but Mommy said somebody stole the gas out of it."

The fact that there was no gas to be had here reminded DJ that his quad was still out on the road. "Nancy, I have to go get my four-wheeler. Can you watch your mom for a minute?"

Again the girl nodded, and DJ grabbed his rifle and went out the door. He carefully scanned from left to right and didn't see anything that looked out of place. It only took a minute to get his quad and ride it up to the house. When he got off, he walked over to the car the attackers had driven. He opened the door and was greeted with the smell of marijuana and alcohol. He leaned over and turned the key. The gas needle moved to halfway between the E and the ¼ marks. DJ walked to the back of the car and opened the trunk. It was full of things that had likely been stolen. Most were worthless items like stereos and DVD players. There was some food, and DJ removed that. He spread the rest of the loot out as evenly as he could and then put the three bodies on top. Looking down at them, he thought he might feel some level of remorse. He didn't. They were old enough to have chosen their paths and got what they deserved. It was a shame, but letting them harm innocent people hadn't been an option. The trunk lid didn't want to close without a good push.

He'd have to get the car out of here, just in case these guys had friends. Plus, doing so would help minimize scrutiny from the law. He would drive it somewhere that it wouldn't be easily found and perhaps set it on fire. Hopefully, the woman would recover and be able to help him. DJ picked up the food and carried it into the house.

The woman was awake and was exploring the knot on her head. DJ could also see welt marks rising where the gangbanger's fingers had impacted her left cheek. She didn't seem startled when DJ walked into the room, which told DJ that Nancy had let her mother know who he was.

"Hi, there. I'm the guy who stopped those guys from hurting you. How are you feeling?" he asked, as he set the food on the kitchen counter.

"I'll be okay, I think," she said as she gingerly touched the bump on her head. "Nancy told me you shot them?"

"I was afraid they were going to kill you and Nancy," he said softly, "after they had their fun with you, of course." He knew they probably would have taken turns at Nancy after they finished with her, but he didn't think she was ready to hear that. "I had to stop them, and shooting them was the only way I could take out all three before they could hurt you."

"Are they all dead?"

"Yes, I'm afraid so." DJ waited for her to lash out at him.

Her eyes narrowed and she furrowed her brow, wincing. "Good," she spat. "I'm glad you killed them. Thank you."

CHAPTER 13

"You're welcome," DJ answered. He was surprised at her response. He hadn't expected her to be thankful. She sat up, and her blouse fell open, exposing her black brassiere and the soft pale flesh that it didn't cover. She quickly pulled the torn material up to cover herself.

"Really, thank you so much," she said in a soft voice. "Since Roger's on the road, I've been worried something like this would happen. If you hadn't come along, there's no telling . . ." Her voice trailed off.

"Where is your husband?"

"He was taking a load to the West Coast; he's a truck driver. I'm expecting him back anytime now."

"I see," DJ said. He knew that if the man wasn't home yet, he was stranded somewhere, or worse.

"I guess I'd better go change clothes," she said. She stood up quickly, then wobbled back and forth for a second before plopping back onto the couch. "Whoa, I guess I hit my head harder than I thought."

DJ stepped toward her and held out his hand. She took it and pulled herself back to a standing position. The hand was soft and smooth. DJ imagined that the rest of her would be the same. Standing next to her, he could see exactly how petite and perfectly proportioned she was. When she recognized how he was looking at her, her face flushed and she removed her hand from his. She and Nancy disappeared into the back of the house.

DJ sat down, immediately realizing how good it felt to sit in a comfortable chair. He thought about how he should already have made it to his bug-out location. It wouldn't be as comfortable as this, but it would be way better than camping out off the quad every day. He'd get whatever gas he could out of the attackers' car and hopefully he could guilt the woman into giving him some. Then, once it got dark, he'd hit the road. Maybe the woman had a guest room, and he could sleep on a bed for a few hours. That would be heavenly.

A minute later, she came back into the room. DJ immediately noticed that she was wearing a baggy sweatshirt.

"By the way, my name's Crystal," she said as she stuck out her hand. "And this is Nancy."

"I've already met Nancy," DJ said as he shook the woman's hand. "She's a very brave little girl, and she's pretty, too, just like her mother." The handshake was short and businesslike. "It's nice to meet you, Crystal." He flashed his best smile and was rewarded with a shy smile from Crystal. "My name's DJ. DJ Frost."

"Thanks again for helping us, Mr. Frost."

"No problem. I'm glad I was in the neighborhood, and please don't be so formal. You can call me DJ." He smiled again.

"Okay, DJ." The woman returned the smile. This time, she seemed a little more relaxed. Suddenly her face screwed up. "Do you think that they might have friends?"

"I doubt it," DJ said as reassuringly as he could. Then he thought that if he could make her a little frightened, she might do whatever it took to keep him around. "But anything's possible. Maybe we should get that car out of here, just in case. I can take it and dump it. Do you feel up to following me in your car?" he asked.

"Shouldn't we call the sheriff and let him get the car and the bodies?"

"Does your phone work?"

"Good point. But we could take the car to town and let the sheriff know what happened," she said.

The last thing DJ wanted to do was to go to the county seat that was out of his way and explain to some country bumpkin of a sheriff why he shot three men. He'd probably get his weapons confiscated until the mess could be sorted out. He could even end up in jail if the sheriff was unreasonable. He couldn't risk it.

"Look," he said, "I'd like to go see the sheriff, but I don't know what will happen if we do. This isn't a normal time for anyone, and there's no telling what he might think. He could end up throwing both of us in jail and putting your daughter in the foster care system. Those guys got what they deserved, but the way things are, it might be better that no one knows we were involved. Does that make sense to you?"

DJ knew she'd agree with him the moment he mentioned foster care. He was well aware no woman could stand to be separated from her children. Her reaction was stronger than he'd expected, though. Her eyes widened and filled with fear at the suggestion. She nodded blankly in response to his question.

"Do you know of a good place, not too close and not too far, where we could take the car?"

She stared at him with glazed eyes for a moment. "What?"

"Do you know a good place to dump the car?"

"There's an abandoned rock quarry about five miles from here," she said.

"That's good." He smiled, and she seemed to relax a little. "Do we have to pass any houses to get there?"

"Just a few."

"Okay, we'll wait until dark, then," he said. "I'll take it, set it on fire, and dump it. You can follow about five minutes behind in your car and pick me up."

"My car won't run," she said. "Someone drilled a hole in the gas tank and stole all my gas."

"Then we'll have to take my quad," he said. He hated to burn the fuel, but at the very least, he'd get to have the woman pressed up against him on the ride back. He could also kiss the idea of her giving him any gas good-bye. "You can drive the car, and I'll bring you back."

"Thank you," she said, sounding more grateful for this than she had sounded for his saving her life. DJ wasn't sure what it was, but there was something more than what met the eye with this woman.

"No problem," he said nonchalantly. "Do you have a place where I could clean up and get some rest?"

"Sure," she said. "Anything you want. I can warm up some water and put it in the bathroom basin for you. Would that be all right?"

"That would be excellent," he replied.

"I could fix you something to eat, too," she said.

DJ wasn't that hungry, but something besides an MRE or freeze-dried food sounded good. "That would be great."

"What would you like?"

"I'm sure anything you fix would be fit for a king." He flashed his best smile again. The woman blushed slightly at the compliment. It was the reaction he'd hoped to see.

"Okay, it'll only take a few minutes to warm up the water," she said.

"I'll go get some clean clothes," he replied.

DJ went to his four-wheeler to grab the duffel bag that held most of his clothes. Back inside the house, he stood silently as the woman put her finger into a pot of water every thirty seconds or so to test the temperature. After several tries, she declared the water ready and removed it from the stove. DJ followed her to the bathroom, where she poured the water into the sink.

"Take your time," she said. "Here's a towel, a washcloth, and some soap. Don't worry about getting the floor wet. I'll clean it up once you're through. If you need to use the toilet, you can flush by dumping water out of that bucket into the bowl. Do you need anything else?"

DJ could only think of one thing, but he shook his head. Crystal closed the door behind her as she left.

Gabe seemed to shrink in size. His eyes glazed over, and Jane was instantly sorry for asking. "Gabe, I'm sorry. If you don't want to talk about it, I understand."

He was quiet for a long moment. He didn't want to talk about it, but somehow he felt compelled to do so. It was as if Jane was some sorceress who had him under a spell. He seemed powerless to deny her. "No," he said, "it's okay." His voice quivered a little.

He got quiet again, staring out the windshield, looking for an answer.

"I know they were in a car wreck," she said, trying to help him.

"It was my fault," he blurted out.

"How could that be? Weren't you at home?"

"Yes, but I should have been with them. Hannah had promised Michael she'd take him to the movies. She asked me to go with them, but I was tired. On the way home, a truck driver fell asleep and crossed the median. Hannah died instantly, but Michael held on for a day and a half. If I'd only gone with them, it wouldn't have happened."

Jane could see that he was almost crying. "Gabe, if you had gone, then you'd be dead, too."

"That's what everybody says, but maybe we'd have been earlier or later, and the truck would have missed us. Maybe I could have reacted faster than Hannah did. If I'd gone, then Michael would've been in the backseat, and he might have lived." The last few words were barely audible.

Jane was at a loss for what to say. She reached over and placed her hand on Gabe's upper arm. He recoiled, and she pulled her hand back, now even sorrier about asking the question. She'd thought he was the way he was because he missed them. She had no idea that he blamed himself, although it now made perfect sense. There were other questions she wanted to ask, but this wasn't the time. Any healing was going to take much longer than she'd originally thought. The main thing now was not to let him fall back into his old pattern.

When they were almost back to his place, she spoke again. "Gabe, why don't you get the rifle and come show Robby how to shoot it? I'll fix dinner while you're working with him."

Gabe didn't say anything. He sat gazing out the windshield, seeing nothing. He was reliving and remembering things he didn't want to remember. They pulled into his driveway, and Jane stopped the truck. He made no move.

"Gabe."

He didn't answer, and she instinctively touched his shoulder and said his name again. The instant she did it, she remembered him pulling away the last time, and she was afraid he'd do it again, but he only jumped as if suddenly awakened.

"What?"

"Get the .22, and you can teach Robby to shoot while I fix dinner."

"Not now," he said as he opened the door and climbed out of the truck.

Jane got out and followed him up the steps. "Gabe, you've got to get over this guilt. I'm sorry for what happened, but you have to stop believing it was your fault."

He continued toward the door as if he didn't hear her.

She refused to let his action discourage her. "We need you, Gabe. Robby and I need your help if we're going to get through this."

He stuck the key in the door and opened it.

"You can ignore me all you want, Gabriel Horne, but I'm not going—"

He shut the door. Damn her. Why couldn't she just leave him alone? How could he have been so stupid to let her into his business? Who did she think she was? This was his problem, and he knew exactly how to deal with it.

*   *   *

Jane drove home disappointed with herself. She'd pushed him too hard. Things had seemed to be going well. There had been a few road bumps, but he had surprised her a time or two, like today in the gun shop. Perhaps she'd read too much into those gestures, and he really wasn't as ready as she thought.

She wondered what she should do now as she pulled into her driveway. Robby must have heard the truck pull up, as he bolted out the door before she could even come to a complete stop. She knew he was waiting for news on the rifle.

"Did you get it, Mom?" he said, almost out of breath with excitement.

She sadly shook her head, and the happy look on his face melted as his shoulders slumped. His transformation broke her heart. She wanted to tell him about Gabe's offer, but she didn't know if that would really happen or not. She had to say something, though.

"We only got to go to one place, and they didn't have anything good. There are other places we can try. It just wasn't possible today. Okay, sweetheart?"

"Okay, Mom," the boy said, painting on a weak smile.

"Help me with this stuff, will you?" she said.

As she looked into the back of the truck, she saw that Gabe had left his groceries. She thought about going back and giving them to him. It would give her an excuse to go down and talk to him again. She decided to wait until the morning. Perhaps he'd be in a better disposition by then. She hoped so.

Once all the groceries were inside, Jane started dinner. She and Robby ate the fish he'd caught while she was in town. By the time the dishes were done, it was dark, and they went to bed.

The sound of chickens squawking loudly woke her up. It was dark, and she didn't know what time it was. It sounded as if a raccoon or possum was in the chicken house. While this wasn't a common occurrence, it did happen from time to time. She got out of bed and pulled on her boots, tucking her flannel pajama bottoms inside the shafts. Grabbing a flashlight, she made her way to the back door. There she had a large garden hoe just for such occasions. She snatched the hoe, opened the door, and started toward one of the large coops. When she was almost there, its door burst open and two men carrying several flapping and screeching chickens appeared. Jane was so shocked that she dropped her flashlight. The two men stared at her for a split second and then spun and ran toward her back fence line.

She was furious. She'd lost some fowl to predators in the past, but they had all been of the four-legged variety. Never had she considered that people would want to steal her chickens. She reached down, picked up the light, and shined it at the retreating thieves.

"Drop those chickens or I'll shoot!" she yelled. One of the men looked over his shoulder for a second, but he and his accomplice continued toward the fence as if they feared nothing. She was about to yell at them again when she saw an orange-yellow flash beyond the fence. An instant later, she felt the searing pain and heard the boom.

CHAPTER 14

As clean as he'd been in over a week, DJ took the time to shave, brush his teeth, and comb his hair. Putting on fresh clothes, he felt like a new man. He stepped out of the bathroom, and his mouth watered. The smells coming from the kitchen were heavenly. He walked to the kitchen table and pulled out a chair. Nancy was on her knees in a chair on the far side of the table, vigorously using crayons on a coloring book. When DJ sat down, she turned the book around.

"Do you like my picture?" she said.

DJ looked down and saw a blue dinosaur eating some orange trees. "I like it a lot," he said, sneaking a peak at the backside of the cook. "That's beautiful."

"Thank you," Nancy said. She beamed as she pulled the book back to her side of the table.

"That sure smells good, Crystal," DJ said.

"It's just chili."

"Well, that's a lot better than what I've been eating." DJ saw that the pantry was open and that the shelves were packed with food. "Did you just go to the store?"

"No. I haven't been for several weeks. Why?" she asked.

"I just noticed that your pantry's almost full."

"Well, the trucking business isn't always steady work. Roger and I buy lots of food when he's working, so we don't have to worry if he doesn't have any jobs for a while."

"That's pretty smart."

"Just practical," she said.

A minute later, she set a steaming bowl in front of DJ. He leaned over it and took a big sniff. His face broke into a smile, and the woman seemed pleased. It didn't take long for him to devour the bowl of chili, and Crystal refilled it for him. He took more time finishing the second helping. When he was done, he pushed the bowl away and leaned back in the chair. Patting his stomach, he smiled. "That might be the best chili I've ever had."

"You're just saying that," Crystal said, "but I appreciate it. I can see you're tired. Would you like to take a nap?"

"Yes, I would."

"The guest room is the door just past the bathroom. There are extra pillows and blankets in the closet. You make yourself at home."

"Thank you, Crystal."

"Don't mention it. It's the least I can do after what you did for us."

DJ agreed. It was the least she could do. He made his way to the bedroom, leaving the door ajar.

Gabe was well on his way to feeling no pain. The bottle was almost a third empty, and the anger he'd felt had subsided in proportion to the level of liquid in it. As he poured another glass, he heard pounding on his door.

"Mr. Horne! Mr. Horne! My mom's been shot!" Robby yelled.

Gabe sprang to his feet and ran to the door. Pulling it open, he saw Robby breathing hard.

"What happened?" Gabe demanded.

"Someone was stealing chickens, and Mom tried to stop them, and they shot her," Robby said, tears streaming down his face.

"Is she okay?" Gabe asked, immediately realizing that it was a stupid question. "Where did she get hit?"

"In the leg." Robby touched his thigh about eight inches above his knee. "She says she's okay, but there's a lot of blood."

"Wait right here," Gabe said as he spun and headed for the bathroom. He prayed the bullet hadn't hit the main artery in the leg. If it had, Jane would be dead by the time they got back to her. Gabe noticed a feeling in the pit of his stomach that he hadn't felt for a long time. He opened the bathroom cabinet and pulled out the tackle-box-sized first aid kit Hannah had assembled when they'd first moved to the country. Walking back to Robby, he wished he hadn't had so much to drink tonight. He felt as though he was forgetting something, but there was no time to stand around and wonder what it might be. "Let's go."

They ran to Jane's truck, and Robby drove quickly down the road to his house. Gabe thought he should make himself puke whatever alcohol was still in his stomach before it made its way into his bloodstream, but he didn't want to do it in front of the boy. When Robby stopped the truck in front of the house, he reached for the door handle. Gabe grabbed the boy's arm. "Robby, I want you to stay in the truck until I come to get you."

"No way. I have to help my mom."

"Robby, please. Just wait here for a minute. I'll be right back to get you," Gabe said with the most authority he could muster. He tried to think of a reason to give the boy that wouldn't scare him to death. "I want you to stay in the truck, so that, just in case the bad guys are still around or something, you can go get more help. If you see or hear anything out of the ordinary, or if I'm not back in three minutes, I want you to take off."

"All right, Mr. Horne, but you better come right back."

Gabe opened his door and ran into the house. "Jane! Jane, can you hear me?"

"I'm in here, Gabe."

Gabe was relieved to hear her voice. "Where?"

"In the kitchen."

Gabe dashed into the kitchen. The room was barely lit by a single candle. Gabe rushed over to Jane. She was holding a blood-soaked dishrag around her leg.

"Let me see," Gabe said as calmly as he could.

She pulled the towel away from her leg. Blood was oozing from both the top and bottom of the outside of her thigh. Gabe was thankful there was no spurt. He remembered reading that the big arteries were on the inside of the thighs. He took her hands in his and placed them back where they held the small towel tightly around her leg. "I promised I'd get Robby as soon as I checked on you. Will you be all right for a minute?"

Jane nodded, and Gabe went back out the front door. The boy was slumped over the steering wheel, his body quivering. "Robby?" Gabe called.

The boy sat up and was out of the truck in an instant. "Is she okay?"

"She's gonna be fine, son," Gabe said as reassuringly as he could. "I need more light. Do you have a big flashlight or a lantern?"

"We have both."

"Go get them for me."

Robby ran into the house. Gabe went to the far side of the driveway and bent over. He stuck his finger down his throat and gagged, but nothing happened. He had to do it three more times before the contents of his stomach took the wrong trip. Once it started, Gabe wasn't sure that it would ever end. The alcohol burned much more coming up than it had going down. Finally it was over, and he made his way back to the kitchen.

"How are you feeling?" he asked Jane. He noticed that her face appeared pale, but he couldn't tell if it was from the bleeding or from the flickering light of the candle.

"I'm okay," she said.

"I need a drink of water," he told her.

If she knew why, she didn't give any indication. "The glasses are in the first cupboard."

Gabe filled the cup and took a small sip. He swished it around in his mouth and spat it down the drain. Then he pulled a long drink out of the mug, and it quenched the fire in his esophagus.

"You should be lying down," he said, putting the cup in the sink.

"I don't want to get blood on the furniture," she said.

"Let's put you up on the table, then. We can clean and disinfect it when we're done."

The woman nodded, and Gabe took her hand and helped her up onto the veneer table.

"You need a new towel. Where are they?"

"Second drawer down next to the sink."

Gabe opened the drawer and pulled out a neatly folded dish towel. He removed the old towel and replaced it, throwing the bloody one into the sink. "Robby, where's my light?" he called.

"I can't find the flashlight," Robby yelled back.

"Then just get the lantern. It'll be better anyway."

"Yes, sir."

"Tell me what happened," Gabe said, turning his attention back to Jane.

She quickly relayed the whole story.

"I dropped the flashlight out back when they shot me," Jane whispered. "It went out when it hit the ground."

Gabe patted her on the shoulder. "It's okay. We can fix it or get another one. You're lucky they didn't kill you. I hope you now know never to threaten to shoot someone, especially if you don't have a gun."

Jane nodded sheepishly. Gabe had started toward the back door to get the flashlight when it occurred to him that the guys who'd shot Jane could still be there. He realized that he'd left his guns at home and mentally kicked himself. That's what he'd forgotten in his haste, or was it his impaired condition? "Jane, did the chicken thieves leave, or is it possible they're still outside?"

"They just fired the one shot and left. I heard them running off toward the east. You don't think they'll come back, do you?" she said.

"No, I don't think so . . . at least not tonight. They already got what they wanted. You don't have to worry about them anymore," he said, hoping he was right. He placed his hand on her face to reassure her and noticed she was cold. "Where are the blankets?"

"In the chest at the foot of my bed," she answered.

"I'll go get you one."

Just as Gabe turned, the boy came in with a kerosene lantern. He set it on the counter next to the candle and grabbed a box of matches out of a drawer. A moment later, the room was bathed in a soft yellow light.

"Thanks, Robby. Will you go get your mother a blanket?"

"Yes, sir."

Gabe turned back to Jane. "Let's have a good look at that leg." He pulled her hands away. The flannel pajama pants were soaked with blood from her knee to her hip. Gabe pulled out his large pocketknife and cut a slash in them about four inches above the entrance hole. He stuck his fingers inside and pulled, neatly ripping the material. Jane moaned.

"Did that hurt?"

"No." She smiled weakly. "It's just that these are my favorite pajamas."

"Sorry. That sure is a good young man you're raising," he said, trying to take her mind off her leg. Jane smiled and nodded. An instant later, Robby reappeared with the blanket, and Gabe wondered if the youngster had heard what he'd said. Robby gave no indication as he draped the blanket over his mother's torso.

The entrance wound was small and clean. There was almost no blood coming from it. Gabe figured it might have come from a .22-caliber weapon. He shuddered to think about what the exit wound might look like, but he had to check it.

"Jane, I need you to roll over on your side. Robby, you help her."

The pair did as instructed. Gabe was surprised that the exit hole looked much like the one on the front of Jane's leg. It was bleeding a little more, but it appeared there was little tissue damage, at least from what he could see. He grabbed some large bandages out of his first aid kit and a roll of wide medical tape along with a tube of antibiotic cream and a bottle of alcohol. He poured some alcohol on one of the dressings and carefully wiped around the wound.

"This is going to sting a little," he said as he got closer to the perforation.

Jane tensed, but she made no sound. Gabe leaned over to where he could see the front of her leg and quickly repeated the procedure. Next he dabbed a liberal amount of ointment on both sites and covered them with clean dressings. Tape was wrapped around the leg and over the bandages several times.

"That should hold you until we get to the hospital."

"Is that really necessary?" Jane asked. "I feel fine."

"Mom, Mr. Horne is right. You've been shot. You have to go to the hospital."

"All right, I'll go," she said weakly. "I can see it's two against one."

"Robby, go pull your truck up as close to the front door as you can get it," Gabe said.

The boy nodded once and disappeared. Jane started to get up.

"Whoa, there," Gabe said. "You're not going to put any weight on that leg until it gets properly checked out."

He put his arms under her and lifted her off the table. She was surprised. It wasn't just that she hadn't expected it, but also that he'd done it so easily. It felt good to have a man's strong body next to hers, but the smell of alcohol brought unpleasant memories.

Gabe carried her through the front door. Robby had opened the passenger door on the truck and was standing next to the idling vehicle.

"Go ahead and get in, Robby," Gabe said.

The boy started to climb in on the passenger's side.

"The other side," Gabe added. "You're driving."

"But, Mr. Horne, I don't have a license. Mom lets me drive on the gravel roads around here, but I can't drive to town."

Gabe thought he'd hurled up most of the alcohol before it had gotten into his bloodstream, but he knew some had made its way into his system. He would never allow himself to drive unless he was stone cold sober.

"Yes, you can," he told the teenager. "Driving on pavement is easier than driving on gravel. You can do it. Just keep your speed down. Now get in, and I'm going to slide your mother in so she can lay her head down on your lap."

"Yes, sir."

The boy climbed behind the wheel, and Gabe put Jane in the truck. He placed a pillow underneath Jane's feet and carefully closed the door. He instructed Robby to stop at his house so he could get his rifle, then climbed into the bed of the truck and knocked on the back window twice to tell Robby he was ready.

When they stopped at Gabe's, it took less than a minute for him to remove his rifle from his truck. Back in the bed, he stayed on his knees, looking through the glass for any sign of trouble ahead. Occasionally, he glanced over his shoulder to make sure no one was closing in from the rear.

The drive to town was uneventful. Gabe noticed lights in a few houses. Probably from candles or lanterns, he thought, but most homes were dark. He wondered if those people were already asleep or if they just didn't have any way to illuminate their homes. It was eerily quiet as they drove down the dark farm-to-market road.

In town, most all of the houses were dark. The only buildings with any electric power were the county courthouse, the jail, and the hospital since they had backup diesel generators. When Robby stopped the truck at the emergency room entrance, Gabe slung his rifle over his shoulder and jumped out of the back. He opened the passenger door and lifted Jane from the front seat.

The doors into the hospital opened automatically as he carried her inside. A nurse saw him and told him to wait right there. She stuck her head through a set of swinging doors and said something that Gabe was unable to discern. A second later, a man dressed in white pushed a gurney through the doors. Following him was a deputy.

"You can't bring that rifle in here," the deputy yelled.

Gabe gave the deputy a quick nod and started talking to the orderly and the nurse as he laid Jane onto the gurney. "She was shot in the leg. It looks like a small caliber, and it went straight through. She lost a good bit of blood, but I don't know how much. I did the best I could to dress it and get her here as quickly as possible," Gabe said in rapid-fire sentences as he set Jane gently onto the gurney.

The nurse pulled back the bandage. "It doesn't look too bad. I'm sure your wife will be fine, sir." She smiled at both Jane and Gabe. "We'll have a doc look at her just as soon as one is free."

"No," Gabe said.

Everyone looked at him quizzically.

"I mean, yes, have the doctor look at her, but she's not my wife. She's my neighbor."

The nurse smiled, and she and the big orderly pushed Jane toward the back. Gabe took half a step in the direction they were going, but the deputy stopped him. "Let's go put that rifle back in your truck," he said.

"Of course," Gabe said.

"And then we'll take a walk down to the sheriff's office," the lawman said.

CHAPTER 15

DJ slowly came to a wakeful state. He could feel the moisture on his face, and his hand came up to wipe it off. He was slightly embarrassed that he'd slept so soundly, not because he'd slobbered on himself, but because he'd let his guard completely down. The bed had been so comfortable that he wasn't even aware of how much time had passed. He looked at his watch, and the tritium hands showed it to be slightly after ten. Through the window, the moon cast just enough light that he could see the trees bordering the back of Crystal's property. He arose and pulled on a tight T-shirt and a clean pair of black BDU trousers.

Walking into the living room, he saw Crystal reading a book by the light of an oil lamp.

"Hi," DJ said.

"Hey," she answered. "You were really sawing logs in there."

"Yeah, I haven't slept in a bed in several days. I almost forgot how good it feels. I think I could get used to all the comforts of home again real quick."

If she caught the hidden meaning of his last statement, she

didn't show it. "I was going to wake you at eleven if you weren't up. The sooner we get rid of that car, the better I'll feel."

"Then let's do it."

"I'll get Nancy up and get her ready."

"I don't know if that's a good idea."

"Well, I can't leave her here by herself."

"There's not room for three people on the quad," DJ said. He knew it wasn't technically true, but if something happened, it would be impossible to maneuver well with that many riders. "Besides, we should be back in thirty minutes or less."

"I don't know," Crystal said.

DJ shrugged. "I guess we can just leave it where it is. Sooner or later, some of those guys' friends will come looking for them, or the law will be by with some questions, and remember, things are going to get real ripe in that trunk in a few days."

Crystal's eyes got big again. DJ wondered which possibility scared her most.

"I guess it'll be okay if we're only gone for thirty minutes," she said tentatively.

"All right, here's what I want you to do. Drive as normally as you can, not too fast and not too slow. We don't want to draw any attention to ourselves if possible. When you get on the road the quarry's on, drive down it normally for a tenth of a mile or so, and then slow way down and turn off the lights. There's plenty of moonlight, so you should be able to see okay once your eyes adjust. If you see someone coming, pull over and turn the car off. Lie down in the seat, and we'll hope they just think it is an abandoned vehicle. I'll be behind you all the time, but you won't see me. Don't worry, though; I'll have you covered if something happens. You understand?"

Crystal nodded.

"Good. Let's go," DJ said.

Less than ten minutes later, they were at the gate to the quarry. It was locked, but DJ made short work of cutting the chain. Crystal drove the car to the edge. DJ looked down and saw that there was water about fifty feet below.

"Do you know how deep the water is?"

"No, but some of the locals fish from the other side where it's not so deep. Rumor has it that they've caught some bass that went over ten pounds."

DJ knew if that was true, then the water had to be fairly deep. It should be deep enough to hide the car. He'd planned on setting it on fire before he pushed it over, but that wouldn't do any good with the water down there. It was probably better, though. If it was deep enough, the car might never be found. He also wouldn't have to use any of his precious gasoline to start the fire.

He removed some tools from his quad and soon had gasoline trickling from the hot rod. He got almost four gallons and was ecstatic, but he didn't let that show. When the last of the fuel dripped from the tank, he and Crystal pushed the car over the edge. It made less noise than he'd expected when it hit the water, and he watched it sink like an old man climbing into a warm bath.

He put everything back on the four-wheeler and climbed on. Crystal hopped on behind him, and they drove back to the gate. He closed it and zip-tied the chain back into place. He noticed that the air was a little chilly and smiled. He remounted his ride and turned on the night vision. Between the speed he was traveling on the bumpy road and the coolness of the night, Crystal had to press herself against his back and hold on tightly.

DJ could feel the softness of her body. He liked his women just like Crystal, on the petite side. Perhaps he'd stick around for a day or two and see what happened.

"And no one got a look at them?" the sheriff asked.

"No, sir," Gabe said.

"Well, Mr. Horne, there's not a lot we can do. I'll have a crime scene guy come by tomorrow to see if he can find any evidence and I'll try to get a deputy to drive by occasionally, but we're stretched pretty thin."

"I understand, Sheriff."

What Gabe didn't understand was the way that the law enforcement officers were treating him. When the deputy had first said that they needed to come see the sheriff, Gabe thought he was in trouble, but as the two men walked the four blocks, something was different. First, Gabe wasn't in cuffs. More than that, the deputy treated him as an equal. When they got to the sheriff's office, the sheriff was actually nice to him. The man had never been unfair with Gabe; however, he'd always treated him like a criminal. Of course, that was before the Smash. Perhaps a guy who got drunk and disorderly on occasion wasn't such a big deal now.

"I'm sure Mrs. Walker appreciates you watching out for her," the sheriff said. "I heard about what happened at the grocery store last week. You did us all a favor that day."

Well, that explains at least part of it, Gabe thought. "Thank you, sir."

"What you ought to do if you really want to help her and the boy is to move in with them."

"I can't do that."

"Why not?"

"Because it wouldn't look right," Gabe insisted.

"And letting her get killed or worse by some scumbags would? I'm not telling you to sleep in the same room with her, but you can't help her with problems like she had tonight if you're not there."

"People would talk."

"Who gives a damn?" the sheriff said as he smartly rapped his knuckles on his desk. "Look, Gabriel." The big lawman took a deep breath. "With the way things are going now, no one is going to cast judgment on you. Lots of families are moving in together to share resources. It just makes sense. We've been pretty lucky around here so far compared to what's going on in the cities, but big trouble is more than likely coming this way, and I can't be everywhere to stop it. Think about it. We need everyone to do what they can to help us by taking care of themselves."

It was the first time Gabe could remember the sheriff using his first name. What the sheriff said did make some sense, but Gabe was used to being by himself. He didn't know if he knew how to live with other people anymore. But at one time, he did. Maybe he could do it again. "Okay. I'll think about it, Sheriff."

"You do that. Now, you better get back to the hospital, and I better get back to this paperwork, or I'll be sleeping here tonight . . . again," the sheriff said with a smile.

"Thanks, Sheriff," Gabe said as he walked out the door with the deputy.

On the way back to the hospital, the deputy quizzed him about his encounter with the thief at the grocery store. "They told me you took the guy out with just one hit. Man, I would have given anything to see that."

"It really wasn't that big of a deal," Gabe said. "He was running with the basket and looking behind. I just stuck my arm out and clotheslined him. He was moving so fast that his feet just flew out from under him."

"Still, it must have felt good to sack him up."

"I don't know. I just reacted without thinking, really. I'm just glad he didn't hurt Mrs. Walker or her son."

"That's true," the deputy said, "but it must have felt a little good at least to know you stopped the guy."

Gabe was still thinking about the deputy's words when he walked back into the emergency room. Jane was sitting in a chair in the waiting area with Robby next to her. "What did the doctor say?"

"He told me basically what you said. It was a clean, through-and-through wound. He cleaned it up a little more and told me to come back in five days unless it starts to look infected. He gave me some antibiotics and some mild painkillers."

"So, you can go home?"

"Yes, I can," she said.

"Let's get out of here, then."

Gabe drove home with Robby sitting in the middle. He thought about bringing up what the sheriff had mentioned, but now didn't seem like the time. Jane was quiet, and Gabe figured that was the painkillers they'd given her at the hospital. When they got to her place, Gabe helped Jane out of the car and into the house. Robby went in ahead of them and lit the lantern.

"Well, I'm going to head home now," Gabe said, realizing his truck was still at home. "I'll just walk. I'll stop by tomorrow and see if you need anything."

"Gabe, I know I'm probably just being paranoid, but I'd feel much better if you'd stay here until morning. You can sleep in Robby's room, and he can sleep on the couch."

"I don't know, Jane. Aren't you afraid people will talk?"

"I don't really care, but if they do talk, I think they'd say 'Look at that nice man, watching out for his neighbors.' Don't you think so?"

"Maybe. I don't know." Gabe looked down and kicked at the floor as if he saw something stuck to it. "I'm just used to being at my house," he said. He saw the look on her face and was instantly sorry.

"Fine. Go on home, then. Robby and I will just have to fend for ourselves," she said, her face noticeably red, even in the pale light.

"I'm sorry, Hannah," he said quickly. "Of course I'll stay, but I'll sleep on the couch. There's no reason to kick Robby out of his room."

Gabe realized what he'd said, but made no effort to correct it. If Jane had noticed, she wasn't letting on.

"That's fine. Robby will get you some blankets and a pillow out of the hall closet. I've got to lie down. This leg is really starting to ache, so I'm going to bed," she said, her tone softer than before.

When she turned to head into her room, and when she knew Gabe could no longer see her, she smiled.

DJ pulled the quad back behind the house. He could still feel the warmth of Crystal's body on his back as they walked into the house. Crystal headed straight for Nancy's room. A minute later, she came back into the living room.

"Is she okay?" DJ asked.

"She's fine," Crystal said. "I really want to thank you for helping me get that car out of here."

DJ wished she meant that she wanted to thank him the way he wanted to be thanked. "It's no problem. Thanks for the grub and the bed. I haven't slept that well since I left home."

They stood quietly for a minute. "Well, I guess I better hit the road," DJ finally said.

"You're not leaving tonight, are you?"

"Yeah, I need to get to my place."

"I was hoping you'd stick around until my husband got home, just in case any more creeps show up," Crystal said.

"There's no telling when or if he'll be back, Crystal. I can't stick around indefinitely."

"Roger will be back! You just wait and see!"

"I hope you're right," DJ said, thinking that it was a long shot at best. He also noticed that her demeanor and tone now seemed more like a young teenager than a grown woman. He would test the water a little more and see how she reacted. "But the longer I stay, the harder it'll be for me to get where I'm going. Besides, there's no incentive for me to stay. If you had some gas or something I really needed or wanted to trade me, then I might consider it."

"I might be able to get some gas."

"How much?"

"Maybe a few gallons," Crystal said.

"Can you get it tomorrow?"

"I can try."

"Tell you what. I'll stay tonight, and we'll see how it goes to-morrow," DJ said.

"Thanks, DJ. Make yourself at home in the guest room. Just turn off the oil lamp when you're done in here. I'm going to bed," she said in a much more adult tone.

"Me, too," DJ said as he blew out the living room lamp, careful not to touch the hot glass chimney.

"Good night, then," Crystal said.

There was enough moonlight coming through the windows that DJ could just make out her form walking down the hallway. "Good night," he said as he headed for his room. Once there, he quickly stripped down and climbed into the comfortable bed.

He could hear dresser drawers opening and closing in Crystal's room. He imagined that she was donning some sexy number from Victoria's Secret. He pictured how nice her feminine figure would look in a slinky silk nightgown, and even better, how she would look out of it. Her body, from what he could tell while she was holding tight to him on the quad, was just the right combination of softness and firmness. He hoped he might hear a soft knock on his door and see her sneaking in to pay him a visit, but the knock never came.

If he was going to get in this girl's pants, he'd have to convince her that her husband was dead. That wouldn't be an easy thing to do with the way she'd reacted earlier, but something about her wasn't quite right. She was strong one minute and needy the next. If he could find the right buttons to push, he might get her to give in to him. Who knew? Maybe if things worked out the way he wanted, he'd just stay here.

CHAPTER 16

The roosters started crowing well before the sun came up. It must have been some kind of contest to see which one could create the most annoying sound. Gabe pulled his pillow over his head in an effort to filter out the morning row, but it was futile. The grand champion irritator let loose with a cock-a-doodle-doo that could have woken the dead. Gabe realized he was but a pawn in that feathered hell-spawn's world. He got up and padded to the kitchen.

He lit the lantern, which illuminated the blood still on the floor and the table. He found a mop and a bucket and set to scrubbing. The dried blood was hard to clean, but the motion wasn't much different from hoeing weeds. It didn't take him long. He cleaned the table with a sponge and some cleanser he found under the sink. It was soon spotless.

He rinsed out the sponge and the mop the best he could with as little water as possible. With the cleaning supplies returned to their places, he leaned back against the counter. His thoughts returned to the sheriff's suggestion the night before. It really wasn't a bad idea. If his neighbors were a man and his son, Gabe would have no problem moving in for the sake of safety. Should it make a difference that Jane was a woman? It shouldn't, but somehow it did.

Gabe saw the old percolator sitting on the stove. Coffee would taste good. He found a can of the black gold in the pantry and started the brewing process. Soon the aroma filled the kitchen. The sky was turning pink, and Gabe shut off the lantern.

"Man, that smells good."

Gabe turned and saw Jane standing in the doorway. She was wearing a long flannel nightgown and a terry cloth robe.

"I can't remember the last time I woke up to the aroma of brewing coffee," Jane said. "Is it ready yet?"

"You shouldn't be up," he said.

"And why not?"

"Your leg. It might start bleeding again."

"The doctor said I could walk on it. Just no running and no heavy lifting," she said. "You cleaned the kitchen. Thanks." She sat down and ran her hand over the table.

"You're welcome," Gabe said as he poured two cups of coffee and sat across from her.

"Thanks for staying last night, Gabe."

"No problem. In fact," he said nervously, "last night when I was talking to the sheriff, he said I should move in here permanently. Isn't that the craziest thing you've ever heard?"

"I don't know. It kind of makes sense with the way things are. I guess the real question is, how do you feel about it?"

Gabe stared at her with a knitted brow. The question reminded him of the therapist he'd gone to see at his boss's insistence. She had asked lots of "feeling" questions. How does this make you feel? How do you feel about that? At one point, Gabe had had all he could take and gone ballistic on the woman. He remembered his last words to her. "I just lost my wife and my son, bitch! How the fuck do you think I feel?" He'd stormed out of the office and slammed the door behind him. On his way home, he'd stopped and bought a fifth of whiskey. That was when he discovered that the alcohol could take the pain away, at least for a little while.

"I think it's a bad idea, Jane. I'm too set in my ways to make a change like that."

"I see."

God, she was just as bad as Dr. How-Do-You-Feel, Gabe thought. "Well, I better get going. My garden isn't going to take care of itself."

"Do you want me to drive you home?"

"No. I'll walk."

Light poured into the room. DJ looked at his watch and saw that it was almost nine o'clock. The smell of breakfast wafted through the house. He got up, dressed, and walked to the kitchen.

"That smells delicious," he said. "What is it?"

"It's eggs and Spam," Crystal said.

"Where did you get eggs?"

"From the neighbor. He has chickens. He gave me a gallon of gas, too."

"Really? Can you get any more from him?" DJ asked.

"He said that was all he could spare, but we can ask the other neighbors. Sit down and eat while it's hot."

"What did you tell him about the guys in the car?" he asked cautiously.

"I told him you showed up and scared them off," she whispered. She looked at Nancy, who was working diligently on a small puzzle. "I didn't want to tell him the truth."

"Good girl," DJ said as he sat. The fried Spam was all right, but the eggs were delicious. They had bright orange yolks that were full of flavor. They weren't like the eggs from the supermarket with their pale yellow centers and bland taste. DJ ate the three eggs on his plate and asked for more. Crystal got up and cooked him two more. He devoured them and felt as if he could eat a whole dozen by himself.

"Those are the best eggs I've ever eaten," he said. "Crystal, you are a wonderful cook."

She blushed slightly at the compliment, a look that suited her well. DJ wondered if she had any other special talents. She certainly looked as if she should. When she got up to wash the dishes, he jumped at the chance to help. Maybe it would earn him some brownie points.

"So, Crystal," he said as he dried a plate with a dish towel, "what kind of truck does Roger drive?"

"It's a Freightliner."

"When did he leave?"

"Eleven days ago. He had to run a load to California. I begged him not to go, but he said we needed the money and that he'd be all right. He took a shotgun with him and a backpack full of food and stuff. He promised me he'd keep enough fuel in the tanks to get home from wherever he was," she said.

DJ could hear some of the same uncertain tone he'd heard last night. He wouldn't say anything to make her believe that Roger wouldn't make it back, but maybe he could make her come to that conclusion herself.

"When was the last time you talked to him?"

"He called me when he got there. He was waiting to get unloaded, but he said he'd probably have to spend the night. The place he was delivering to only had half of their crew, and it was taking them a long time. The next morning when I got up, the phones were out."

"How long ago was that?" DJ asked, trying to sound as if he was concerned.

"Eight days," she answered. DJ saw a tear roll down her cheek. He almost felt sorry for her, but he pressed on.

"And when did you expect him back?"

"A couple of days after that." The single tear was followed by a torrent, like the first fat, cold raindrop of a summer squall.

"I see," DJ said as sadly as he could. He reached out and gently put his arm around her shoulders. She seemed to melt into him, and a river of sobs and indistinguishable words poured out of her. DJ held her tightly and slowly stroked her hair. It was soft and smelled like strawberries.

After a couple of minutes, the flood of tears slowed some, and she slowly lifted her head. "He could still make it, right?"

DJ thought about his answer. He didn't want to give her any hope, but he had to look sympathetic. "Anything's possible," he said, "but . . ."

"But what?" she sniffled.

"But you might want to start thinking about what you and Nancy are going to do if he doesn't."

The river began to flow again, and this time seemed as if it might rival the Mississippi. "I don't know what we'll do. I don't have any family and Roger's family is too far away. He's my whole life. If he doesn't come home, I don't know what I'll do. Tell me what to do."

"There, there," DJ cooed. This had been easier than he had thought. "We'll figure it out. I'll stay another day or two, and we'll come up with a plan. Don't worry. Everything will work out." *For me,* he thought.

Gabe was mentally kicking himself. Why was he such a jackass? He didn't used to be this way. Why couldn't he just tell Jane how he felt? What would be so wrong with that? He didn't have an answer. He just knew he didn't want to let the words come out. As he walked down the road with his rifle slung over his shoulder, he wondered what else he could screw up.

"Mr. Horne! Mr. Horne!" a voice called out. Gabe looked and saw an old man waving at him and shuffling down his driveway. The name "Blake" was crudely painted on the mailbox in white in a juvenile, freehand style. Gabe wondered if he knew this man, but he didn't recognize the name. The elderly man looked slightly more familiar as he got closer, and Gabe looked up the driveway and recognized the late-model truck. He'd seen it pass by his house on many occasions, but the driver had always acted as if Gabe was invisible.

The fact that the men had never talked before didn't seem to bother Mr. Blake now. "Mr. Horne, I heard about what happened to Mrs. Walker. Is she all right?"

Gabe's first impulse was to tell this old goat—who'd never given him the time of day before—to go pound sand, but he thought about what the sheriff had said last night and decided to be civil.

Besides, I've probably already pissed off my quota of people this week.

"Yes, she's going to be fine," he said.

"Nasty business, getting shot over a couple of chickens. I hope it was an isolated event," the man said, his eyes so wide they pulled half the wrinkles out of his face.

"Me, too."

"Well, she's lucky she had you to help her out. It must be really hard for a woman without a man in times like these."

"I reckon it is."

"It's smart you're carrying your rifle, too. After what happened, I'm not going anywhere without a little protection." The man pulled up his shirttail and revealed the grip of a small semi-automatic pistol.

"I guess we should all be prepared for the worst," Gabe said as the two men nodded in agreement. "I'm sorry, but I need to get on home."

"Sure. Listen, we're planning to butcher a steer later in the week. I don't have enough hay to feed all the cows over the winter. It'll be way more meat than we can eat before it spoils. I was wondering if Mrs. Walker would be willing to trade us some eggs and if you'd trade us some of those tomatoes of yours. My wife has bought some of them from Mrs. Walker at the farmers' market before, and they're the best I've ever tasted. I'll make you a really good deal."

"I'm sure we can work that out, Mr. Blake. Thanks."

"No, thank you, Mr. Horne. It's nice to know we have good neighbors like you to count on," Mr. Blake said with a smile as he extended his hand.

Gabe took the hand and shook it. "Likewise. I'll see you later this week," he said, feeling his own mouth turn up on the corners.

"See you later. You have a great day."

Gabe continued his walk home, and noticed that his mood was much improved by the encounter. Maybe someone should get all the neighbors together and see what everyone needed or had to trade. He'd talk to Jane about it. She knew more people around here than he did. He needed to go back and apologize for leaving so quickly anyway. Maybe once he was done with his chores, he'd drive over and check on her. Maybe, if it was early enough, he'd take Michael's .22 over and show Robby how to shoot it.

Gabe approached his driveway, and the hair on the back of his neck stood up. He didn't know why, and he tried to convince himself that he was just being silly, but the feeling only got stronger as he got closer. Mentally laughing at himself, he unslung the rifle and peeked around the corner toward his trailer. There, backed up to the front porch, was a strange pickup. A man was seated behind the wheel.

Gabe's face went hot. He stepped into the drive and began to walk quickly toward the truck. "Who the hell are you, and what are you doing?" he yelled.

He saw a man behind the wheel jerk his head around and look at him. He honked the horn and nervously looked into one side mirror and then the other. A second later, a man appeared out of

Gabe's open front door. He jumped into the bed of the truck, and the driver floored it. The truck leapt toward Gabe, showering the front of his mobile home with gravel and dust. Gabe stood dumbfounded for a moment, as the implications of what was happening sank in. At what seemed the last second, he jumped out of the drive as the truck rocketed past him. He kicked at it, as if it were some stray dog he was trying to run off. Gabe saw his Rototiller stashed in the back. A man was crouched down next to it, an evil grin on his face.

Gabe went from mad to furious in a millisecond. It wasn't that the old tiller was worth that much. It was that it carried a sentimental significance to him, being the last thing he and Hannah had bought together.

The truck squealed out of the driveway and onto the road so fast that Gabe thought it would roll onto its side. He ran the few steps back to the road and saw the goblin in the back still smirking at him over his tiller. Gabe realized he was holding a rifle in his hands, and he brought it up to his shoulder. He aimed at a tire and began to squeeze.

The smile on the thief's face vanished. Evidently, he hadn't noticed the rifle until Gabe shouldered it. Gabe continued to squeeze the trigger, but the gun wouldn't fire. Upon quick examination, he realized the hammer was on half-cock. Not that cocking it would have done any good since there wasn't a round in the chamber. Gabe dropped the rifle off his shoulder some and jacked the lever. As he was bringing it back up, he saw his tiller roll off the truck. It seemed to take forever, but it finally hit the road and began to roll. The man in the back must have pushed it out to distract Gabe, and distract him it did. He held his breath as the ma chine tumbled over and over. Gabe said a prayer for its safety and cursed the men who had done this all in the same breath. He fired a shot at the retreating truck, but he knew it was in vain the instant the rifle barked.

At long last, the tiller stopped, lying on its side, half on and half off the road. The truck disappeared around a bend. Gabe took a step toward the wrecked machine. He could see that the handles were bent down as if two giants had used them for a wishbone. He felt his throat close. A second later, he was able to convince his other leg to move in the direction of the contraption. Perhaps it would be okay. Another step and then, though he wasn't aware of it, he was running toward it. When he got there, it looked like a total loss.

It was the worst thing the men could have done to him. If they had stolen it, at least someone would have gotten use of it. Now it was nothing but scrap metal. Gabe knelt down beside the lifeless appliance on the side of the road. He felt a tear on his cheek. It was stupid to cry over a machine, but he couldn't stop, and he didn't understand why.

CHAPTER 17

It was sophomoric, he knew, getting a thrill out of holding Crystal while she cried, but it was the closest thing to a date he'd had since before the Smash. Finally her body stopped heaving against his, and a minute later, she pulled away.

"Thank you, DJ," she said as she wiped her nose with the back of her hand.

DJ thought it was unattractive and a little immature, but he could get past it. After all, his goal had nothing to do with perfect personal hygiene, and his plan was working better than he had hoped. She was thanking him.

"It's no problem. I'm glad to help," he said.

They returned to the dishes and finished them in silence.

"What do you want to do now?" she asked.

DJ almost slipped up and said the first thing that came to his mind. "Why don't we go and see if the neighbors have any gas?" he said.

"Okay."

They put their jackets on, and bundled Nancy up since it was a little chilly. DJ decided that he wouldn't take his rifle since it might make the neighbors nervous. Instead, he slipped his compact pistol inside his waistband and put two extra magazines in his pocket. They left the house, each holding one of Nancy's hands, and walked down the driveway like a happy young family.

Crystal turned them to the right once they reached the road. They bypassed the first house since it had been where she'd gone for gas that morning, and the man had said he had no more to spare. The second house was small, similar to Crystal's. They walked up to the door and knocked. After a minute, a man looked through the window beside the door. DJ heard the dead bolt unlock, and the door opened just an inch or so.

"What do you want?" the man asked.

"Hi, I'm Crystal Jones from up the road."

"I know who you are. What do you want, and who is he?"

"He's my cousin, Bob," Crystal said. "Someone stole all the gas out of my car, and I was wondering if you had any I could borrow or trade for."

"Is that what all the shooting was about yesterday?"

"Yes," she said. "Bob got to my place just as they were sneaking off with my gas. He scared them so bad that they shot at him, and he shot back. Nobody got hurt, thank God. The guys took off like a bat out of hell."

"Hmm," the man said. He looked at DJ. "So, don't you have gas in your car?"

"No, sir. I walked here," he answered respectfully.

"So, do you have some gas? I can pay you back later," Crystal said.

"No." The door snapped closed.

Crystal turned toward DJ and shrugged.

He was amazed. She had lied so easily and convincingly that he almost believed his name was Bob. She seemed like such a goody-goody, but DJ knew that lying skills like hers had to be developed. She was an enigma, but as far as he was concerned, it only made her more attractive.

They walked farther down the road and stopped at each house along the way, but they had no luck. Some people were friendlier, but they either didn't have any gas or wouldn't part with it. Crystal told the same story to everyone. DJ thought that Nancy might spill the beans, but she just stood and smiled brightly, not batting an eye as her mom told the fib.

They did find one man who wanted to trade some gas for a rifle, but that would have been out of the question even if DJ did have one to spare. He tried to bargain away one of the gang-banger weapons, but the man said he already had a pistol and wanted a long gun.

Some people wouldn't even open their doors. DJ thought one family wasn't home, and he considered looking around the place for some gas, but upon further consideration he realized it wasn't worth getting shot.

It was getting close to lunchtime, so they opted to head back. When they were almost home, DJ decided that he'd like to talk to the man Crystal had gotten the gas and eggs from. He obviously had more since he'd said it was all he could spare. Perhaps DJ could convince him to part with some, though Crystal thought it was a waste of time.

"He already told me it was all he could give me," she said.

"Yeah, but maybe he'll sell me some or trade with me," DJ said.

They turned down his driveway and walked up to the house.

Crystal knocked, and an older man answered the door with a shotgun in his hand.

"Hi, Crystal."

"Hi, Mr. Scott. This is my cousin, Bob, I was telling you about."

"Nice to meet you, Bob. It's lucky for Crystal that you showed up when you did. I'm sorry we weren't home when it happened, or I would have come over and helped you with those creeps," the man said, patting the bird gun in his arms.

"I told him not to worry about it," Crystal said, turning to DJ before he could speak. "I told him you ran the guys off before he could have gotten there anyway."

"That's true," DJ said with a big smile. "It's very nice to meet you, Mr. Scott. I told Crystal that the eggs you gave her were the best I'd ever eaten. Thank you so much for them."

"You're more than welcome. What brings you folks by?" Mr. Scott said.

"I was wondering if you had any more gas that I could buy or trade you for," DJ said.

"All I have left is what's in the pickup. What I gave you should get you to town, though," the older man said.

DJ was a little confused. What would going to town accomplish? Could he get more gas there? And what had Crystal told the man? He didn't want to blow her cover story.

"Uh, Bob just wasn't sure it was enough to get us to town," Crystal said, looking at DJ through the corner of her eyes.

"I figured that little car of yours would get at least twenty-five miles to the gallon, Crystal," Mr. Scott said, "and it's only about twenty miles to the gas station. If you get your five gallons, that should get you back home easily."

DJ shot a glance back at Crystal. It seemed the neighbors weren't the only ones she was lying to.

"Did the J-B Weld work on the gas tank?" Mr. Scott asked DJ.

"Oh, uh, I haven't gotten to try it yet," DJ answered. He and Crystal needed to have a talk. "Thanks for all your help, Mr. Scott. Anything we can get you in town?"

"We got our gas and groceries yesterday, but if you find any D batteries, I could use a couple of packs."

"We'll keep an eye out for them," DJ said as he took Crystal by the arm and turned to leave.

"Thanks," Mr. Scott said. "And remember, I need that J-B Weld back when you're done with it."

Gabe felt something touch his shoulder. He jumped, snapping his head around. The tears stopped immediately, and his eyes grew wide as he tightened his grip on the lever gun. A neighbor was standing there holding a scoped bolt-action rifle.

"Gabe, are you all right?" It was Harold Wilkes, Gabe's next-door neighbor. They had visited often before the accident and the funerals, but since then it had mostly been short waves or perhaps a few awkward words when they saw each other.

"Uh, yeah," Gabe said as the back of his hand wiped his cheeks.

"Are you sure you're not hurt?" Harold asked, his voice full of concern.

"Yeah, I'm okay. I just got a bunch of dirt in my eyes." It wasn't a total lie.

"It was those guys in the tan truck, wasn't it?"

"Yes, it was," Gabe answered. "How did you know?"

"They came and knocked on the door at our house. Said they were looking for work. I had a strange feeling about them, but I didn't think they were really dangerous. Did they shoot at you?"

"No. That was me."

"Did you hit the truck?" Harold's eyes were wide.

"No. I know I missed."

"Well, I'm sorry I didn't do anything, Gabe. I should have known they'd cause trouble."

"What could you have done, Harold? You can't shoot someone for asking for work, and it's not like you can pick up the phone and call the law to report a suspicious person, is it?" Gabe said.

"I guess not," the other man replied slowly. "Did they get anything? Besides the tiller, I mean," Harold said, nodding toward what remained of the machine.

"I don't know. One was in the house when I walked up, but he came out empty-handed. The other was sitting in the truck and keeping a lookout, I guess. I reckon I better go check."

"You want me to go with you?"

"That would be nice, Harold. Thanks," Gabe said. He pulled the mutilated tiller completely off the road. "I'll come back for this later."

The two men walked in silence to Gabe's house. Beside the door was a medium-sized crowbar that had been used to jimmy the frame. The door and jamb had been severely damaged. Gabe and Harold observed it for a few seconds, then entered the house. Gabe felt the hot blood rush back to his head. The home had been torn apart. There were cans of food strung across the living room like fallen soldiers. All of the cabinets in the kitchen were opened. Gabe stepped over the cans and into the kitchen. He saw that almost all of his food, along with the alcohol he kept in the kitchen, had been stolen. He was a little surprised that he wasn't that upset about the whiskey, probably because he knew he had his emergency stash in the bedroom.

The thought that the thieves might have made it in there flashed through his mind. He quickly walked to his bedroom and pulled open the bottom drawer of his dresser. There, sitting in a neat row, were the three bottles. Gabe breathed a sigh of relief. Happy that the whiskey was safe, he examined the rest of the room. He saw that Hannah's jewelry box was right where it should be. He opened the drawer that held his pistol and found it was still in its place. Opening the closet door revealed that his long guns were also safe. It looked as if he had interrupted the thieves before they could get past the kitchen. He was at least a little thankful for that as he walked back into the living room where his neighbor was waiting.

"What all did they get?" Harold asked.

Gabe decided not to say anything about the stolen liquor. "Looks like they just got my food, almost all of it. The son of a bitch must have been on his last trip from the kitchen when his buddy honked the horn," Gabe said, his face twisted tight.

"That's horrible," Harold said.

"Yes," Gabe said, realizing that he couldn't just run to the store and replace everything. He thought he should be angrier, but he wasn't. The hurt of losing the tiller was most on his mind.

"I guess it could have been worse, though."

"I reckon so," Gabe said, trying to convince himself that it was the truth. The food was probably worth about a hundred dollars before the Smash. Now, on the black market, who knew? You could get groceries, but some things were hard to come by, and you could only buy so much even if you did find what you wanted.

The alcohol, on the other hand, might be priceless. Gabe had noticed that the liquor store had been closed when he'd gone to town last. He kept a stockpile of the expensive bourbon. It was really the only luxury he afforded himself. There had been nine and a half bottles of it in the cabinet. Gabe always stocked up over the months that he was able to sell his produce at the farmers' market. The small life insurance policy he'd had on Hannah and Michael through his work had paid off the land, with just enough left that the interest from the small nest egg would usually pay his basic bills. If he didn't stockpile like this, he'd end up drinking rotgut over the winter. The three bottles in his bedroom would hold him for a while, but he didn't like to get into them since they were for an emergency. *Well, I guess this is an emergency,* he thought.

Perhaps it would be okay and the three bottles would hold him until he could get some more. After all, he hadn't been drinking as much lately. Before the Smash, if something like this had happened, he would have run straight to the liquor cabinet. He couldn't do that with Harold here, though. He noticed with a little surprise that he didn't really want a drink right now. All he wanted to do was to clean up his home.

He set about the task and soon had everything back in its place. Harold tried to help, but he didn't know where anything went and just ended up slowing Gabe down. Gabe appreciated the gesture, though.

"I don't know what we can do about the door," Harold said as Gabe closed the last cabinet door.

"I'll just have to nail it shut for now and go in and out the back."

"You need some help?"

"Sure," Gabe said. "I've got some plywood out back. We can cut a strip of it and cover the damaged part of the door and the frame."

The two men walked out to the shed, and Gabe retrieved a hammer, some nails, and a saw. Then he pulled out a large piece of three-quarter-inch plywood from the stack of scrap lumber. They carried it around to the front, and Gabe used his hands to measure how big the piece of plywood needed to be. He began sawing as Harold held the wood.

Either the teeth were dull or the wood had hardened—possibly both—because the sawing was painfully slow.

"Don't you have a circular saw?" Harold asked.

"Sure, but without electricity it's worthless."

"I have a portable generator."

"Really?" Gabe said.

"Yeah, let's go get it. We can pick up your tiller on the way back, too."

"Let's go," Gabe said, dropping the old saw as if it had suddenly grown warts.

"So, what the hell's the deal, Crystal?" DJ said just as soon as Nancy had been sent to her room to play.

"I'm sorry, DJ," she said, tears beginning to well up in her eyes. "I was afraid if I told you that you could get gas in town, you'd leave. I'm so stupid. Now you're probably pissed off at me and will leave for sure."

Good guess, sister.

DJ wondered if the tears were real, or if she was just using them to continue lying to him. It was most likely the latter, he thought. He had to admit, the bitch was good at it. Well, one good turn deserves another. He put on his sweetest voice.

"No, I wouldn't just leave you and Nancy here defenseless, and I'm not angry about you lying to me, since I know you're worried about Nancy's safety and your own. I figure that's why you did it, but if you want me to stay here, I expect nothing less than the truth from you from here on out. Understand?"

Crystal nodded like a three-year-old, caught with her hand in the cookie jar.

"When did you learn to lie so well?" he asked.

"When I was growing up. My dad ran off when I was just a baby, and my mom had a lot of problems. I was in and out of foster homes my whole life. I don't know what was worse, being in the system with people who pretended to care for you just so they could get the money, or being at home with mom and her druggie boyfriends who would take turns on me when Mom was passed out."

The tears were still in her eyes, but they were from anger now, not fear. DJ didn't believe she could fake the trembling in her voice, either. He could only imagine the horrors this girl had seen and experienced. It all made sense now. No wonder she was scared shitless when he had mentioned foster care before.

"And the part about your husband, is that true?"

"Every word," Crystal said emphatically. "Roger saved me from that nightmare when I was seventeen. I owe him my life."

"Okay. Give me the epoxy that Mr. Scott gave you, and I'll try to patch the hole in your gas tank. By the time it dries, it will probably be too late to head into town today, but we'll go first thing in the morning. All right?"

"Okay, DJ. Thank you for not being mad at me," she said as she handed him the two tubes.

DJ gave her his million-dollar smile. He was better at this than she was. He turned and headed out to her car.

And the Academy Award goes to . . . me.

CHAPTER 18

"It's butt-ugly, but I guess it'll hold," Gabe said as he looked at the patched-up door. "At least until I can get to town and get a replacement," he added. Hannah wouldn't have liked it, he thought. He'd have to fix this properly as soon as he could.

"What are you going to do for food?" Harold asked.

"I can just eat out of my garden until I get back to town, and Mr. Blake wants to trade some beef for vegetables. I may also try to shoot a feral hog. It's been a long time since I hunted, but there's not much choice now."

"I guess to get by, we're all going to have to do things that we're not used to doing," Harold said thoughtfully. "Do you need to use the generator for anything else while it's here?"

"No," Gabe said. "I don't, but if you don't mind, could we take it down to Jane Walker's place and use it to run her well for an hour or two?"

Harold paused for a long moment, his face pensive. "That wouldn't be a problem, Gabe, but I don't really have enough spare gas to run it that long."

"How much will it need?"

"It burns between a half and three-quarters of a gallon an hour, depending on the load," Harold said.

"I'll siphon whatever it burns out of my truck and give you some fresh vegetables to boot."

The neighbor smiled. "Then what are we waiting for?"

The two men loaded the generator into the back of Gabe's truck. Gabe ran into the trailer and came out with a long box under his arm. He put it behind the seat of the truck and climbed in. He locked his gate behind him this time. It wouldn't stop anyone from breaking into his house again, but they'd have to carry whatever they stole back out to the road. When they pulled into Jane's driveway, a sheriff's car was there.

Gabe tensed and swallowed hard at the sight of the cop car, but relaxed as Robby appeared in the door and came running out.

"Mr. Horne, the sheriff's office is here trying to see if they can figure out who shot Mom," he said. He noticed the other man in the truck, and Gabe could see the question on his face. As the two men climbed out of the truck, Gabe introduced Harold and Robby.

"Nice to meet you, sir," Robby said.

"The pleasure's all mine," Harold said with a smile.

"How's your mother feeling?" Gabe asked.

"She says she's all right, but she's limping some. When she thinks I'm not looking, I can see her wincing."

"Let's go check on her, then."

They went into the house and found Jane sitting at the table with the sheriff's investigator. The two of them were drinking coffee. Jane knew Harold, and she introduced the newcomers to the deputy.

The lawman stood up and shook both their hands. "The sheriff had some nice things to say about you, Mr. Horne. Said you were a real take-charge kind of guy."

"I was only in the right place at the right time at the grocery store," Gabe said meekly.

"Well, most folks would've just watched the thief run on by. I was just starting to tell Mrs. Walker what I found." He bent over, reached into his briefcase, and pulled out a plastic bag with an expended shotgun shell in it. "This was by the back fence. It's a Magnum 'T' waterfowl load. It had a bunch of .20-inch steel shot in it." He reached down and brought out another baggie. It had several small round balls in it. They looked like ball bearings. "I pulled these out of the siding on the back of the house. It's a good thing they were so far away. Any closer and you might've caught five or six of these, Mrs. Walker."

"Can you tell where they went, Deputy?" Gabe asked.

"No. I tracked them to the road, but there are too many sets of tire tracks to tell which ones belonged to them. My best bet is to get a print off the shell, but with all the lawlessness we're starting to see, I wouldn't hold my breath that we'll catch these guys."

"Speaking of lawlessness, two guys broke into my place this morning and stole all my food and my garden tiller. I got home as they were carrying things out to their truck, and they took off," Gabe said.

The deputy squinted, and his lips pressed together so hard that they almost disappeared. "Did you get a plate number?" he asked.

Gabe's hand smacked his forehead. "No. I'm sorry. I was so mad that I wasn't thinking clearly."

"Where'd they break in at?" the deputy asked.

"Through the front door. They used a crowbar."

"Well, I'll head over there and see if I can pull some prints off the door."

Gabe rolled his eyes and sighed. "I'm sorry, Deputy, but Harold and I patched the door up before we came over here. I'm sure we messed up any prints they might have left."

"Anything else they might have touched?"

Now Gabe felt like a real idiot. He'd hit the trifecta. He hated to admit it, but he told the deputy anyway. "One of them dropped some canned goods in my living room, but I picked them up and put them away. They also pushed my Rototiller out of their truck while they were getting away, but Harold and I brought it back home. It might be your best bet, though. I'm sure both of them had to lift it into the truck."

"Why would they push it out?"

Gabe wasn't sure how the deputy would feel about him taking potshots at the truck. He thought about making something up but decided to tell the truth. "I took a shot at the truck's tire. I think the guy pushed it out so I wouldn't shoot at them again," he said sheepishly.

"I see," the deputy said in a disapproving voice. "I'll go see if I can get anything off the tiller. Where is it?"

"It's behind my house. The gate's locked, but there's a key under the rock next to the second fence post to the left of the gate."

"All right. Mrs. Walker, I hope you get to feeling better. Mr. Horne, can I have a word with you outside?"

Gabe just nodded and followed the deputy out the front door.

When the deputy got to his car, he turned around. The look on his face told Gabe that he was in more trouble than he'd thought. He was afraid that he might be headed to jail.

"Mr. Horne, I'm going to give you some advice. It's the same advice the sheriff gives all the deputies when they start working for him. When you fire your weapon, you don't miss."

Gabe blinked. He didn't know how to respond. After a moment he said, "I thought I was in trouble for shooting at them."

"No," the deputy replied quickly, "I'm upset you missed. First, you don't know where the bullet you fired went. Second, it's much easier to find a truck or a perp with a hole in them." The deputy paused a second. "Mr. Horne, the sheriff's department is doing its best to keep order, but it's getting to be a losing battle. We need to rely on the citizens of this county to help us if we hope to succeed. I know that shooting at someone for stealing some canned food seems extreme, but it sends the message that we will not tolerate thieves and other lawbreakers. Food is a precious resource right now, and anyone who would steal it might just be killing the person they stole from. Do you understand what I'm telling you?"

"Yes, Deputy, I do."

"Good. I'm going to look at your tiller. I'll lock the gate behind me when I leave."

"Thank you, Deputy."

"No. Thank you, Mr. Horne."

Gabe turned and walked back into the house, wondering why the deputy would thank him. Jane was still sitting at the table when he got back to the kitchen.

"Did you get into trouble?" she asked as Robby and Harold looked on with interest.

"No. Well, yes, but not for what I thought. He wasn't upset that I shot at the guys; he was upset because I missed." Gabe shrugged.

"Go figure," Harold said.

"What did he say exactly?" Jane said.

Gabe told them word for word, or at least as close as he could remember.

"It makes sense," Jane said. "They must know things are getting out of control. I mean, look at what's happened to us in just the last twenty-four hours. If things keep getting worse, someone's going to get killed. We need to figure out how we're going to stay safe."

"That's true," Harold said.

"You know," Gabe said, "when I was walking home this morning, Mr. Blake stopped me to check on you and to tell me that they were going to butcher a steer. He wanted to trade some beef for some eggs and some vegetables. I was thinking that someone should get all the neighbors together to see what everyone has to trade and what everyone needs. We could talk about safety, too."

"That's a great idea, Gabe," Jane said. "We could meet down at the little Baptist church on the corner."

"We should do it soon," Harold said. "In fact, the sooner, the better."

"What would be wrong with tomorrow?" Jane asked.

"Nothing, but how can we get the word out?"

"I have an idea," Jane said with a smile.

DJ checked the J-B Weld. It was hard and dry. He poured the gallon of gas into the car and looked under to see if it was leaking out. It seemed to be holding, so he got into the car, put the key into the ignition, and turned it. The little Japanese four-cylinder engine started almost immediately. It was too close to dark to go to town now, but they could go first thing in the morning.

"The car's fixed," he announced as he walked into the house.

"That's great!" Crystal squealed, jumping out of her chair and giving him a quick hug.

He tried to get his arms around her, but she pulled back away before he could return the embrace.

At least she seems to be warming up to me a little more.

Crystal fixed dinner, and after the dishes were done, the three of them played a game of Monopoly. Nancy won with only a little help from the grown-ups.

DJ retired to his room, thinking about the gas he'd be able to buy tomorrow. The neighbor said that the station was limiting everyone to five gallons per week and that they wouldn't fill a can. That was all right; he knew how to siphon gasoline out of a car. Two trips would give him more than enough to make it to his retreat. He'd see what else he could find in town, as well. Maybe there was something Crystal needed. He'd be willing to spend some money on her if it would help him get closer to her.

Just as he was about to doze off, he heard a tap on his door. His mind came to full alertness. The door groaned almost inaudibly as it was pushed open. DJ felt a smile spread across his face.

"DJ," Crystal whispered.

"Yes, Crystal," he said.

"I heard a noise outside in the back. Would you take a look?"

Damn it.

Well, at least it was a chance for him to be her knight in shining armor. "Sure," he answered. He threw the covers back and reached for his clothes. He knew exactly where each piece was, and it took less than a minute to dress, even in the blackness. "What did you hear?" he asked as he found her waiting on the other side of the door.

"I thought I heard voices whispering."

DJ suspected it was more than likely just the wind whistling through the trees. "Stay here and be quiet," DJ told her, just in case there really was something, "and don't use a flashlight or light a lamp."

"Okay," she answered quietly.

DJ took the three steps he knew it was from the door to the chair that held his rifle and vest. His night-vision goggles were also there. He felt for the device and pulled the headgear on so that the infrared scope was in front of his right eye. He turned it on and easily donned the vest and grabbed his carbine. He could see that Crystal was wearing a thick bathrobe, which she was clutching together right under her neck. As he passed her, he squeezed the back of her arm.

He decided to go out the front door and creep around to the back. When he opened the front door, his heart jumped into his throat. Two men were pushing his four-wheeler through the front yard and toward the road.

CHAPTER 19

DJ's mind raced for the best solution. He could easily shoot them with his carbine, but that would make a lot of noise and might bring more attention than he wanted. His pistol would be a little quieter, but probably not quiet enough. He could just scare them off with a couple of shots over their heads. It would work, but they might come back later with friends. Besides, they were stealing from him. They had to pay.

If he had a baton like the one he carried at the mall, it would have been easy to take them down and apply a little mostly silent justice. He had taken several classes—out of his own pocket, of course—on the proper way to use a PR24. It was a devastating weapon in the right hands. Unfortunately, the only quiet weapon he had was his knife, but would the punishment fit the crime?

His mind flashed to the Old West, where horse thieves were hanged for their crimes. The big quad was sort of like a horse, and the current events weren't unlike those of the frontier days. Besides that, he'd always thought that if he'd been born a hundred and fifty years earlier, his name would have been synonymous with Reeves, Masterson, and maybe even Earp.

DJ didn't have any offensive knife training, and that made him a little nervous. He'd seen plenty of movies and had read some accounts on the Internet about using a knife, though. They all agreed that if you clamped your hand over the victim's mouth and inserted the blade into the base of the skull, the results were not only instant but silent.

He set his carbine down by the door, as well as his goggles. He couldn't afford for them to get damaged. There was enough moonlight that he'd be able to operate up close.

His hand found the handle of the big knife, and he pulled his expensive cutting tool out of its Kydex sheath. The Tanto blade was made for this kind of work. The strong point, hardened steel, and curved blade made this knife a favorite of black operators the world over.

The blade was flat black, but the scalpellike edge glinted in the moonlight. The rubber handle filled his hand perfectly. The pommel nestled in the crease of his palm between the ball of his thumb and heel of his hand. It wouldn't slip if he hit a vertebra as he pushed it in. He felt his face tighten into a grin as his gaze moved from the instrument to the two men making off with his property.

He moved like a cat, quickly and quietly closing in on them. The man pushing on the back of the quad was the logical choice to take first. If things went bad, DJ could always pull his big Glock out of the thigh holster and use it. He took a deep breath and sprang onto the man. He clamped his left hand over the man's mouth and inserted the blade just below the bump where the man's neck and skull met. The thief went limp without making a sound, and DJ let him go, allowing the weight of his body to pull the knife free. *That was better than shooting Crystal's attacker in the head,* DJ thought.

The man pushing on the handlebars didn't notice a thing except that he was no longer getting any help. "Damn it, Chuck," he whispered without turning around, "would you stop screwing around and push?"

DJ grabbed the rear rack and began to push.

"That's better," the thief said.

DJ worked his way from the back of his machine around to the side while still helping the bandit. He let go of the rack he was now pulling on to grab the perp and give him a taste of what his buddy had gotten. Before he could grab the man, though, the bandit started cursing and spun around.

"How many fuckin' times do I have to tell . . ." The man saw that it wasn't Chuck who was behind him. DJ and the thug both froze for a second, each unsure of what to do. The rustler was the first to move. His right hand sped toward his waistband, where DJ could see he had a pistol stashed. He was clumsy, though, and the pistol wouldn't come out, as it seemed to be hung on his clothing. DJ thought about drawing his own pistol, but he'd have to drop the knife first.

DJ had almost forgotten that he already had a weapon in his hand. He looked at it for a split second as if he was trying to convince himself that it was real. His eyes then traveled back to the man in front of him and found their way to the triangle of neck that sat between a stain-filled shirt and an unkempt beard.

DJ's hand followed his eyes and traced a horizontal line across the man's neck. The razor-sharp blade seemed to glide through the soft tissue. DJ saw the man's eyes go wide as he quit jerking on his trapped handgun and brought his hands up to cover the thin red line across his neck. A split second later, a stream of blood shot from between the man's fingers and painted DJ with spurt after spurt like some abstract artist who slung his media onto an oversized canvas in an attempt to create a so-called masterpiece.

DJ watched in gleeful horror as the color blanched from the man's face and he fell to his knees. His eyes looked up at DJ's face as if he expected DJ to run the knife backward and heal the fatal wound. DJ was fixated on the copious amount of blood pooling at his feet and the sucking noises coming out of the wound, as the man's lungs tried to keep working. He finally fell onto his back, his mouth uselessly opening and closing and his body thrashing in vain. After what seemed an eternity, the man's mouth finally opened for the last time, and his body came to an awkward rest.

DJ didn't know how much time had passed while he was watching the man bleed out. What he did know was that the euphoria he'd felt on the slash had given way to repulsion as the smell and taste of the sticky blood overtook his senses. The lump of stone that his dinner had suddenly become started rushing upward, and he retched uncontrollably. The aroma of half-digested food and bile was preferable to the stench of death. He wished he'd used a firearm, as he had to admit to himself that this was indeed a very personal method of exterminating someone. He hoped he never had to do it again.

As he stood erect again and wiped his mouth with the back of his sleeve, he noticed his hands shaking. *It's just the adrenaline,* he thought to himself as he clasped his hands together. He tried to spit the vile taste from his mouth, but it was to no avail.

The two bodies lay on the lawn, one with little blood pooled under him, the other in a lake of it. He wondered if the ground would soak up the syrupy fluid before daylight. That was unlikely, given the amount of rain that had fallen recently. Another wave of nausea attacked him, but he beat it back this time, barely. He knew the first thing he had to do was to get rid of the bodies. These wouldn't be like the gangbangers, not missed by anyone. These were probably local boys. Good or bad, someone would want to know what happened to them.

He could dump them in the quarry as he'd done with the car, but they'd float. How could he weigh them down? Even if he tied some kind of anchor to pull them under, would it hold? Maybe the quarry wasn't the best answer.

He could bury them. In the woods somewhere would be good, but he didn't know if there was a good-sized patch of woods around. He'd have to ask Crystal. He turned back toward the house and spat out a small amount of bile that had found its way into his mouth. He picked up his carbine at the front door and walked into the house.

"Is that you?" Crystal whispered.

"Yeah," DJ answered.

He saw the strike of a match and then Crystal's pretty face behind it as she lit a candle. A second later, the room was bathed in the soft light. DJ saw Crystal's eyes open wide.

"Oh my God!" she screeched. "Are you okay? Is that your blood?"

"No. I'm fine," he answered, his voice raspy and low.

"What happened?"

"Two guys were stealing my quad."

"How did you get covered in blood?" she asked.

"I didn't want to draw the neighbors' attention by firing any shots. I used my knife to take them out. I'm going to have to bury them somewhere. Do you know of a good place? Oh, and we need to clean up the blood in your front yard somehow."

Crystal just stood frozen, staring at DJ as if he were a ghost.

"Crystal, did you hear me? Do you know of a place to bury the bodies?"

"You killed them?"

"Yes. They won't be able to hurt you or Nancy."

"But they were just taking your four-wheeler?" she asked more than said.

"Yeah," he answered, not liking the direction the conversation was going.

"And you killed them?"

"What the hell did you want me to do? Invite them inside for some hot chocolate and a sing-along?"

"Well, no, but I don't think killing them was the right thing to do. Why didn't you just fire a couple of shots over their heads and scare them off?"

"So they could just come back with their own guns and kill us in our sleep?" he shot back. "What's your problem, Crystal? You didn't have any problem with me killing the gangbangers who at- tacked you."

"Those guys were probably going to kill us. These guys were just stealing something. They didn't deserve to die."

"And how do you figure that?"

She didn't answer.

"You know," he continued, "in the Old West, they hung horse

thieves. That quad is like my horse. Without it, I can't get to my bug-out location, and I might die. So what I did was justified."

Crystal's eyes narrowed, and she stared at him. Finally, she turned and headed for her room. She hadn't told him where to bury the bodies, but he no longer needed help. He knew where to dispose of them. Going back outside, he tied the dead thieves to his quad, one on the front rack and one on the rear. It was only a short drive back to the old shed he'd been in when he'd first heard the shots at Crystal's house. The dirt was soft there, too.

"I think that's enough," Jane said.

"Do you think so?" Amanda, Harold's wife, asked.

"It should be. Besides, I'm tired. If we need any more, we can make them tomorrow."

Gabe looked at his watch. It was twelve thirty. Everyone looked tired. Robby had been doing his best to keep his eyes open for the last fifteen minutes, but it looked as if he was about to lose that battle. The Wilkeses stood up, and hands were shaken all around.

"It was so nice to meet you," Amanda said to Jane.

"The pleasure was all mine," Jane replied, "and thanks so much for the help with the flyers."

"No problem at all. It's too bad that it took something like this 'Smash' for us to meet our neighbors."

"I know what you mean."

"Well, we'd better get home and let you get that boy to bed," Amanda said with a smile. "Let's go, Harold."

"Okay. You want a ride to your house, Gabe?"

"No. I think I'm going to sleep here on the couch again, just in case those chicken thieves come back."

Gabe noticed the quick eye contact Jane and Amanda shared. He wondered what it meant.

"If that's okay with Jane, of course," he added quickly.

"No, no, that's fine. In fact, I'd appreciate it."

"Then I'll see you in the morning," Harold said.

"Okay, see you in the morning," Gabe said, still wondering what the women's looks meant.

Harold and Amanda showed themselves out the door while Jane busied herself leading her zombielike son to his room. Gabe picked up one of the flyers. It looked almost like a ransom note since each of them had written a different section of the flyer.

ATTENTION

Neighborhood meeting at the Calvary Baptist Church at
6:00 PM today, June 29th.
Topics of discussion will include Neighborhood Security,
Bartering, and anything else you want to talk about.

Jane walked back into the room with an armload of blankets and pillows. She set them on the couch. "Thanks for staying, Gabe."

"No problem," he mumbled. "How's your leg?"

"It's still a little stiff, but the medication is keeping the edge off the pain."

"That's good," he said, noticing that she was looking at him as if she expected him to say something else. He just stood there for an uncomfortable moment. "Well, good night."

"Good night," Jane said.

Gabe arranged the blankets on the couch and then climbed into them. He wondered what was going on with Jane. What did she want from him? Was it what he suspected?

Christ, I need a drink.

CHAPTER 20

DJ woke up with a start. He looked around the room. Nothing seemed out of place in the pale dawn light that was just beginning to illuminate the room. He listened for a minute, and except for the cheerful chirping of a couple of birds, he heard nothing. He threw the covers back and rose out of the bed in one motion.

"Ahh," he groaned, grabbing his right shoulder. He grimaced as that motion brought pain to his other shoulder, though not as much as his right shoulder and back were experiencing. The digging had been harder than he'd thought it would be. He gingerly lowered his left hand so he could see his watch. It was just after six a.m. After burying the two bodies and then cleaning up his quad and himself, he had only gotten a couple of hours' sleep.

Moving as carefully and slowly as he could, he dressed and headed out to the spot where he had stopped the thieves. There wasn't as much blood as he'd expected. The ground seemed to have soaked up quite a bit of it. The patchwork of grass and weeds that made up Crystal's front lawn was somewhat discolored by the red substance, though. How could he cover it up? He thought about washing it off with a hose, but there was no water pressure. He could get some water in a bucket, but how far would he have to carry it? Crystal was getting low on water in the house. She probably wouldn't appreciate him using it to wash the grass.

He thought about getting some dirt and sprinkling it over the area. His muscles protested at the mere thought of a shovel. Besides, the fresh dirt might look suspicious. He walked around to the backyard and looked into the storage shed, hoping it would inspire him. An almost new lawn mower with a bagger was sitting next to the shed. If he cut the lawn short, most of the blood-stained grass would be removed. He decided to give it a try.

He unscrewed the gas cap and saw that the tank was nearly empty. He figured it would only take a quart or so to mow the front lawn. He could spare that much, especially since they were going to town to get more.

Once he'd carefully put gas in the mower, he pushed it around front. His shoulders were still sore, but he'd just have to live with the pain for now. He couldn't wait and take the chance that someone would find the bloodstains. He wondered if the mower would wake any of the neighbors and cause them to come over. It might, but he decided that the sooner he got this done, the better.

He started mowing in the middle of the lawn where the blood was just in case someone came to see what was going on. The mower not only cut and bagged the bloody grass, but it also seemed to make the red dirt disappear. DJ figured that it stirred up whatever dust there was and deposited it over the sticky red substance. However it was happening, he was pleased with the results.

It didn't take long to finish. He pushed the mower back to the shed and went into the house. Crystal was sitting at the table, her eyes bloodshot. She stared at DJ as he walked in, and he felt a little uncomfortable. "Good morning," he said.

"I think you should go," Crystal said.

"Why?" he asked with genuine shock.

"You know why."

"Crystal, try to look at this from my point of view. That quad is my survival. Without it, I can't get to my retreat. Maybe I could have scared the thieves off, but what if they came back with more guys or with guns? They could have killed all of us. Or worse, they could have finished what I stopped the bangers from doing to you and Nancy."

"I don't care. I want you out of here."

DJ felt his face go hot. He'd done everything for this woman and she didn't appreciate it. "Fine," he spat. He still needed the gas, though. Five gallons probably wasn't enough to make it to his retreat, but it would get him close, and he could beg, borrow, or steal enough to get him the rest of the way. He could take the car and go get the fuel himself, but what would Crystal do? As mad as she was, would she go to the neighbors and tell them what had happened? He couldn't take that chance. "I'll leave, but first we're going to town to get some gas."

"You can go to hell, for all I care, but I'm not going anywhere with you."

DJ had half a mind to backhand her, but he kept himself in check. He knew it would only strengthen her resolve not to go to town with him. He lowered his voice and spoke only a decibel or two above a whisper. "If you want me to leave, then you will go to town with me. I can't leave without more fuel. So make up your mind what you really want."

He could see that his words had the desired effect. Her icy stare gave way to a pensive look. "We can go to the grocery store, and I'll buy you some food," he added to sweeten the pot.

"Well," she said slowly, "I guess if that's the only way to get rid of you, but you buy me whatever I want and then leave as soon as we get back."

DJ wouldn't leave until dark at the earliest, but he could argue about that once they got back. "Agreed," he said with his best smile.

"That's the last house," Gabe said as he wiped his brow. He, Harold, and Robby had spent the morning walking down the roads in the area and passing out the handwritten notices they'd made the night before. All the people they had talked to were excited about the meeting and promised to be there. Gabe was surprised by how friendly they all were and how they all wanted to talk about current events. It would have normally taken only a couple of hours to walk around to all the houses. If Gabe and Harold hadn't excused themselves from several of the houses, they wouldn't have finished until well after dark.

The two men and the boy headed back home. The noontime sun was warm, but not hot. The sky was blue, and a light breeze blew steadily. It was a great day for being outside. Gabe would have been in his garden if he hadn't needed to pass out the flyers. There were still a few hours of daylight left, and Gabe thought about putting them to good use.

They said good-bye to Harold when they reached his driveway, and then Gabe and Robby continued on quietly down the road for a few minutes. Finally Robby broke the silence.

"What was his name?" the young man asked.

"Who?" Gabe said.

"Your son. I know he died, and that's why you're sad all the time."

A black hole opened in Gabe's stomach. He hated this feeling. The only thing that would stop it was the whiskey. It upset him that the boy had reopened the wound, though he knew that he wasn't really angry at Robby. It was more that he felt vulnerable. He thought back to some of the difficult questions Michael had asked him. Questions he didn't know the answers to, or questions with answers that he couldn't put into words a boy would understand. Gabe had always tried his best, though, and Michael had always seemed satisfied.

The answer to Robby's question was easy, though. At least it should have been. It was only seven letters, two syllables that formed a simple, common name, but Gabe could not get his mouth to move. It was almost as if saying it would cause the world to end.

The trip to town was a quiet one. Other than Nancy humming softly in the backseat, no one made a sound. When they got to the gas station, DJ saw a large hand-painted sign.

5-gallon limit per week per family. NO CANS.

He noticed two men armed with rifles at the front of the building. When he pulled up to the pump, he saw that the nozzle was locked with a padlock. A second later, the attendant came out.

"Driver's license please," the young man said.

"What for?" DJ asked.

"We have to put it in the database and make sure no one from your address has gotten gas in the past week."

"You have a database just for that? That seems a little extreme, doesn't it?"

"It's not. You wouldn't believe what people try to pull just to get some extra."

"I guess so," DJ said as he reached for his wallet. He pulled out his license and handed it to the man. Just as he did, it occurred to him that he should have made Crystal give her license. Then he could come back later and get more gas with his four-wheeler.

The man looked at DJ's card for a second and then handed it back. "I'm sorry, but you're from out of town. We only sell to locals."

"I'm staying with my cousin," DJ said as he tipped his head in Crystal's direction. "Give him your license, Crystal."

Crystal didn't say a word. She handed her license to the attendant without turning her head. The man took it, looking curiously at Crystal and then the license. "Ma'am, are you all right?" he asked.

DJ turned to see what she would say. She continued to stare straight ahead and simply nodded once.

"She's not feeling well," DJ said sadly.

"Okay, then," the young man said slowly. "This address is fine. I'll be right back." He walked back toward the office.

"You better chill, Crystal. You're going to blow this, and if I don't get my gas, I can't leave. Now, act normal."

She turned her head only slightly toward him and stared at

him with eyes full of hate. DJ decided to push her no further. A minute or two later, the man came back out of the office. He handed Crystal's license back to DJ.

"Do you want the whole five gallons?"

"Yes," DJ said.

"That'll be fifty bucks."

DJ whistled. "Wow, ten dollars a gallon. Well, we have to have it."

"You're lucky we have any. We ran out yesterday, but a truck came first thing this morning," the attendant said as he took DJ's cash. "Fire it up," he hollered at one of the guards.

DJ watched as the guard set his rifle against the building and pulled the rope on the generator he'd been standing in front of. The attendant unlocked the nozzle, and soon the five gallons of liquid gold was in the little economy car. DJ thanked the man and drove across the street to the grocery. It was an old store with huge glass windows. DJ parked the car. There weren't many other cars in the lot, but there was a considerable line of people leading into the store.

A man was sitting at a card table with a laptop computer in front of him, an armed guard standing right behind him. Someone had cobbled together some wires that ran from the device down to a car battery. The man was recording information from people's driver's licenses just as DJ imagined they'd done at the gas station. He seemed in no particular hurry.

After thirty minutes of standing in line, DJ and Crystal were at the front. The man asked for an ID, and DJ nudged Crystal. He didn't want to show his license and was glad the man at the gas station hadn't taken his ID. He didn't want any record of having been in the area. Crystal fished it out of her purse and weakly smiled at the man. He took Crystal's license and entered her address. "You can buy one hundred dollars' worth of merchandise," he said. "Not a penny more, and you have to pay in cash."

"No problem," DJ said. He wondered what people who didn't have any money were doing. They grabbed a basket and went into the store. The large front windows, plus windows along the side of the building and skylights, made it seem as if they had expected that the power would go out one day. Of course the building might have been constructed before they had electricity in this area, DJ thought. It certainly was here before power became reliable.

"Whatever you want," DJ said to Crystal.

She finally looked at him and almost smiled.

"Well, that's better," DJ said.

"I'm sorry, DJ. I guess I was afraid after what happened that you might hurt us. I'd been getting a vibe that your motives toward me might not be so pure, that you really didn't care about Nancy or me. I figured you lied about buying the groceries just to make me come to town with you. Now I see that I was wrong."

DJ was a little surprised. Was he that easy to read? It's funny how perceptive women could be at times. His motives toward her were not pure, and if the money meant anything to him, he would have lied about the groceries. But cash was one thing he had plenty of, and he figured it would soon be worthless, so he might as well spend it.

"Really?" he said, trying to sound shocked.

"Yes." Crystal hung her head.

"Don't worry about it. I understand." But he didn't understand.

Crystal's mood swings were unpredictable. He wondered if she was one of those women who could, out of the blue, just kill someone. Probably not, he told himself, but she did need to be watched. "Does this mean you don't want me to leave?" he asked.

"Not now."

"Hmm," was all he said.

"What do you think we should get?" Crystal asked cheerfully, interrupting his wish.

"Are you short of anything?"

"Not really."

"Then just buy whatever you usually eat," he said.

She smiled weakly and began to push the cart down an aisle of canned food. DJ noticed that while the shelves weren't full, they were better stocked than he would have thought. Also, each can had a price tag on it. He couldn't remember the last time he'd seen every item in a grocery store with a price sticker. As Crystal began to pick things off the shelf, it was obvious that prices were not what they used to be.

"These were three for a dollar last month," she whispered, holding a can of corn. "Now they're a dollar each."

DJ nodded. He wasn't too surprised. As they continued to shop, it became clear that nearly everything was at least double the price it had been pre-Smash, and that all the products were priced in even dollars. It didn't take much to reach the hundred-dollar limit. They pushed the cart to the front, paid, and were soon on their way back to Crystal's.

"DJ?" Crystal said.

"Yes."

"Are you still mad at me?"

"Why?" he said.

"You were so quiet in the store that I was afraid you were still angry and that you're going to leave as soon as we get home."

"I haven't really made up my mind, Crystal," he said flatly. He was lying. He knew he wanted to stay for at least another week.

"Please stay," she blurted. "I don't know what Nancy and I would do without you. I heard those women talking in the line about what's happening in the bigger cities. If the gangs get out here in force, well . . ." Her voice trailed off.

"I can stay, but we're going to have to get a few things straight if I do."

"Whatever you say, DJ."

"We'll talk about that when we get back to the house," he said.

CHAPTER 21

Gabe walked the boy home in silence and then drove his truck back to his trailer. The ugly patch on the door made him feel even worse. Damn them, he thought as he walked around to the back, not sure which "them" he really meant. There, next to the back steps, sat the broken tiller. Its bent handles and badly scuffed engine taunted him.

He opened the door and headed straight for his bedroom. Removing one of the precious bottles from the bottom drawer, he took it to the kitchen. Gabe poured a glass of the sweet poison so expertly that not a drop was wasted. He took the glass and the bottle and walked to his favorite chair. He plopped down and stared at the liquid gold, rolling the glass between his fingers and thumb.

This wasn't his fault. It wasn't like the accident. They wanted things from him. He wasn't sure what or why, but they did. He had enough to deal with without them. Didn't they know that? Maybe they did, and they didn't care, or maybe they were just too wrapped up in their own needs to know what he needed. Well, right now he needed a drink.

The glass was almost to his lips when the sound of knuckles rapping on his door reached his ears. He lowered the glass and bent his neck around toward the door. Maybe he should ignore it. Maybe it would go away. No, there it was again, longer and louder than last time. They wouldn't go away. He'd have to get rid of them.

He set the glass next to the bottle and wearily rose from the chair. The walk to the back door seemed as if it were a trek of a thousand miles. He opened the door, and there she stood.

"What?" he asked.

"Are you drinking?"

"I would be if you'd just leave me the hell alone."

Jane pushed past him. He knew he shouldn't let her in, but he was too tired to stop her. It would be twice as hard to get rid of her now. She saw the whiskey on the coffee table and looked at him.

"You know you can't drink. We've got the meeting down at the church in a couple of hours."

"I'm not going," he said. "I did my part. I passed out the flyers. Now, just leave me alone and let me do what I do best."

"The hell I will," she said. Jane walked over to the table and took the top off the bottle. Then she picked up the glass and clumsily poured the whiskey back into the bottle, spilling almost half of it. Each drop that hit the table ripped a section of Gabe's guts out. "If this wasn't so valuable, I'd pour it down the drain," she said.

That was all that Gabe could take. "Get the fuck out!" he screamed. "Get the fuck out and don't ever come back!"

Her stare burned a hole in him, and her hands rapidly opened and clenched. He felt a little uncomfortable with her being so angry with him, but he told himself he didn't care. She took a couple of steps in his direction, and he thought she was going to hit him. He wished she would, and he hoped the woman really knew how to punch. He didn't need some halfhearted, open-handed, sissy slap right now. Jane closed to striking range, and he prepared himself for the wonderful pain.

Her hands moved so quickly that it surprised him even though he was waiting. There was pain, but it wasn't at all what he'd been expecting. Her arms were wrapped around him, and her lips were pressed so hard against his face that they mashed his lips onto his teeth. He didn't know what to do. As hard as she was kissing him, he noticed that her body seemed to melt into his. He hadn't felt anything like this in a long, long time. His body reacted against his will. What was she doing? Without thinking, he found his arms circling around her and noticed he was kissing her, too. What was *he* doing?

His hands found her shoulders, and he pushed her away. "What are you doing?" he demanded.

"I'm just trying to show you that people care about you, you big, stupid son of a bitch. We need you, Gabe, and, believe it or not, you need us, too."

"Rule number one . . . I make all the security decisions. If we have to defend ourselves or our property, I don't need you second-guessing me," DJ said.

"All right," Crystal said quietly.

"Next, we keep up the charade that I'm your cousin. We don't tell the neighbors anything that we don't discuss first."

She nodded.

"Here's the last thing. If Roger isn't back in a week, then we have to assume he's not coming. You have to accept that, and we'll figure out what's best for you and Nancy from there."

A tear formed in her eye. "What do you mean by that?"

What he really meant was what was best for him, but he couldn't tell her that. "I mean we need to figure out how to keep you two safe. Maybe it means I stay until this thing blows over. Maybe it means we need to try to find somewhere for you to stay, or maybe you end up going with me, but we'll worry about that in a week. Right now we just hope Roger shows up, all right?"

"Okay," she said with a sniffle. "I really appreciate your staying, DJ. I don't know how to thank you enough."

I know, he thought.

They spent several minutes making out like a couple of teenagers. Gabe felt impulses and sensations he thought had died with Hannah. What was he doing? He couldn't do this. He was still in love with his wife. He brought his hands up to Jane's shoulders and, this time, gently pushed her back. She looked into his eyes.

"What's wrong, Gabe?"

"I don't know," he stammered. "I'm just not ready for this."

"Something is telling me you are," she said with a smile.

He'd never noticed how beautiful she was, not like some runway model, but a deep inner beauty that manifested itself through her whole being. Her eyes were warm and inviting. The little laugh lines around the edges only made them prettier. Her laugh was infectious, and all of Gabe's troubles seemed to drown in the sound. Her body was firm and muscular from work, but it melted like hot butter in his arms. He was lost for a second just staring at her.

He shook his head quickly as if he were trying to clear the cobwebs out after a blindsiding sucker punch. "No, I mean, uh, it's just been a long time."

"I understand," she whispered. She rocked up on her toes and gave him a quick peck on the lips. "I'll see you at the church in a couple of hours."

Gabe stood there like a statue. He watched her leave, and even though he desperately wanted to tell her to stay, he couldn't get his mouth to move. When the door closed behind her, he wished it would reopen and she'd come back. Then he prayed she wouldn't. He stared at the portal as if his life hung in the balance. He realized that his fingers were touching his lips where hers had been only seconds before. He could taste the sweetness and feel the warmth. He felt something, something he hadn't felt in a long time. He felt alive.

DJ sat in the comfortable chair and watched Crystal put the groceries away. The kid was coloring at the table and humming softly, as she often did. Sunlight streamed through the window and made the room just a little warm. His eyes began to get heavy as he contemplated his options. Maybe he should just stay here. The chances of Roger showing up were slim, and sooner or later Crystal would come to grips with it. DJ had often wondered what it would be like to have a family. He figured it would be nice. And why leave? Yeah, there was lots of stuff buried at his bug-out location, but what else was waiting for him there? At best, nothing, and at worst, well, he didn't want to think about that. No, he could get real comfortable here.

A voice brought him back from the edge of slumber. "What would you like for dinner, DJ?"

"I don't know," he answered, truthfully for a change. "I'm sure whatever you fix will be delicious."

Gabe was at the church before anyone else. He opened the windows and propped open the door to get some airflow through the small sanctuary. Then he stood on the landing in front of the main doors to wait. A few minutes later, the Blakes showed up. Gabe remembered that they were the ones with beef for trade. He shook their hands and exchanged pleasantries until another couple with two small children walked up. He introduced himself.

"So you are Gabriel Horne," the man said as he shook Gabe's hand. "My name's Jerry Strickland. This is my wife, Deb, and our two kids, Gary and Hope."

"Pleasure to meet you," Gabe said. "Ma'am."

The Stricklands made their way into the church, and Gabe looked back toward the road. It seemed as if everyone was coming at once. Almost everyone was walking, although some were on bicycles and a few others were driving their vehicles. Many were pulling wagons loaded with children or pushing strollers. Clearly word about the meeting had spread. He wondered where they had all come from and if they'd all fit in the little church.

Gabe saw her in the crowd. She was walking beside Robby, the limp barely noticeable, and talking with Harold and Amanda.

Jane's beauty struck him again. His fingers absentmindedly touched his lips before he realized what he was doing. He forced his hand back down to his side, but the thought of her kiss stirred something inside him.

Gabe followed Jane into the church and sat beside her on the third pew from the front. After a few minutes, the chatter quieted and there was an uneasy silence. Jane poked an elbow into Gabe's ribs. He looked at her with wide eyes and shook his head almost imperceptibly.

She leaned over and whispered, "Just go up and welcome everyone, then get the discussion going. That's all you have to do. Things will go on their own from there."

Gabe stared at her in disbelief, but something compelled him to stand up anyway. As he walked to the podium, it was dead quiet.

He turned and faced the assembly. He'd never spoken to so many people before. His hands reached out and grabbed the lectern tightly. His throat was the Sahara.

"Uh, we want to welcome everyone to the meeting," he said slowly. "It's good to see you all. I guess we have a lot to discuss. Who wants to get us started?"

The silence seemed as if it would go on forever. Finally someone in the back spoke up. "How are we going to make sure we don't have any more attacks like what happened to Mrs. Walker, or any more thefts? I lost almost five gallons of gas out of my barn two nights ago, and I've heard about others losing things, too."

A murmur of approval for the first question seemed to quickly emanate from the whole room. Then it was quiet again, and all eyes were on Gabe. He felt the weight pushing down on him.

Do I look like the Shell Answer Man to you? he wanted to yell.

"I, uh, really don't know. Other than being a lot more cautious and making sure everything is locked up all the time, does anyone have a suggestion?" he said.

"What about roadblocks? We could let only those who live in the area come through," a person on the left side said.

"I guess that would be one thing we could do. Does anyone have any experience with that sort of thing?" Gabe prayed that someone would hold up their hand so he could turn the floor over to that person. Everyone just looked around. Gabe wished he could take a little shot, just enough to calm his nerves. "How about law enforcement experience? Anyone been a police officer?" Still no hand was raised. Gabe was scraping the bottom of the barrel now. His hands were clutching the podium tightly to stop them from shaking, but he could feel the tremors begin to move up his arms. Surely several people would have to raise their hand for this one. "Anybody have any military experience?"

Gabe breathed a sigh of relief when three hands went up. He was sure that more than these three had been in the service, but this was enough to get him out of the hot seat. He pointed at the man closest to him. "What did you do in the military?"

"I was a flight mechanic in the air force," the man said. "If you need an F16 fixed, I'm your man, but I don't know squat about roadblocks."

"And what about you?" Gabe pointed at the next closest man. He was thin and distinguished looking with short gray hair.

"My name is Paul Lozano, and I was an army captain during

Vietnam. I was assigned to the Pentagon as a gofer for most of my career, though. I don't have much field experience."

"You must have had some training in officers' school, right?" Gabe was almost pleading.

"Yes, but that was a long time ago, Mr. Horne. Surely someone has more recent combat experience."

"All right, Paul, thanks. How about you? Do you have any combat experience?" Gabe pointed at a middle-aged man in the back.

"I have a lot of combat experience, but I don't think it's going to help. I was a navy corpsman assigned to the marines during Desert Storm. All my training has to do with patching holes in people and treating heat exhaustion."

"Well," Gabe said, "let's hope we don't need your expertise, although it's good to know you're around, Mr.?"

"Easton," the man said.

"I guess you're our ranking military man, Captain. Would you care to come up and give us some ideas of what we can do?"

Gabe had already taken half a step away from the podium when Captain Lozano started to speak. "I'd be happy to meet with the other vets and brainstorm with them about this. We could try to have some suggestions for your next meeting. How would that be?"

Gabe froze in his tracks. This wasn't his meeting; he'd just come up to get the ball rolling as Jane had said. Someone else needed to take over. He returned to the lectern. "It's not up to me," he said. "Would that be all right with everyone?"

A chorus of affirmative answers rang out.

"Good. Now, does anyone else have anything they'd like to come up and discuss with everyone?"

"What about bartering like your flyer said, Mr. Horne?" It was Mr. Blake, the man who wanted to trade beef. "Do you think you could make that happen?"

Gabe had had enough. He wanted to lash out, but at the last second, he saw Jane's face. It stopped him. She gave him a little nod of encouragement, so he took a deep breath and controlled his frustration.

"I'm really not the man to facilitate anything," he said. "I'm glad to help out wherever I can, but this is not my meeting. I just handed out the flyers with Harold and Robby. This is your meeting, so if someone has an idea, come on up."

"Let's just have our own farmers' market," someone shouted.

"That's a great idea. Why don't you come on up and lead the discussion?"

"What's to discuss? Just tell us which day and where, and let's do it," the voice said, not quite as strongly as before.

Gabe's shoulders dropped. He placed his hands back on the podium, noticing that they weren't shaking anymore. He sighed. "What day would be good for everyone?"

"Ever since the lights went out, I've lost track of what day it is!" Jane yelled out, smiling up at Gabe, as if she was enjoying his uneasiness. The whole auditorium laughed.

"Thursday," Gabe replied seriously. A second later, he laughed uncomfortably, realizing Jane was trying to lighten the mood or pulling his leg. Probably both, he thought.

"What's wrong with Saturday?" someone asked loudly.

"Nothing, I guess," Gabe said. "I figured we could just do it here in the church parking lot. Say we start at about eight. Is that all right with everyone?"

Gabe only heard positive responses. "All right, then, is that all, or is there anything else?"

It was quiet for a moment as everyone looked around. Just as Gabe was about to adjourn the meeting, a woman from the center of the sanctuary spoke. "What's everyone doing about school? I've been too afraid to send my kids for a couple of weeks now."

"Me, too," someone else said.

"I stopped sending mine last week when there was a shooting less than a block from the school," another voice said.

"What about homeschooling them?" a man in the front said.

"I would, but I don't have the materials," the lady who started the conversation said.

"Does anyone here homeschool their kids?" Gabe asked.

Two people raised their hands.

"Good. How about teachers? Do we have any here?"

Two other people raised their hands.

"That's excellent," Gabe said. "How about the four of you get together and come up with some suggestions for the next meeting, just like the roadblock guys?"

It seemed as though everyone was in agreement. Gabe decided not to ask for any more questions. He just wanted to finish up the meeting.

"Then what does everyone think about getting back together on Saturday evening, same time as today?"

Everyone agreed.

"Then we're adjourned." Gabe gave a quiet sigh, and felt as if a weight had been lifted off his shoulders.

CHAPTER 22

The knock on the door woke DJ up from his nap with a start. He jumped out of bed, grabbed his pistol, and headed toward the door of his room. Before he could get there, Crystal appeared.

"It's the sheriff," she whispered, her eyes wild. "What should we do?"

"Do you know him?"

Crystal shook her head.

DJ turned and placed his pistol on the bed. "I'll answer it," he said. "Will you just go along with me, no matter what happens?"

She nodded.

He made his way to the front door as quickly as he could, but not before the authoritative knock was repeated. DJ unlocked the door and pulled it open before the man on the outside could put his hand down.

"Hello, Sheriff," DJ said, painting on his best smile.

"Uh, it's Reserve Deputy Johnson actually."

The man was a little shorter and much wider than DJ. He was older, too. His eyes didn't hold the icy stare the professional peace officers in the city had. DJ had dealt with many of his city's finest when he caught shoplifters at the mall. The cops all had a certain air about them as if nothing escaped their notice, but not Reserve Deputy Johnson.

This guy looked more like a manager of a fast food joint. His uniform was shabby and worn sloppily, the shirttail hanging out around his ample midsection. His pistol was an inexpensive model DJ wouldn't have used for a trotline weight, and it was in a cheap nylon holster he'd never seen professionals use.

"I'm sorry, Deputy. Won't you come in?"

"No, no," the man said. "I don't want to bother you folks, Mr. . . . ?"

"Clark," DJ said. "It's on the mailbox." He pointed toward the road.

The deputy looked over his shoulder in the direction DJ was pointing. Of course, the letters on the mailbox weren't big enough to read from this distance. The man turned back. "We're looking for two brothers," he said, holding up two pictures. "Have you seen them, by chance?"

Despite his best effort, DJ felt his eyes widen and his face go hot as he recognized the two quad thieves. He knew that an experienced lawman would have picked up on it. He hoped this guy wouldn't since he was obviously just some hick wannabe who probably wasn't able to make it on a real force. DJ reached out and took the pictures, pretending to study them. After a moment or two, he extended them back toward the substitute lawman.

"Sorry, Deputy. I don't recognize either one of them."

"Perhaps your wife has seen them?" the deputy asked.

DJ walked over to Crystal and held up the pictures. "Honey, have you seen these men?"

Crystal immediately shook her head no. DJ walked back to the door and gave the pictures back.

"I'm afraid neither of us has seen much of anyone the last couple of weeks," DJ said. "Why are you looking for them?" he asked, feigning mild interest.

"That's a good question," the man said in exasperation. "They're just a couple of local punks, but they're the sheriff's second cousins or something, so he has us out looking for them. Supposedly, they've been missing for a couple of days. We found their truck on a side road not too far from here, and now the sheriff has us going door to door. It's a big waste of time if you ask me. We've got a lot worse problems than a couple of overgrown delinquents. They're probably holed up in some crack house or whorehouse, or something. Anyway, if you see them, tell them their mama's looking for them, okay?"

"No problem," DJ said in a cheery voice.

"Thank you, Mr. Clark," the deputy said. He turned and walked back to his car. DJ shut the door but watched as the deputy backed out of the driveway and drove off.

"Does he know anything?" Crystal asked as DJ turned from the door.

"I don't think so. He's not a real cop."

"Good," she said. "I was scared."

"No need to be, Crystal. Even if he did know something, it would all be on me. I'd tell them you didn't know anything about it."

The tension on her face melted. "Thanks, DJ," she said as she stepped up and gave him a hug.

He returned it. "You're welcome, girl. How about I help you with dinner?"

*   *   *

Jane set the large pot of soup in the middle of her kitchen table. The smell of the chicken wafted over the room. She filled the three bowls, then sat next to Gabe. He detected the scent of her perfume over the aroma of the soup. It made his mind race and he wondered what might happen if they got some time alone tonight.

"What do you think?" she said.

"This looks great," he said quickly, hoping she was talking about the soup and not what he was thinking about.

"Thanks, but I was talking about what you thought about the meeting."

"Oh, I guess it went okay. I was hoping a leader would show up and take over. Maybe once people get a little more comfortable, someone will step up to the plate."

"I'm sure we'll find someone," she said. "How's your soup, Robby?"

"This is delicious, Mom," Robby mumbled with his mouth half-full.

"Yes, Jane, you really outdid yourself. The chicken tastes so fresh," Gabe said.

"It should. One of the hens quit laying a few days ago. I told her that everyone had to contribute one way or another. Today was her last chance."

Gabe looked at Jane with surprise. "Oh," he said. "Well, I hope I'm contributing. . . ."

"We'll see," Jane said with a smile.

When dinner was over and the dishes were done, the trio retired to the living room. Jane and Robby sat down, but Gabe looked nervously toward the door. Jane noticed, but didn't say anything. After a minute, he spoke.

"I'll be right back."

He headed out the front door and went to his truck. He removed the box containing the .22 rifle from behind the seat. When he came back in with it under his arm, Robby's eyes lit up. Gabe looked at Jane, and she gave him a soft smile and a gentle nod of her head.

"Robby, this is a .22 rifle you can use," Gabe said, as he set the box on the coffee table. "Tomorrow morning, I'll show you how to shoot it and how to care for it. This is not a toy. If I see that you don't respect how dangerous even a .22 can be, I will take it back home. Understand?"

"I promise, Mr. Horne, I'll be careful."

"I know you will." Gabe smiled. He opened the box and lifted the little rifle from it. He opened the bolt and looked to make sure the rifle wasn't loaded. "Tonight, I want us to go over the rules. First, you must treat every gun as if it is loaded, whether it is or not."

"Treat every gun like it's loaded," Robby said as he stared at the .22 as if it were some magic talisman.

"Second, never point a gun at anything you aren't willing to destroy."

Robby repeated word for word.

"Next, finger off the trigger until the sights are on the target," Gabe said.

"Finger off the trigger until sights are on target."

"And last, always make sure of your target and what is behind it." Robby parroted the last rule.

"Good, we'll go over these again in the morning." Gabe motioned the boy over. When he was close enough, Gabe handed the .22 to him. Robby took it cautiously and looked it over from end to end, careful to keep the muzzle pointed at the ceiling.

"Thank you so much, Mr. Horne! I can't wait to shoot it tomorrow. This is going to be so much fun."

"You're welcome, Robby. I'm sure you'll have a great time with it, but I'm not just lending it to you for fun. Your mother and I are going to expect you to provide us with some meat. There are lots of rabbits and squirrels in this area, and I don't think your mother has enough chickens to cook one every day."

"You can count on me," Robby pledged.

Gabe laughed at the wide-eyed oath. "I know we can, son. Now you take this owner's manual and read it, cover to cover."

"Yes, sir," Robby said enthusiastically.

He handed Gabe the rifle and took the booklet. Before he returned to his chair, he had the cover open and was studying the first page. Gabe returned the rifle to its box and looked at Jane. She was smiling. She mouthed the words "thank you."

Gabe nodded at her and closed the box. He slid it under the couch. "I guess I'd better get home," he said.

"You're welcome to the couch again," Jane said.

"I don't know. I think it might be better if I go home tonight."

"As you wish. I'll walk you out."

"Robby, you wait until I get here to get that rifle out, all right?" Gabe said.

"I will, Mr. Horne," Robby said excitedly. "What time will you be here?"

"I'll come for breakfast if your mom will have me."

"You're welcome any time, Gabe. You know that," Jane said.

Once out the door, Jane reached for Gabe's hand. The press of her flesh onto his gave him goose bumps. They walked silently to his truck. He opened the door of the old Chevy and then turned to face her. Leaning down, he kissed her, and time seemed to slow down until their lips finally parted.

"I love you, Gabriel Horne," Jane said softly.

"I . . ." Gabe began, but something stopped the next three words. " . . . better get home," he said instead.

DJ lay in the guest bed staring up at the ceiling that he couldn't see in the dark. He was weighing the risks versus the benefits of staying at Crystal's. The benefits—or at least the potential benefits—were obvious. He'd known he would probably move on at some point, but the promise of hooking up with Crystal, along with the ability to get more gas in town, had kept him hanging around.

But now he realized he needed to get the hell out of Dodge. If those two thieves really were related to the sheriff, it was only a matter of time before someone else came around asking questions, and next time, it might not be some overweight, under-trained, reserve deputy.

DJ thought about his retreat. Would the group be there? Did they still even own it? He'd heard that they had put it up for sale. It really didn't matter. He knew his stuff was still buried. No one but he knew where it was, and if he did find them there, they'd most likely be very happy to see him, considering the circumstances. In fact, if anyone should be holding a grudge, it should be him. He had started the group, found the property, and organized them.

He figured he had enough gas to get at least two-thirds of the way there. He'd have to siphon what they'd bought in town out of Crystal's car. Whatever he couldn't get out would probably leave enough for her to get back to town for some more. He was sure he could scrounge up another five or six gallons along the way to complete his trip. He made a mental note to take a siphon hose with him.

He was disappointed he hadn't made the progress with Crystal that he'd hoped. If he had another week, who knows what might have happened? As he thought about it, he started to get angry. Who was he kidding? That bitch was probably never going to put out. She was more than likely just stringing him along to keep him around.

Maybe he just should take what he wanted. After all, he had saved her from a fate much worse than that, probably twice. If his quad hadn't been there for the rednecks to take, who knows what they might have done? She owed him. He had not only protected her and her daughter, but helped out around the place and had bought food for them. If he tore a little piece off as repayment, who would it really hurt?

No, I can't do that. If I did, I wouldn't be any better than those gangbangers. I'll just leave tomorrow night once it gets dark.

Gabe was kicking himself for what he'd almost said. He did have feelings for Jane, but he still loved Hannah. He picked up the picture of her and Michael, the one he'd taken at the beach. Her eyes told him that she would love him forever, no matter what happened. He just couldn't do this to her.

He'd been stupid, sneaking around like some teenager with his first crush. He would end it tomorrow. Jane would be upset with him, but it had to be done. He appreciated how she and Robby had befriended him and how they'd worked together for the whole neighborhood's benefit. However, that was as much as he could give. If she couldn't accept that, well, it didn't really matter. That's just the way it had to be.

Gabe gently placed the picture back in place. It struck him as odd that looking at it this time hadn't left a burning hole in his guts.

CHAPTER 23

Gabe knocked on the door lightly. The sky was just turning pink on the eastern horizon, and the air was crisp. A few seconds later, the door opened. Jane's face appeared behind the screen on the outer door, and she smiled at him.

"I wasn't expecting you so early," she said as she swung out the screen door. "I haven't even started breakfast yet." Before he could say anything, she was embracing him and stretching herself up for a kiss.

"Is Robby up yet?" he asked, standing stiffly.

"No, not yet. He stayed up pretty late last night reading the manual on the rifle. What's wrong?"

"We have to talk," he said.

The look on her face changed, and her arms fell to her sides. She turned and walked to the couch and sat down. "What is it, Gabe?" she said, extending her hand toward the chair opposite where she was sitting. She already knew the answer.

"Well, um, I just think we need to cool it," he said as he sat.

"And why do you think that?"

"I'm still in love with Hannah," he said. "It's not right for me to be carrying on like some starstruck high school kid. I really want us to remain friends. I appreciate all the help you've given me over the past couple of weeks, but we just can't continue with the romantic stuff."

Jane sat with a pensive look for a moment, clearly thinking hard about what she wanted to say. "You were very happy with Hannah, weren't you?"

"Yes." He was glad to see that she wasn't upset.

"Was it love at first sight?"

Gabe chuckled. "Not at all. In fact, we had a big fight the first time we met."

"But you grew to love each other and be happy together?"

"Yes," Gabe said, wondering where this line of questioning was going.

"Do you think that Hannah would want you to be unhappy now that she's gone?"

"Well, no."

"And have you been more happy or less happy the last few days?" Jane asked.

Gabe paused. "That's not a fair question."

Jane opened her mouth but then closed it for a second. "Then let me ask you this. Would Hannah be happy with the way you've lived your life since she died?"

It was Gabe's turn to be silent. The color blanched from his face. It felt as if he'd been punched in the gut, but from the inside out. He hung his head and shook it slowly. He'd known this but had always pushed it to the back of his mind. Hearing it out loud made it seem so much worse. He wished Jane would say something else, but it took forever before he heard her voice again. It was soft and quiet.

"Listen, Gabriel, I'm not trying to run your life for you, but I think Hannah would want you to be happy, and I think you've been happier the last couple of days than you have been in quite a while. I know you love her. You'll always love her, no matter what happens. In some ways, I still love Robby's father, even as bad as he was to me. I know I could never live with him again, but it doesn't change some of the feelings I have for him.

"However," she continued, "that doesn't mean I don't want a meaningful, healthy relationship with someone who can love me back. You are a caring, loving man, Gabriel Horne. You have drowned yourself in that whiskey since Hannah died. I think maybe you hoped it would kill you, but I've seen a change in you over the last couple of weeks. I'm not asking you to commit to anything, just to give our relationship a chance to grow, like you did with Hannah. Having a relationship with me doesn't diminish what the two of you had in any way. If anything, it shows that you value what you shared with her and that you want and need a companion—not to take her place, no one can do that, but to help you be happy like she did.

"We don't always understand the curves life throws at us, but sometimes good comes out of bad. Just consider that life has given you a second chance to be happy," she finished.

Gabe continued to stare at the floor. Finally he nodded. "I hear what you're saying, and it all makes sense, but we're going to have to take things real slow. I need to think this through."

The light streamed into DJ's room. He'd slept as long as he could since he knew he'd be riding most of the night. He got up and dressed, then pulled out his map. He was fifty or sixty miles from his original route. With a little luck, he could be back on it and well on his way to his retreat location by this time tomorrow. He found one of his camping spots about thirty-five miles from where he'd get back on track. *That should be an easy ride for the first night back in the saddle,* he thought.

He organized the gear in his room and made mental notes of the things he needed to do before he left. He'd decided he wouldn't tell Crystal until just before he left. No need to have her pissed all day. He'd just play it cool until dark.

When he walked into the living room, both Crystal and Nancy were reading.

"Hi, sleepyhead," Crystal said cheerfully. "I thought you were going to sleep all day. Want some breakfast?"

"Yeah, that would be great," he said.

She got up and walked to the kitchen. Even in the ratty old sweatpants she was wearing, the sway of her hips made his mouth water.

"Now just squeeze the trigger. Don't jerk it," Gabe said.

Bang.

"That was a lot better," Gabe said. "Where were the sights when the rifle went off?"

"They were just a little to the right of the bull's-eye," Robby said excitedly.

"All right, let's go look."

Robby carefully set the rifle on the table, and then he and Gabe walked down to the homemade paper target that was pinned onto the fence at the back of Jane's property. There was a small hole just to the right and slightly below the black circle in the center of the paper.

"Not too bad," Gabe said. "Let's go back and shoot three shots this time."

They turned to walk back to the table they were using as a shooting bench. Gabe watched as the boy hurriedly walked back to Michael's rifle. Gabe felt a pang at the fact that it wasn't his son he was teaching to shoot. Michael would have been close to Robby's age if the accident hadn't happened. Gabe wondered if the boys would have been friends.

They probably would have. Maybe I would have taught Robby to shoot at the same time I taught Michael. Maybe this is the path my life is supposed to take now.

They reached the table, and Robby loaded three rounds into the magazine and fired them at the target with Gabe coaching him. Then they'd examine the target and repeat the process again. With each group, Robby got closer to the center of the target.

As Gabe guided Robby along, he thought more about the things Jane had said. It was likely she was right. Maybe this was his second chance. He was going to do his best not to screw it up.

After a few more groups from the bench, Gabe had Robby shoot some from a standing position. The first group was all over the target, but with a little more instruction, even this improved dramatically. When they'd been at it for a little over two hours, Gabe felt it was time to take a break.

"Do we have to stop, Mr. Horne?" Robby asked.

"It's almost lunchtime, and we both have chores to do," Gabe said. "Maybe we can shoot a little more this afternoon."

"Can I just shoot one more group?"

"Okay, one more," Gabe said, trying not to smile.

After lunch, Robby attacked his chores with a vigor his mother couldn't recall him ever having. He was waiting anxiously when Gabe drove up with several buckets of vegetables in the back of his truck. Robby helped him carry them into the house.

"Gabe, this is way more than we can eat before it goes bad," Jane told him.

"Then I guess we better trade some off or can some of it. I have almost twice this much back at my place."

"Canning it sounds like a good idea, but I don't know how. Do you?"

Gabe shook his head. "Hannah used to do it. I still have her pressure cooker and a bunch of jars at home, but I don't think there are any lids. We might be able to get some in town, and I think there's a book that tells how to can all kinds of things in her stuff. I hope there is, because I don't have a clue," he said.

"We could go back to your place, and I could help you look for it," Jane said.

Gabe saw the happy look on Robby's face melt. He decided to have some fun with the youngster.

"Well, I promised Robby we could shoot some more once all the chores were done." The smile returned to the teen's face. "But I was also thinking we really shouldn't waste any more ammo on target practice." The corners of the boy's mouth were starting to resemble a yo-yo. "So I guess we could go look for it. Or . . . Robby and I could go back to my place and try to get some squirrels for supper."

Robby's mouth dropped open, and his eyes looked as if they

might pop out. "Please, Mom, let me go hunting with Mr. Horne. I'll help you look for whatever you need later if you let us go. Please!" he said.

"Please!" Gabe added, tipping his head to one side and putting on a big smile and his best little beggar boy look.

"All right," Jane said. "I can see that you boys would be useless anyway, but you'd better bring home some meat. I'm getting sick of chicken."

"We will, Mom. You'll see. Thank you!"

"Get your rifle and a hat," Gabe told Robby.

"Yes, sir."

After Robby left the kitchen, Gabe said, "That's a good boy you've got there, Jane."

"You just make sure you teach him to be safe, and I'm serious about the meat." She gave him a peck on the cheek.

"I will, and I know you are," Gabe said with a wink.

Gabe and Robby were soon walking into the woods that made up the back of Gabe's acreage. Gabe reminded the boy of the safety rules and told him it was important not to let the excitement of the hunt cause a lapse in the adherence to those rules. He showed the young man how to move slowly and quietly and how to watch for squirrels. Before long, they spotted one, and a few minutes later, it was in the bag. Gabe encouraged Robby only to take head shots, so none of the meat would be wasted. He also explained that it was best to take fully grown animals and only to kill what they needed.

It didn't take long for them to have six bushy-tails. They walked back up to Gabe's house and cleaned them; Gabe first showed the young man the process, then had him do it. As they drove back to the Walker place, it was hard for Robby to contain his enthusiasm about the hunt. They pulled up in front of the house, and the boy was out of the truck and running for the front door with the squirrels before Gabe could bring the vehicle to a complete stop.

Gabe smiled as he walked into the house with the rifle case Robby had forgotten.

"It was so cool, Mom. We got six squirrels. See? I got four of them. I only missed the head on the first one. Mr. Horne showed me the tricks of how to get them. It's pretty easy if there are two of you. One of us just has to go to the other side of the tree, and the squirrel will come to the other side, but if you're by yourself, you have to be really patient. The squirrels are curious, and if you wait real quiet, they'll stick their head up to look at you. Like Mr. Horne said, he didn't know if curiosity killed the cat, but it sure has done in a bunch of squirrels."

"I see," Jane said. "So I guess you had a good time."

"It was great! Mr. Horne said I did really well! He said maybe we could go hog hunting one night, if it's okay with you, of course."

"We'll talk about it," she said. "I'm sure we can work something out. Now I need you to go get the eggs before it gets completely dark."

"Okay, Mom. Thanks," Robby said as he ran out the back door.

Jane looked at Gabe with a big smile on her face. "I can't remember the last time he was this excited about something, but what do you expect me to do with these tree rats?"

"We men killed and cleaned the ferocious beasts; all you have to do is cook 'em, woman," Gabe said with a sarcastic smile on his face. A split second later, he was ducking to dodge the wet sponge Jane hurled at him.

By the time he stood back up straight, she had closed in to put her arms around him and had pressed her lips to his.

It was almost dark. DJ had tried to sleep, to no avail. His mind kept racing about getting ready to go. He really had gotten comfortable here and hated to leave, but he couldn't chance being caught for killing the two quad thieves. He got up, went outside, and cut a section of garden hose from one hanging in the shed. Crystal was in the kitchen cooking and hardly noticed him go outside. He siphoned all the gas he could get out of her car into one of his jerry cans. He was only able to get a little over three gallons, so he figured there should be enough for Crystal to get back to town for more. If there wasn't, she could always borrow another gallon from the neighbor. Going around back, he filled the tank of his quad with the last of the fuel he'd brought with him. There was a little left in the can, and he poured it in with the gas from Crystal's car. He turned the key on the big machine, and it fired immediately. He inspected it quickly and determined that it was ready to go, so he turned it off. All he had to do was load his stuff.

"What are you doing?" Crystal said as he walked into the house.

"Nothing, just checking on my quad," he replied.

"Well, dinner's almost ready. Why don't you get washed up?"

"All right."

He was sad that this would probably be his last home-cooked

meal for a long time. Crystal wasn't just nice to look at; she was a hell of a cook.

Dinner was quiet. Crystal and Nancy talked some, but DJ was detached as he thought about getting everything ready to go. After the table was cleaned off, Crystal sent Nancy to her room to play.

"What's the matter, DJ?" she said as she started washing the dishes.

"I have to go, Crystal," he said.

She dropped the plate she was scrubbing back into the water. "No. You don't have to. I'm not mad at you anymore."

"It's not that, Crystal. It's the cops. They're not going to stop until they find out who killed the sheriff's cousins."

"They won't find out," she insisted. "I won't tell them, and nobody else knows."

"They'll find out if they keep looking. I was sloppy and told the deputy I was your husband. Sooner or later, someone's going to tell them I'm not, and when they discover that lie, they'll start digging. They'll interrogate us both until one of us cracks." DJ knew all they'd have to do was tell Crystal they were going to take Nancy, and she'd tell them everything. "Then I'll be in jail, and you'll be without me anyway. It's better if I go now."

"But we need you to protect us until Roger gets back. Can't you just stay a little while longer?"

"I can't. If it had been a regular deputy who'd come to the door instead of the reserve, I'd probably already be in jail. I have to leave tonight," he said.

Crystal started to cry. "Who's going to take care of us?"

"You are. I'm leaving one of the guns we got from the guys who attacked you."

DJ spent a few minutes showing Crystal how to use the Desert Eagle. He knew it was way too big for her hands, but she should be able to scare a few goblins with it. There wasn't much ammo; otherwise he probably would have taken it himself, but it was better than nothing. She cried the whole time he was showing her how to load, unload, and shoot the huge handgun, but hopefully she'd remember. When he was done, he went to his room and started carrying his gear out to the quad and securing it in place.

He was on one of his last trips when Crystal met him at the door.

"Please stay, DJ," she pleaded. "I'll do anything."

"Anything?" His mind went into overdrive.

She blushed. "Well, not that, but almost anything," she said quietly.

"Look, Crystal, I have everything I need where I'm going. Everything but one thing," he said with emphasis. "Now, if you're willing to give me what I don't have, then we can talk about me staying. Otherwise, I have to go."

She stared at him blankly. After a moment, he pushed past her and went into his room. He picked up what was left of his stuff. It was more than he would normally carry, but he didn't want to face her again. When he turned toward the door, she was standing there looking at him.

"Okay," she whispered, a tear running down her face.

"Okay what?" he said a split second before he realized what she meant.

"I'll do it. Just let me put Nancy to bed first."

It was all DJ could do not to drop the armload of gear and rub his hands together like a hungry man sitting down to Thanksgiving dinner.

"Dinner's almost ready," Jane called into the living room.

"All right," Gabe said. "Robby and I are almost finished cleaning our rifles. We'll be right there."

Jane heard them zipping up the rifle cases and then tromping into the bathroom to wash up. She smiled. Robby had long needed some male guidance. She hoped Gabe would remain the man he'd become and that he'd help Robby become the man she knew he could be.

DJ was waiting outside Nancy's door when Crystal came out. She turned and headed for her bedroom without saying a word or even acknowledging his presence with her eyes. He closed and locked the door behind him. She stood silently by the bed. He wrapped his arms around her and began to kiss her. She didn't return the kiss.

I guess she doesn't want any foreplay.

He pushed her down onto the bed.

Jane was washing, and Gabe was drying and putting away. Dinner had been good. The fried squirrel was a little tough, but at least it was different. Jane promised that if the guys would get more, she'd cook them slowly to tenderize them and make squirrel and dumplings. Gabe and Robby promised to go hunting again as soon as possible.

"How do you think the meeting will go tomorrow?" Gabe asked.

"What do you mean?" Jane replied.

"Do you think the small groups will have plans for the things we talked about?"

"I'm sure they will be. The question is whether they'll be acceptable to the whole group."

"I guess so," Gabe said. "I hope they are."

"I'm sure they will be. It seems like you got some good people to work on the committees."

"Yeah. I hope one of them will step up and take over the meetings. I think that army captain would make a good leader."

"I guess," Jane said, as if her mind were somewhere else. "So, are you spending the night here?"

"I don't think it's a good idea. People might get the wrong idea about what's going on with us."

"And what is going on with us?" she asked with a coy smile.

"I guess we're kind of going together."

"Wow! How romantic. You really know how to sweep a girl off her feet."

"You know what I mean," Gabe said.

"I guess I do, but it's not like we're in high school, Gabe. If you spend the night over here on the couch, what difference does it make?"

Gabe had to admit that she had a point, but somehow he just wasn't comfortable with it. "I see what you mean," he said, "but I think it's best if we just sleep in our own homes for now."

"Whatever you want, Gabe." She seemed agreeable, but Gabe couldn't help wondering if he'd hurt her feelings.

DJ picked up the last armload of his stuff out of the guest room. She was nuts if she thought he was going to stay if that was what he could expect. She had just lain on the bed like a dead fish. Sure, it was better than nothing, but not much. He'd built up in his mind that she would be so good, and then it was as if she weren't even in the room.

He carried the stuff out to his quad and strapped it into place. He looked at his gear. Everything seemed to be there. It wasn't quite dark, but it would be in ten or fifteen minutes. He thought about going ahead and leaving, but it wouldn't do for someone to witness him leave on his quad. It might give the law too much to go on.

He decided to recheck everything since he had a few minutes. He heard the door open behind him.

"What are you doing?" Crystal said.

"I'm leaving."

"But you promised you'd stay."

"I never promised," he said.

"But—but I did what you asked me." Tears began to run down her cheeks.

"Yeah, right! That was horrible, Crystal. It's no wonder Roger hasn't come home. He's probably shacked up with some little truck stop tramp who really knows how to screw."

DJ smiled as he saw her eyes open wide and the tears suddenly stop. All the color blanched from her face as what he said sank in. She turned and ran into the house.

She deserved it. She was no better than a used car salesman, selling him on some fancy sports car that looks great on the outside but has all kinds of mechanical problems and barely runs.

He checked the sky again. The pink was turning to purple. It wouldn't be long now. He climbed onto the big four-wheeler and fired up the motor. It would feel good to be on his way again. He was about to put the machine into gear when he heard the shot.

Gabe looked at the gas gauge. It read a quarter of a tank. He should go to town and get some soon, he thought. Maybe he'd invite Jane to go with him. It would be kind of like a date. Well, not really, but at least they'd be spending time together. Maybe it would somewhat make up for him not staying the night as she wanted.

As he thought about the gas, he realized he really shouldn't be driving from his house to hers so much. He'd have to start walking more and save the gas.

His thoughts turned to the farmers' market. He had lots of stuff ready to trade in the morning. He wondered what and how much he might trade for. Other than what he grew, he didn't have much food in the house. He was well aware that whatever he got would be a good trade.

DJ turned off the bike and pulled his pistol out of the holster almost without thinking. He slowly pushed open the door, watching and listening for a moment, his mind going a million miles a minute. He made out rustling toward the back of the house, and then Nancy's voice could be heard.

"Mommy, Mommy, are you okay?"

A second later, DJ heard the little girl begin to cry. He crept down the hall to her room and looked in with the aid of his flashlight, but she wasn't there. He moved down to Crystal's room and peered around the corner.

Crystal was sitting on the bed with the enormous pistol in her hand. She was just staring at the wall in front of her, unresponsive to Nancy's pleadings. DJ saw a hole in the ceiling. Its location indicated that she probably hadn't tried to harm herself. More than likely it was a ruse to get his attention. Well, he wasn't going to leave her a weapon if she had any thoughts of hurting herself. He walked over to retrieve the monstrosity and she looked at him. He could see the hate burning in her eyes. She lifted the handgun and swept DJ with the muzzle.

He realized she probably had no intention of shooting him, but he couldn't take a chance. His left hand came down in a karate chop on her right wrist. The gun went flying across the room and crashed into the dresser mirror. His right hand came across to push her down, but he ended up hitting her harder than he intended. She fell over and hit her head on the footboard of the bed.

Nancy retreated into a corner and began to cry. "You hit my mommy," he barely made out between the sobs.

"No, sweetie, I pushed her to make sure she didn't hurt us with the gun."

She cried something else, but he could only make out the word "bad." He started to explain to her that it was only an accident, but before he got halfway done, he realized there was little point in justifying himself to a five-year-old. He turned back to Crystal.

She was still lying in the same position she had landed in. He turned her over and she appeared unconscious. He reached down and checked her neck for a pulse. It was strong. He walked over to retrieve the pistol and saw that it had cracked the mirror at chest level. His reflection was disjointed and looked monsterlike. He chuckled to himself. *I hope this doesn't bring me seven years of bad luck,* he thought.

He walked out to his bike and stowed the pistol in his gear. A minute later he was driving down the road. He felt bad about hitting Crystal and leaving this way, but what choice did he have? The more he thought about what had happened, the angrier he became. *Stupid bitch,* he thought, *she probably got what she deserved.*

CHAPTER 24

Gabe woke up before daylight with the meeting on his mind. How would it go? Would the solutions the groups came up with be acceptable to everyone? Would Paul Lozano, the former army captain, assume command? If not, who would? This last question concerned Gabe more than the others. He didn't like being in front of all those people.

When he couldn't will his mind to slow down enough to get a little more sleep, he decided to get up. He got out of bed, dressed, and fixed a quick breakfast. By the time he was finished eating, the sky was just showing the first hints of dawn. There was an hour or so before he had to be at the farmers' market at the church. He could see if there was anything ripe enough to add to his produce. He went outside and headed to the garden.

DJ could see the sky getting light. He'd pushed hard all night and had gone faster than he would have liked. The GPS said it was still a few miles to the spot he wanted to reach. It was back on his original route, and more important, it was across two county

lines from Crystal's house. DJ didn't know what kinds of communications were still available to law enforcement, but he figured it
was likely that the sheriff where Crystal lived would only contact
the surrounding counties. He wondered if Crystal had gone to
the neighbors' yet. He hoped not, but even if she had, chances
were they wouldn't even be on their way to town yet.

He just needed another five or six minutes to get to his waypoint. He pressed a little harder on the throttle. The trip so far
had been uneventful. He hadn't even seen another person or vehicle. He hoped there were no early-rising farmers who might
spot him out and about.

A few minutes later, he came on a large patch of woods. It no
doubt belonged to someone, but it appeared as if no one had been
to it in years. It sat right next to the road, but was so overgrown
you couldn't see into it more than a few yards. DJ slowed the bike
and pulled through the ditch next to the old rusted fence. The
barbed wire, much tougher when it was new, effortlessly yielded
to his multitool. He eased the big bike into the thicket and soon
was unable to see the road. There was a small, open spot he'd
discovered on one of his scouting trips, and the GPS took him
right to it. He unloaded what he needed, set up his tent, warmed
up an MRE—he was running low. His hunger satisfied, he
climbed into the tent for some sleep. Even though he wasn't as
comfortable as he was in the guest room at Crystal's, he was soon
asleep.

Gabe pulled into Jane's driveway and stopped the truck. The
front screen door opened before he could get out of the car. She

stood there, wiping her hands on her apron. He wondered what she was thinking. When he got out of the truck, her smile told him all he needed to know.

"Good morning," she said.

"Good morning to you, too. I thought you might be mad at me," he said.

"For what?"

"You know, for not staying last night."

She waved her hand. "Don't you worry, Gabriel Horne. If I'm mad at you, you'll know."

Gabe recalled the time she'd been mad at him for the drunken words he'd spoken to Robby. Her feelings were more than obvious. He was glad they'd forgiven him. Most folks wouldn't have given him even the first chance when he was drinking, let alone a second chance.

"Are you ready to go?" he asked.

"Almost. Are we going in my truck or yours?"

"I think we should take mine since it uses less gas. I was thinking last night that we need to start being really careful with the gas we use. I don't know how long we'll be able to get more. I'm going to start walking unless I really need to take the truck."

"Sounds like a plan to me. Maybe you should talk to all the neighbors at the meeting tonight about that," Jane said.

"I'm sure most of them have already thought about it."

"Perhaps, but it can't hurt to mention it. Robby is getting the tables and the canopy. Can you help him?"

"You bet," Gabe said.

Soon the trio was at the church with eggs and vegetables displayed on the tables. It was a little slow at first, but by nine, people were starting to arrive in droves. It appeared that news of the market had spread beyond the small area Gabe considered the "neighborhood." Even the preacher showed up. He lived in town but heard about the event. He eventually made his way to Gabe and introduced himself.

"Are you Mr. Horne?" he asked.

"Yes," Gabe said.

"It's nice to meet you, Mr. Horne," the short, stocky man said, extending his hand. "I'm Reverend Washington. I understand you organized the farmers' market."

"No," Gabe said, a little surprised that he'd been singled out as the planner. "We all just agreed to do it when we had a meeting here the other night. I'm sorry we didn't get permission to use the church, first, though. I hope you aren't upset."

The pastor laughed. "No reason to apologize," he said. "This is exactly what the church is for, to bring people together. In fact, I've tried for years to get the congregation to host something like this to involve us in the community. I couldn't get anyone interested. I guess it took a real crisis for it to happen, and no one from the church had a thing to do with it. I guess when people are ready, God will send a Moses."

Gabe didn't fully comprehend what the preacher was saying and felt a little awkward, but he nodded politely.

"Is this your family?" Reverend Washington asked, nodding in Jane's and Robby's direction.

"Uh, no. This is my, uh, this is Mrs. Walker and her son, Robby. We're just friends."

Jane shot Gabe a look.

"Oh, please forgive me. Mrs. Walker, are you the one who got shot?"

"Yes, Reverend."

"I assume by your presence at this event that you're doing well."

"I am. Thank you for asking," Jane said as she shook the man's hand.

"That's good to hear. My, what a fine-looking young man you have there," the preacher said, smiling at Robby.

"Thank you," Robby said shyly.

There was an uncomfortable pause in the conversation. Gabe wondered what he could say, but no words came to mind. Finally the preacher broke the silence.

"I also heard you're the man to see about vegetables," Reverend Washington said. "Someone told me to make sure to get some of your tomatoes. My wife puts up preserves. I brought a few jars, and I'd be glad to trade with you."

"Sure thing. What do you need?" Gabe said, understanding the trading part. He grabbed a grocery bag and started stuffing it with vegetables.

"Well, I can use a little of everything, to be honest with you. I have some blackberry preserves and some peach. Which would you prefer?"

"Peach," Gabe replied as he started filling another bag with tomatoes. He handed the two bags to the preacher.

"Mr. Horne, this is too much for just one jar of preserves. I insist that you take a blackberry, as well."

"Thank you, Reverend. We'll really enjoy these."

"As will I, Mr. Horne," the man said with a smile as he lifted the two bags. "I heard you have another meeting planned for this evening. If you don't mind, I'd like to stick around for it. Would that be all right?"

A plan whirred in Gabe's head. "We'd be honored, Reverend."

DJ woke up and stared at the top of his tent. He sat up and felt the stiffness in his back. This certainly wasn't the nice soft bed at Crystal's. He wondered if there'd be a bed for him at the retreat. Would Thomas forgive him? He might since they probably needed his expertise. Maybe he wasn't even married to Sheila anymore. There were too many possibilities to worry about it now. He'd just have to see what the situation was when he got there. Most likely, the rumor he'd heard was true and they had sold the place. Outside the tent, he pulled out his maps and his GPS. He knew exactly where he was, but he liked lining up the data from both sources and making sure. It also allowed him to see if there was something he'd missed before. That was highly unlikely, but he had nothing better to do.

He traced the route with his finger and estimated that he could make it in another two days. He'd need a little gas, but nothing else stood in his way. He thought about his retreat and how nice it would be to finally get there. Although he hadn't been in several years, he knew his large cache would still be there. Word had traveled through the grapevine that the group had put the property up for sale after he'd quit associating with them. He wished he would have been able to buy it, but there was no way he could afford it on his salary. If it hadn't sold, who knew whether some of them might be there? He'd bet that they'd be glad to see him now.

Hungry, DJ pulled out one of his last MREs. Using the included chemical heater, he warmed up the entrée while he ate the M&M's that were supposed to be dessert. He noticed a slight chill in the breeze and wondered if the weather was going to change. He hoped not, but if it did rain, it would only delay him a day or two at most. The wind switched directions for a moment and DJ smelled gasoline.

He walked over to the quad and opened the cap on the gas tank. It had the amount in it that he expected. He found that the smell was stronger at the back of the quad. He saw a small wet spot beneath the jerry can. Then he saw the drip. It was small but was no doubt the source of the smell. It had come from the bottom seam. He figured it must have happened when the trailer had been wrecked. He lifted the can and found that it was now way less than one-third full.

"Son of a bitch!" he yelled. He opened the top and looked inside. It held only about a gallon, maybe a gallon and a half. He poured it into the quad and threw the empty can against a tree. It bounced off harmlessly, taunting his anger. Walking over, he stomped on the side and was surprised that it only dented in a little. "Yeah, now you're tough, you piece of shit."

DJ walked back over to where his entrée was heating and kicked it into the woods as hard as he could.

Gabe was pleased with how the market was going. Everyone seemed to be having a good time, and he'd made some good trades. Not only had he traded for beef with the Blakes and preserves with the preacher, but he'd swapped his vegetables for two boxes of .22 ammo, a folding skinning knife, some homemade candles, and a few other odds and ends. He'd also sold some vegetables outright for cash. A few of the people didn't have any money or anything he was interested in, but looked as if they could really use some fresh produce, so he gave quite a bit away. Jane was doing the same with her eggs, and it looked as though some of the other vendors were following suit.

Gabe was happy everything was going so smoothly. He had his revolver and rifle in the truck, just in case trouble showed up, but nothing bad happened. In fact, Deputy Armstrong came and made a few trades himself. He briefly spoke with Gabe, but he spent most of his time talking to the preacher before he resumed his patrol. Gabe wondered what the two men were talking about for so long. It was probable that the deputy was a member of the church. Gabe didn't really know since, even though he could see the church from his place, he was usually too drunk or passed out to notice who was there on Sunday mornings. Gabe did know that Deputy Armstrong had always treated him with more respect than most of the white deputies had.

By three, the market was winding down, and soon Jane, Robby, and Gabe folded up their tables and headed back to Gabe's house for a late lunch.

Jane fried up some steaks she'd acquired, Gabe made a salad with the little produce he hadn't sold, and Robby set the table. The three of them sat down to eat, giving thanks for the bounty they had.

After lunch, Robby and Gabe decided to try their luck at rabbit hunting. They took their rifles and walked to the back of Gabe's fifty acres. Gabe was pleased to see Robby carefully following the safety rules. The young man raised his rifle and shot. Gabe hadn't seen the rabbit until Robby fired, but the report of the .22 kicked the animal into high gear, and Gabe saw him disappear into the woods.

"I missed," Robby said.

"You shot too fast," Gabe said. "Always take your time. Aim for something specific, like the eye. That's a good target on a rabbit."

Robby nodded, and the two continued their hunt. A few minutes later, Robby spoke again.

"Thanks for teaching me to hunt, Mr. Horne. I always hoped my dad would show me, but he was too busy."

"You're more than welcome, Robby," Gabe said.

The boy had a pensive look on his face for a long moment. He finally spoke. "Are you and my mom going to get married?"

Gabe was dumbfounded for a minute. "Why would you ask that?"

"I don't know. I've seen you guys kissing a few times, and I was just wondering."

"Well, you don't have to worry about that right now, Robby. Your mom and I are just kind of dating. You know, getting to know each other. I think it will be a while before we're ready to think about marriage."

"I understand," the boy said. "I just wanted you to know it's all right with me if you do decide to get married."

Gabe would have laughed if Robby hadn't been so serious. "Tell you what, if we do decide, you'll be the first to know. Okay?"

"Okay."

The pair continued their hunt for another hour or so, but they didn't see any other rabbits so they decided to head back. It was about time to get ready for the meeting anyway. Jane was disappointed that they came back empty-handed, but she still promised them a good dinner after the meeting.

The preacher was already there when they arrived. Gabe walked up and shook the man's hand. "Thanks for staying, Pastor. I was wondering if you'd be so kind as to chair the meeting tonight."

"I'm honored you would ask, Mr. Horne, but this is a meeting for the residents of this community, and it should be led by one of the residents."

Gabe's shoulders dropped at the preacher's response. "Okay," he said, dreading the fact that he'd have to start the meeting again. Perhaps, if Gabe was lucky, Captain Lozano would take the reins. He could only hope.

"You know," Pastor Washington said, "when I first started preaching, I was nervous about speaking in front of a crowd. Someone gave me good advice. He told me to imagine that I was only talking to one person, a trusted friend or loved one. It really helped me."

"Thanks, Reverend," Gabe said, wondering if he was that transparent.

Soon the small sanctuary was filled, and Gabe trudged to the front. "Welcome, everyone. We'll just get right to it, if that's all right. Captain Lozano, would you and your committee like to come up and start us off?"

"Actually, Chief Easton isn't here yet. We realized we needed an easel to display a map, and he ran home to get one. We'll be ready as soon as he gets back."

"All right, then." Gabe exhaled. "How about the education committee? Are you all ready?"

"Yes, we are," a man said as he stood up. Gabe recognized him as one of the two people who had raised their hands when he'd asked for teachers the other night.

"Come on up, Mr. . . . ?"

"Evans," the man said, making his way forward.

Thank God, Gabe thought as he relinquished the lectern. He stepped down from the podium and squeezed into the pew in the front row.

"We actually have two solutions," Mr. Evans began. "First, Mrs. Cook and I, both certified teachers, along with Mrs. Bell and Mrs. Nguyen, the homeschoolers, can teach forty or fifty kids in a modified, one-room-schoolhouse-type of setting. We thought we could use the church here, if that's all right with the preacher. We'd need to see exactly how many and what ages the kids are, but basically we'd divide them into four groups, and each of us would teach the ages with which we're most comfortable. Mrs. Bell has even volunteered to teach a music class."

A murmur of approval rose behind Gabe followed by a short round of applause.

"Of course, we would expect to get paid for our services," Mr. Evans said as the din diminished. A different murmur shot through the crowd.

Mr. Evans raised his hands to quiet the assembly. "We know that many don't have cash, but we'd be glad to be paid in goods. We aren't looking to get rich, but if we're going to be away from our families to do this, it only seems fair to us that we receive some kind of compensation. Even if someone has nothing of value to trade, we'd be willing to accept some help with tending our gardens or something similar. We would negotiate with each family depending on how many kids they had and what they could afford to do."

"That seems reasonable," someone called out.

"What's your other option?" another asked.

"Mrs. Nguyen has the complete homeschooling curriculum from kindergarten through twelfth grade. She's willing to check out one section at a time, at no charge, to anyone who wants them, as long as they promise to take care of them."

The sound of applause again filled the church. Gabe turned around to see that everyone seemed happy with the two solutions the education committee had recommended. Out of the corner of his eye, he caught movement and turned back to see Mr. Evans heading back to his seat.

Gabe rose and reluctantly marched back to the front. He hated this. It made him wish for a drink. He recalled the advice Reverend Washington had suggested and decided to give it a try. What did he have to lose?

He considered thinking about Hannah, but he saw Jane's face in the audience and focused on her. "I guess the first thing we need to know is if we can use the church. Would that be okay, Reverend?" He diverted his eyes to the pastor.

"Other than worshipping the Lord, I can't think of a better use for this building," the preacher said. "Of course it's okay."

"Thank you, Reverend Washington," Gabe said, looking back at Jane. She smiled, and the gesture relaxed him. "Does anyone have any comments about what Mr. Evans proposed?"

The group remained silent.

"How many of you are interested in bringing your kids to the church for school?" Gabe said.

At least thirty-five people raised their hands.

"How many of you are considering homeschooling?"

Five or six hands went up.

"I guess you can get with Mr. Evans after the meeting and sign up with him. Is that all right, Mr. Evans?"

"Yes," the teacher replied. "All four of us will be in the back if anyone has any questions."

"Thank you," Gabe said, noticing that concentrating on Jane made him not nearly so nervous. "Captain Lozano, is your group ready?"

"Yes, Daniel just got back with the easel." The three vets rose and walked toward the front. Gabe walked down the steps back to his seat, but he didn't feel as if he was sneaking out this time. One man carried the easel, another had a medium-sized whiteboard, and Captain Lozano had a spiral notebook. The captain stepped up behind the podium while the other two set up the visual aid and stood to the side of it.

"In case you don't know, my name is Paul Lozano. I am retired army. Standing beside the map is Daniel Easton, a former navy corpsman."

The man closest to the map waved.

"Beside him," Paul continued, "is Jerry King, a former air force aircraft mechanic, who is still in the reserves."

Jerry nodded.

"We have cussed and discussed several plans to protect our little slice of heaven here. The biggest thing we need to do to secure our homes and neighborhood is restrict access to the area to only those who live here. Without controlling who can come and go, we can't control anything." Paul stopped for a second to let his words sink in.

"If you look at the map we've drawn up, you can see the area we have marked off as being our AO, or area of operation. As you can see, there are four roads that lead into and out of our AO. There's Cotton Creek Road that leads in from the north. Prairie Road goes through the southern part of our AO and enters on both the east and west sides. Then Wilke Road comes in from the northwest." Jerry pointed to each road as Paul named it.

"We could set up a roadblock at each location," Paul continued. "The problem is manpower. To do this right, you'd need five or six men at each location. If you ran eight-hour shifts, that's three shifts a day times four locations times six men. That is seventy-two men a day, and that doesn't give anyone a day off. What we're suggesting is that we only have one way in and out of the area. That should give us plenty of manpower, and no one should have to man a roadblock more than every other day. There's a natural choke point on the west side of Prairie Road where it cuts through a small hill, and we're recommending that for the checkpoint. Jerry, will you point to that location? We think that by eliminating the Wilke Road, Cotton Creek Road, and east-side Prairie Road entrances, we can secure the neighborhood from those who don't belong here. We realize this may mean some people have to drive a little farther to get to town, but it's the best compromise between convenience and security we could find." Paul smiled.

"What do you mean by 'eliminate'?" a large man in the back of the church asked.

"Just that," Paul answered. "We can take out the bridge on Wilke Road where it crosses York Creek, and we can do the same thing with the old bridge over Cotton Creek. We'll have to block off Prairie Road by pushing or blasting dirt over it where it passes through the big hill on the east side of the Jacobs place."

"You can't destroy bridges and roads like that! They belong to the government," the man said.

"Yeah," another man said. "I live on the other side of the Cotton Creek Bridge. If you destroy it, I'll have to drive an extra eight or ten miles to town. I can barely afford the gas it takes now."

This started everyone talking at once. Some were only whispering to their neighbors, while others were shouting out toward the front, but little could be understood. Paul held up his hands to quiet the crowd. It worked a little, but many were still talking, and he had to raise his voice to be heard.

"Listen, everyone, please. I realize that what we're proposing will create some hardships. There are no easy choices to be made if we really want to secure our homes and neighborhood. We've discussed all the options, and this is really the only way we see to make sure the riffraff stays out."

"Why do you need so many men at each checkpoint? Why can't we just put two or three men at each place and keep all the roads open? Can't two guys check everyone coming and going?"

"Yes, they can," Paul said. "The problem comes if someone wants in who doesn't belong. It would be easy for a small group to overpower two men. With six, two can do the checking, and the other four can cover them in case something happens."

"Cover them?" a woman asked. "What could happen? You think this might be dangerous?"

"It's a possibility, and we want to be prepared," Paul said.

"Well, if it's dangerous, I'm not letting my husband do it."

"Would you prefer that we just let the murderers and rapists drive right up to your front door?" Paul said flatly.

It got quiet for a minute.

"You're overreacting!" the woman said loudly, breaking the silence. "No one is going to come here and do that. You just want to play Rambo!"

The room filled with voices, as the sounds of bickering seemed to come from everyone. Gabe looked around, a little sorry for Paul and his committee but glad it wasn't him on the hot seat. The arguing went on for a while, and everyone ignored Paul's pleading to come to order. Finally the din settled to a mild clamor and then quieted to where Paul could speak again. Gabe could see that he was trying to remain diplomatic.

"If anyone has a suggestion on how to secure the neighborhood without taking out the other entrances, we would be more than glad to listen."

"What if we just blocked them off with junk cars or something instead of blasting them?" someone said.

"That doesn't solve my problem," the man who lived across the Cotton Creek Bridge said.

"It also doesn't really stop anyone," Paul said. "Unless a barrier is watched, and the watchers have a way to discourage people from taking it apart, it will only slow down the interlopers. With time, any obstacle can be overcome."

"Then there's no way to guarantee that destroying the bridges will keep everyone out," the man argued.

"That's true," Paul said, "but it's much harder to rebuild a bridge or dig a road out from under tons of rubble than it is to push a bunch of junk cars off it. The undesirables we're trying to discourage would not likely take the time to repair a bridge."

"They could still find a place to wade or swim across."

"I agree, but again, we're talking about people who wouldn't do that. Criminals are lazy by nature and want a way to make a quick getaway. Walking in won't appeal to them."

"Well, I still think it's stupid to destroy government property."

"Why don't you just put a couple of guys at each entrance and keep them all open?" a woman in the back called out.

Paul blew out a long, deep breath. "Let's say we do exactly that," he said. "Suppose a pickup truck full of guys who have no good on their minds comes up to the two guys manning the checkpoint. What do you think is going to happen?"

"Well, couldn't they call for help?" the woman said.

Gabe could see that Paul was at the end of his rope. "Sure," the retired army officer said sardonically, "they can just call 911 on their cell phones. I mean, besides the fact that the phones don't work anymore and that the sheriff's department's response time is ten minutes or more before all the shit starts hitting the fan, that should work just fine. You know, maybe after a couple of us get killed, you people will take this shit seriously!"

It was quiet as Paul glared at the crowd.

Gabe didn't want to, but something made him stand up and walk up to the podium. He turned and faced the audience while he placed his hand on Paul's shoulder. He hoped the gesture would both show his support for the angry man and calm him down some.

"Perhaps we all need some time to think this over," Gabe heard himself say as he painted on a smile. "Paul and his group are only doing what we asked them to do. How about we get back together on Monday evening and talk about this again? Is that agreeable to everyone?"

Everyone murmured their approval, and the meeting was

over. As everyone was beginning to file out, the preacher stood and made his way to the podium and stood next to Gabe and Paul.

"I want to invite everyone to church in the morning. It doesn't matter to me or to God what church you usually attend, or if you normally go to church or not. You are welcome here," he announced. "I hope to see you all here."

CHAPTER 25

As the last of the people exited the church, Gabe, the preacher, and Paul stood on the podium and watched. After a long, uncomfortable moment, Paul spoke.

"I want to apologize for getting angry and using foul language in your church, Reverend Washington."

"Brother Lozano, getting angry is not a sin. Christ did it when he drove the money changers out of the temple. What we must be careful about is losing control of our words and actions. You did a good job presenting the case for what your committee proposed for all but the last minute or so of the debate. However, the damage you did with just a few words might have undone all the good up to that point."

Gabe saw Paul's head drop and nod weakly. "You're right," the retired officer said.

"What we need to do is to find a way to convince these people that you're right, and you *are* right." The preacher paused, and Paul's head came back up. "I spoke with Deputy Armstrong for a while today, and he told me of unspeakable acts happening not far from here. Our sheriff's department has done a fantastic job keeping this plague of crime out of our county, but they're fighting a losing battle. He's afraid it's beginning to overwhelm them, and we're going to be no better off than the big cities. We must convince these people that we have to take care of our own."

So that's what they were talking about, Gabe thought. "Pastor, why didn't you say something about what Deputy Armstrong said during the debate?"

"Because, brother Horne, just like I told you when you asked me to chair the meeting, I'm not a resident of this community, at least not yet. I drive out here once a week to preach to a small congregation, most of whom don't live here, either. Many of the people here see me as an outsider. Some won't listen to me because of that. Others won't hear me because I'm just an old black man to them."

"No one thinks that," Gabe said.

"You may not think it, brother Horne, but many do. You're open-minded, and that's one of the reasons these people look to you. I heard about how you'd changed. It sounded like a miracle, too good to be true. I decided to see for myself. Even though I didn't know you before, I knew the stories. You are not the man you used to be. You remind me of the story of Saul. While your transformation may not have been the result of a blinding light from God, it is no less a miracle. Saul became Paul, the leader of the church. You, brother Gabriel, have become the leader of this community, and you are the man who can convince the people to do the right thing."

"But I don't know what the right thing is, preacher," Gabe protested. "Right now you talking to me about this stuff makes me want a drink. How do you know I won't go home and get drunker than Cooter Brown when I leave here?"

"I don't know, brother Horne, but I have faith in God that you'll do the right thing, the same way these people have faith in you."

It was getting dark, and DJ was ready to go. The quad was loaded the same as it had been when he had arrived this morning with one notable exception. DJ looked with disdain at the jerry can in the failing light. "Piece of shit," he said under his breath as he double-checked everything on the quad.

He had perhaps four gallons of fuel. It wouldn't last through the whole night. If he was lucky, he would get seventy-five or eighty miles. He went over his plan in his head again, detouring off his course toward the nearest medium-sized town. Hopefully, he'd be able to buy some gas there. If not, then he'd do whatever he had to do.

It was finally dark. He pulled on his night-vision goggles and eased the big quad out onto the road. It was just one problem after another, he thought. He wondered if he'd ever make it to his bug-out location.

"So, what were you and Paul and the preacher talking about?" Jane said as they walked back to Gabe's house.

"Just about how to get everyone to go along with Paul's plan. Reverend Washington told us that Deputy Armstrong said we've been lucky so far, but that things are getting worse, and we'd better be ready to take care of ourselves."

"Anything else?"

"Yes, the preacher has some fool notion that everyone will do what I say. He said I'm the leader. Isn't that silly?"

"It's not, Gabe. People do listen to what you say. They see the things you do, and they know you'll do what's best. It started when you saved our food at the grocery store, but since then, you've looked after Robby and me, you organized the market, and you got everyone together to have the meetings."

"I just passed out the flyers," Gabe said defensively. "I never wanted to be the leader."

"That's just it. Anyone who wants to be the leader is probably doing it for the wrong reasons. They want to be important, or to do what's best for themselves, or some other selfish reason. You don't want any of that stuff. That, combined with not being afraid to do what's right, is what makes you the best man for the job."

"You mean if I wanted the job, no one would want me?"

"Yes," she answered.

Gabe shook his head. "I don't believe it. I got the job because I *don't* want it?"

"That's right," Jane said with a smile.

"Well, remind me not to 'not want' any more jobs."

DJ was still fuming about the jerry can, so he didn't see the truck on the side of the road until he was much closer to it than he would have preferred. If anyone was in it, they might be able to see him with just a cheap night-vision scope, or they might have heard him. He quickly pulled the big quad into the ditch on the opposite side of the road and grabbed his rifle. When he was twenty yards or so from the four-wheeler, he eased out to where he could see the truck. It was probably out of gas, as were most of the cars abandoned alongside the road, but perhaps it simply broke down and had some of the precious fluid DJ so desperately needed.

DJ eyed the truck for several minutes and saw no sign that anyone was in it. Of course, it could be that the owner was watching from a distance to ambush any unsuspecting passersby. It was probably just an abandoned vehicle, but it paid to be careful, he told himself. He wished he had infrared equipment, as that would be very hard to evade.

Finally he ran across the road in a crouch to the ditch on the other side. After scouring his surroundings from his new vantage point, he cautiously approached the truck. He placed his hand on the hood and pulled it off immediately, as if it were too hot to touch.

It was only slightly warm, but the fact that it had been running in the past few hours made him overreact. He looked around again, trying his best to spot anything out of the ordinary. The night-vision goggles made everything an eerie shade of green, but DJ had become accustomed to this in the past few weeks. There was nothing out of place.

Squatting down in front of the truck, DJ took his helmet off, removed his goggles from it, and balanced it on the muzzle of his rifle. He stuck the helmet up where it would be visible to anyone watching the truck. Nothing happened. After a minute, he pulled the decoy back down. Since the truck was still warm, there was a chance it held some fuel.

Putting his gear back on, he worked his way to the passenger door and carefully looked inside. No one was there. Checking the bed revealed nothing special. There was a spare tire, a jack, a pair of bolt cutters, some other assorted tools, and a bit of canned food. DJ was a little surprised someone would leave food behind. He looked around again, wondering if it might be a trap. However, he reasoned, he'd given anyone who might be lying in wait every opportunity to take a shot at him. Plus, how likely was it that someone who drove an old beat-up truck like this would have the quality night-vision gear it would take to execute an after-dark ambush? In a way, he wished it was a trap because then the truck would have fuel for sure.

He made his way back to the cab and pulled open the door. The dome light came on and activated the auto shutdown on his goggles. Lifting them up, he saw that the keys weren't in the ignition. At least that was a promising sign. He pulled the plastic cover off the interior light and removed the bulb. No sense making it easy for someone. Lowering the goggles and switching them back on, he looked around one more time.

If anyone was going to take a shot at him, surely they would have done it by now. He drove his quad between the truck and the ditch. Then he removed the siphon hose he'd cut at Crystal's and stuck it down into the gas tank. Blowing through the hose only created the sound of rushing air, not the sound of bubbles he was hoping to hear.

Damn it, I never have any luck. He remembered the hole someone had drilled into Crystal's tank to remove all the gas. Was it possible there could be a little gas left that the hose just couldn't reach? He didn't have a drill, but there was a punch and a hammer in his tool kit. He grabbed them, along with a small flashlight. Removing his helmet and night-vision goggles—since he couldn't take a chance on damaging his best asset next to his quad and rifle—he climbed under the truck. He put the punch on the lowest point on the gas tank and drew back the hammer.

Dumb-ass, he thought. If there was gas in the tank, he had to have something to catch it with. He climbed back out and removed the last good gas can he had. It wouldn't fit under the truck in the upright position, but by rotating it ninety degrees he was able to make it fit. Climbing back under, he resumed his operation.

It took a couple of whacks with the hammer before the punch defeated the metal skin of the tank. Gas began to drip down as soon as the puncture was made, and DJ placed the jerry can's opening directly under the hole. When he pulled the punch out, he was rewarded with a stream of liquid gold. It ran for several seconds and then reduced itself to a slow drip. Finally DJ pulled himself out from under the truck. He figured he had recovered around half of a gallon of fuel.

He happily poured it into the big quad, recovered his tools, confiscated the food in the truck, and strapped everything onto the four-wheeler. Back on the road, he smiled. A half gallon of fuel might not be much, but it would get him another nine or ten miles.

Gabe had to catch his breath and unkink his back. He sat up on the edge of the couch.

"What's the matter?" Jane whispered, leaning up next to him.

"My back is all twisted. I'm not a teenager anymore, you know." The taste of her lips was still on his.

"Could have fooled me." She smiled in the soft candlelight. "I know I haven't felt this way since I was a teenager. Of course, at this age I don't have to worry about my dad catching me making out with my boyfriend."

"Well, I guess that's good."

"It's good for you. There's no telling what my old man would have done to you if he caught us like this." Jane paused. "On the other hand, I don't know what Robby would think about this behavior."

"He told me it was all right with him when we were out hunting this afternoon."

"He did?" she asked, sitting up all the way.

"Yes. He said he'd seen us kissing before, and that if we wanted to get married, it was okay with him."

"Robby really said that?"

"No. I just made it up," Gabe said, smiling sardonically at the alluring creature sitting next to him on the couch.

She slapped his arm playfully. "Really, did he say it was okay with him?"

"Yes."

"Did you ask him?"

"No," Gabe said, now serious. "He brought it up on his own. I almost choked when he asked me."

"What did you say?"

"That we weren't thinking about that right now, but we'd let him know if we were."

"Hmm," she said.

Gabe could see the wheels turning in her eyes. He almost hated to ask, but he knew enough about women to know he should. "Hmm, what?"

"I was just thinking, well . . . I don't know . . . what do you think?"

"Think about what?" he asked innocently.

"About getting married, silly!"

DJ was humming a song he couldn't remember the name of as he drove along. It felt like rain, and that usually would have put him in a foul mood, but for some reason, it didn't. He'd traveled a couple of miles since he'd gotten the gas. The road was straight here, and lined by field after field. The openness let him relax a little and look around. Of course, everything was green through the night-vision monocular, but it struck him that green was a happy color.

In the distance, he saw four animals in a field. *Cattle, probably,* he thought, although they seemed too small. He strained his eyes a little trying to make out the green blobs. Perhaps they were deer. No, they were too tall. As he closed the distance, it became apparent they were humans. DJ could also see that they were moving toward a farmhouse. He slowed the big quad a little to get a better look. It didn't help much at first, but as he got closer, he could see that they were carrying rifles. The one in the back was carrying something else, but he couldn't make out what it was.

He stopped the four-wheeler and stared on as the men crossed the large field. It didn't appear that they had any kind of night vision because each of them occasionally took an unsteady step, and one actually fell at one point. It was also clear that they'd had no tactical training. They were walking so closely together that one well-thrown grenade or one well-aimed burst from an automatic weapon would take out all four. As he watched them, he finally figured out that the last man was holding a gas can.

DJ realized these must be the guys who'd left the truck. What he wasn't sure of was their intentions. It was obvious that they were headed to the farm to get some fuel, but how were they going to obtain it? And they had no idea there was a hole in their gas tank. That can, once poured into the leaky tank, wouldn't take them far. He snickered at their bad fortune.

He sat and watched with interest. If the farmer traded with them, then perhaps he'd trade with DJ, as well. *Hell*, he thought, *if I could just fill up the quad, I could probably make it without any more gas from here.* DJ unzipped his jacket some. It wasn't hot, but the air was getting thick, and he was starting to sweat a little. Finally the men were nearing the house. They huddled up for a minute, and then one of them approached the front of the house while the other three ducked away in hiding.

The hair on the back of DJ's neck went up. Were they planning an ambush? DJ's mind went into overdrive. They could be, but it was more likely that they were just being careful. If DJ had been part of the group, he wouldn't have exposed all of them, either, although he might have sent two to the door instead of just one. Well, these guys were obviously not strategic geniuses, so they were probably honest. DJ hoped so. He wanted to see if they got some gas.

The man went to the door and knocked. A few seconds later, a light came on upstairs. DJ pulled off his night vision and got his binoculars. He could see the light moving through the windows, its glow floating ghostlike toward the front door. With the field glasses, he could make out the middle-aged man who opened the door. He held a hurricane lantern in one hand and gestured with the other in an animated fashion. DJ could see that he wasn't happy, his head shaking from side to side. Clearly the four men, and DJ, would have to look elsewhere for fuel. The farmer closed the door, and the light began to reverse its path. Once on the top floor, the light extinguished.

DJ put his night vision back in place and saw the men grouped up on the edge of the complex. The man who had knocked was obviously telling the others what had been said. Then the four spread out across the front yard. A few seconds after that, the firing began.

The color drained out of Gabe's face. He turned and bolted through the front door so rapidly, the screen door closer popped off the doorframe with a bang. Jane stood frozen for more than a minute.

She wondered if she should go after him. He hadn't been gone very long. She could drive the truck and easily catch him before he got home. On the other hand, the long walk might give him enough time to think things through. She was praying he wouldn't drink. If he did, it would be her fault.

Get married, she thought, scoffing at herself. She didn't know why she'd said it; it had just kind of come out on its own. She should have held back, but things had seemed so good between them. The look on his face when she asked was the same one she would've seen if she'd driven a stake through his heart. She mentally kicked herself again. She should've known he wasn't ready for that.

Earlier she'd headed off a relapse by kissing him. This time, in

a way, that was what had started the trouble. What could she do?
She had an idea, but was it right? It didn't matter, she told herself.
He was back on track, and it was her job to keep him that way.
"Whatever it takes," she whispered.

She went to her room and opened the bottom drawer of the
bureau. It had been a long time since anything in it had seen the
light of a flickering candle. As she pulled out the long silk gar-
ment, a wave of doubt swelled up inside her. She sat down on the
bed, bringing the soft material up to her face and feeling a tear
form in the corner of her eye. She made herself look deep into her
motives. Was she just using him because he gave her and her son
some security in these troubling times? Was that fair to him?
More important, was it fair to her? Was she willing to sacrifice
her principles for a little security? She forced herself to stare
deeper into the abyss, past all of the justification and reasoning.
Past the second-guessing and doubts, the trepidation and the
fear, like a distant lighthouse, was the answer. She loved him.

Everything zoomed into view. She loved him. He was the best
man she had ever known, and she loved him. Of course he'd been
blown off course by the deaths of his wife and son. Who wouldn't
have been? But she loved him, flaws and all, and she wanted to
make sure he knew it, even if it did drive him away.

She quickly packed the nightgown and a few other things into
a small bag. She wrote a quick note to Robby, in case she wasn't
back by the time he woke up, and left it on the table. Grabbing her
keys, she headed for the truck. The broken screen door banged
the side of the house again as she hurried through it.

*   *   *

DJ was pissed. Who did these guys think they were? He jumped off the quad and quickly cut the fence with his multitool. Climbing back on, he mashed the throttle open and started toward the house. The fact that the four men were attacking told him there was gas at the farm and the farmer just didn't want to part with it. If they killed the occupants and took what they wanted, he could get gas after they left.

DJ brought his quad to a halt and looked toward the house. The farmer was returning fire from a window on the second floor. DJ wondered how many people were inside. One would have a hard time holding off four. With nobody watching the back of the house, it would only be a matter of time before one of the raiders slipped in and blindsided the farmer.

The farmer wasn't shooting nearly as much as the raiders. *He's either pretty smart or doesn't have much ammo,* DJ thought. One of the raiders had disappeared from DJ's view on the far side of the house. Another was creeping toward the back on the near side. Then DJ saw a bright flash out of an upstairs side window and an instant later heard the unmistakable sound of a shotgun. So there were at least two people in the house. DJ saw the raider drop to the ground and squirm. A second shot came, and the squirming stopped.

DJ cranked the bike up and resumed his course toward the house. It was clear that, more than likely, the occupants of the house would win. If he helped them, maybe they'd give him some gas. Besides, it was the right thing to do, he reasoned, even if there was no gas.

He drove as fast as he safely could toward the back of the complex, finally parking behind a barn, and removed his rifle from the custom scabbard. Switching on the sight to the night-vision setting, he began making his way to the back of the main house. When he came around the barn, he saw one of the raiders trying to kick in the back door. DJ raised the rifle and centered the man in the glowing sight circle. He squeezed the trigger, and the rifle barked. A second later, the kicker was lying motionless on the back steps.

DJ worked his way toward the front of the house, careful to stay well away from the building. He didn't want to be mistaken for one of the raiders. It took a couple of minutes, but soon he could see one of the attackers shooting at the house from behind the cover of a large tree. The man wasn't covered from DJ's angle, however. He raised his rifle, and a quick double tap ended the man's assault. The last raider broke cover and ran back toward the field. A shot from the rifle upstairs ended his retreat.

DJ was wondering if the people in the house knew they had help. Should he call out to them? Before he could decide, a man's voice shouted down.

"Who's there? What do you want?"

"My name is DJ Frost. I was driving by, heard the shots, saw these men attacking your house, and came to help. I don't really want anything. Maybe just a place to hole up for a day or two, if that's all right."

"How do I know you're not one of them?"

"Well, you just saw me shoot one of them, and there's another one on the ground outside the back door. Why would I shoot them if I was with them?"

"Maybe you saw you were losing, and you turned on your own men to get what you wanted."

This guy has his tinfoil wrapped a little tight.

"That's not very likely," DJ said. "Five guys with any kind of intelligent plan would have no problem taking the house." That was probably an exaggeration, DJ knew, but he needed to convince the man that he was a good guy. "If I hadn't helped you, you might be the one dead right now. Besides that, I can prove I wasn't traveling with this scum. I have a quad parked behind your barn. There's no way five guys would fit on it."

"That might be true, but I still don't know if I can trust you."

DJ decided to try a little reverse psychology. "Well, there's no way I can absolutely prove I'm trustworthy. I'll just continue on my way," he said, attempting to sound disappointed.

"Wait," a female voice called out.

DJ could hear the two voices going back and forth for a minute. He couldn't make out the words, but it was obvious they were arguing. Finally the man called out.

"Please stay right where you are. I'm going to the barn to check out your story. If you're telling the truth, we'll be happy to let you stay for a few days. My wife has you covered, so don't try anything funny."

"No problem," DJ answered. He saw the light being carried down the stairs again.

"Thank you so much for you help," the woman said. "I'm sorry my husband is so suspicious."

"He's only being as cautious as I'd be," DJ answered in as pleasant a voice as he could muster. "What did those men want?" he added with feigned curiosity.

"They wanted gas. Peter told them we didn't have any extra, but they didn't believe him. The only gas we have is in my car, and we need that to get back and forth to town. I never thought anyone would be willing to kill for a few gallons of gas." The woman's voice was starting to shake. "I—I never thought I'd have to shoot someone."

"You only did what you had to," DJ said reassuringly.

"You seem so calm. Have you had to do this before?"

"Once."

"How did you, you know, deal with the guilt?" she asked.

"It helps if you think of them as the animals they are. Humans don't prey on each other, no matter how bad things get. They were rabid dogs, and you only stopped them before they hurt and killed lots of people. Just remember that."

"I will. Thanks, DJ."

Neither spoke for a minute or two. DJ wondered where they kept the car. Maybe he could just siphon the gas he needed when the couple went back to bed. If not, he'd have to play nice for a while. It might be a day or two until he could talk them out of a couple of gallons.

"So, DJ, where are you from, and where are you headed?"

DJ figured that the silence might be awkward for her, and that was why she started the small talk.

"I'm from the big city," he said, careful not to give out too much information, "and I'm heading over to a place in the boonies that some friends of mine own."

"I heard it's awful in the cities," she said.

"Yes, ma'am. It's getting really bad."

After another awkward pause, she spoke again. "What does DJ stand for?"

"Devlin James," he answered.

"That's a nice name."

"I never liked my first name. The kids in school used to tease me about it. That's why I go by DJ."

"Well, then, DJ it is," she said in a cheerful tone.

About that time, DJ saw the light coming to the front door. It opened and the man stepped out on the front porch holding the lantern up high, making himself visible. "Your quad is right where you said it was. I appreciate your help, and we'd be glad to put you up for a day or two."

It's a good thing I'm one of the good guys, DJ thought. *Otherwise I could have easily killed this guy.* "Thanks," he said in his friendliest voice. "I'm only happy I was passing by."

Jane knocked on the door, fearful of what she would find. It seemed like an eternity until the door opened. He stood there, straight and rigid. Most important, he didn't have a glass in his hand.

"I'm so sorry, Gabe. I'm so stupid for just blurting that out. I don't know why I said it. I just wanted you to know—"

She was surprised that his arms were around her and his mouth pressed against hers before she even saw him move. They'd been making out for a while now, and she had really enjoyed the closeness, but this was a kiss on a whole other level. It was warmer, softer, and more passionate than anything they'd shared up to this point. Was it just because she'd come to grips with her feelings? She pushed the thought aside and just enjoyed the moment, hoping this was a good omen for them. At the very least, it put off the risky confession she had to make.

Before she was ready to stop, his hands clasped her upper arms, and he gently pushed her back. Why had he stopped? She looked in his eyes for the answer. They were different. The cold, steely gray had turned soft and warm. What was it? It looked like happiness. Could that be right? Her mind began to race through the countless possibilities.

"Okay," he said quietly, before she could even begin to sort the probable from the improbable.

"Okay?" she asked, confusion in her voice and on her face.

He nodded gently. "Yes, okay. Let's get married," he whispered with a smile.

CHAPTER 26

"Do you mean it?" Jane said.

Gabe's head tipped slightly to one side, and his eyes opened wider.

"Of course you mean it," she stammered. "I just mean, are you ready for this?"

"When you asked me what I thought about it earlier, I didn't think I was, but on the walk home, I realized I've been happy for the first time since Hannah and Michael died. I think I was feeling guilty about that, and that's why I haven't wanted to admit it to myself, but there's no reason to feel guilty about being happy. I want to be with you. I want you and Robby to be a part of my life. I really do want to marry you, if you'll have me."

"Of course I'll have you." She stood on her toes and gave him a kiss. "I love you."

"I love you, too."

"I can spend the night here if you want me to," she whispered in his ear.

"I do want you to," he said, "but let's wait until we're married." He gave her a kiss on the forehead.

"I don't know if I want to wait that long."

"Me, either. That's why I thought we might get married next Saturday. We can talk to the preacher about it after church tomorrow."

"Oh, Gabe!" She threw her arms around his neck.

"If you need another blanket later tonight, they're in the chest at the foot of the bed," the woman said.

"Thanks, Margaret," DJ said.

"And the bathroom's right down the hall on your left. If you need to flush, there's a five-gallon bucket of water in there," Peter said.

"Okay," DJ said. "Thanks again for putting me up."

"Well, we really do appreciate you helping us out. I think we would've stopped those bastards, but you never know."

"You were using tactics," DJ said, trying to sound authoritative, "and you have good fire discipline, too, I noticed."

"Learned that in the army a long time ago," Peter said.

"You see any action?"

"No. I was too young for Korea and too old for Vietnam. How about you? Looking at your gear, you must have some military experience."

"No," DJ said, "I'm in law enforcement."

"You're a cop?" Margaret said.

"Yes."

"That explains why you were so cool," she said. "I was a nervous wreck. The blasts of the guns and sounds of the bullets smacking the house were way different from what you hear on TV."

"That's very true, but you did fine, Margaret."

"Thanks, DJ, and thanks again for rescuing us."

"No problem. Good night."

"Good night," the couple chimed in unison.

DJ heard them climb the stairs and shuffle around for a while. When it had been quiet for forty-five minutes, he slipped out of bed and pulled his boots on. The old wooden screen frame was held in place with a simple latch. DJ had no problem removing it and slipping it in through the window. Climbing out the window, he pulled his night vision into place.

He looked up at the second story of the house, and all appeared to be still. He walked behind the house to the detached garage. His quad was in here, and so was Margaret's car. The garage door was locked from the inside, but luckily he'd been the last one out of the regular door on the side when Peter had let him put the four-wheeler inside. DJ had feigned locking the door. He'd left everything except his rifle, pistol, and a small duffel bag on the quad. They were with him now. His plan was to siphon enough gas out of Margaret's car to fill the quad and his last good jerry can, then leave.

DJ turned the knob and slowly pushed the door open. Walking to his vehicle, he laid down his rifle and bag and removed his last good fuel can and the siphon hose. He walked to the other side of the car and opened the fuel door.

"Damn it," he whispered under his breath. A locking fuel cap was covering the tank. He could try to remove it, or he could just punch the tank as he'd done on the truck, but that might make too much noise. *I'll have to wait until the old couple is away or find a way to get the keys,* he thought. He exited the garage, really locking the door this time, and made his way back through the guest room window.

Gabe had heard a few hellfire and brimstone preachers in his life, but all of those paled in comparison to Reverend Washington. The preacher's voice trembled with passion as he spoke. "And the Good Book says in Proverbs 22:3 that 'A prudent man foreseeth the evil, and hideth himself: but the simple pass on, and are punished.' Can I get an amen?"

"Amen!" the crowded sanctuary boomed.

"Brethren, God is admonishing us to be prudent and wise. He says we must foresee the evil that might come our way. Some of us would rather look the other way and hope that evil passes us by. That is the easy thing to do. It is the simple thing to do. But if evil does not pass us by, and we are unprepared, then we will be punished according to the Word of God!" The preacher's fist smacked the pulpit with a resounding report.

Reverend Washington went on to talk about David and how he'd protected the sheep from predators with his sling. He preached about the watchman in Ezekiel 33 and how if someone ignored his warning, his blood was on his own hands. He read a few more passages from different books of the Bible and related their meanings to the congregation.

Gabe smiled at the wisdom of the white-haired orator. He'd found biblical support for all of the things Paul had suggested last night, and with most of the neighborhood here in the church, Gabe was sure the defensive plan would pass the next time they voted on it.

*   *   *

The bed wasn't as comfortable as the one at Crystal's had been, but it was sure better than sleeping on the ground. The smell of coffee tempted his palate as he rose, dressed, and headed down the stairs.

"Good morning," Margaret said. "How did you sleep?"

"Pretty well, Margaret," DJ said. "How about you?"

"Not too good. I guess I had too much adrenaline pumping to sleep much."

"Yeah, that happens. Where's Peter?"

"He's wrapping up the bodies of those guys who attacked us and putting them in the barn. He plans to go to town after breakfast to get the police to come pick up the bodies."

"He should just dig a hole with the tractor, dump them in, and cover them up. Then, if anybody comes looking for them, you two should say you don't know anything."

"We couldn't do that. Those boys might have families. I feel bad about killing them, but they would have killed us for the gas in the can. I can't believe they died for a few gallons of fuel," she said as she put her hands over her head and face. She began to sob.

DJ could see that the reality of what had happened last night was just starting to dawn on her. He wondered if Peter knew what he was doing, going to the police. More than likely, the police would come get the bodies and not press charges on the old couple, but DJ couldn't take that chance. If he couldn't change Peter's mind, he'd have to leave. If the cops came and started asking questions, who knew what might happen? DJ figured he'd better get some gas and get out of there.

"There, there," he said as he patted the older woman on the back. "Everything's going to be okay."

The woman sniffed a couple of times and painted on a smile. "Thanks, Dev . . . I mean, DJ. You really are an angel."

DJ smiled at the compliment. "I'm going to go out and see if Peter needs any help while you fix breakfast."

"Okay."

As he walked outside, he saw a tractor with a front-end loader on it parked next to the barn. DJ made his way there, getting his first view of the complex in the daylight. Behind the barn was a very large fuel tank. It looked as if it might hold three or four hundred gallons of gas. He wondered if it was empty. If it was even half-full, there was plenty of gas for Peter to give him five gallons or so. In fact, DJ wondered why Peter would even risk a gunfight by turning down the guys last night if he had any extra fuel.

"Peter," he called as he approached the barn.

"In here," the answer came.

DJ entered the barn and saw Peter pulling the fourth body, wrapped neatly in a sheet, next to the other three. "I came to help, but I see I'm too late."

"Thanks," the man said. His brow was deeply furrowed as he looked at the four carefully placed bodies.

DJ could see that Peter wasn't in much of a talking mood, but he couldn't wait. "Peter, Margaret told me you were going to the police this morning to report what happened."

"Yes," the man said, looking up. "I'd really appreciate it if you'd go with me."

"Are you sure involving the police is the right thing to do?" DJ said.

"Of course it is. I'm a little surprised to hear a cop ask that question, DJ."

"Well, things are different now. Who knows how the police will react? One of those boys could even be a cop's son or something," DJ said, recalling his encounter with the deputy at Crystal's house.

"Well, I know the sheriff, so we won't have any problems, especially if you back up my story. We can do some shopping in town if you need anything. No sense wasting the gas."

"Speaking of gas, I noticed a huge tank behind the barn. Isn't there any gas in that?"

"It's a diesel tank for the tractors. It's almost full, but little good it does unless we drive one of the tractors to town," Peter said.

"I see. You don't have a truck that runs on diesel?"

"Yes, I have a Dodge one-ton, but as my farmer's luck would have it, it's broken."

"What's wrong with it?" DJ said.

"The injection pump went out just as things started to go south. I had it towed to the shop, and they ordered a new one, but who knows when or if it'll ever come in? Come on, let's go eat, and then we can go to town."

The two men walked out of the barn and back toward the house. DJ was thinking about what to do. If Peter really did know the sheriff, and there was no reason to think he was lying, then everything might end up all right. He could possibly even buy the gas he needed to get to the retreat. On the other hand . . . he just couldn't risk it.

"Listen, Peter, I just can't go with you. The sheriff knows you, but he doesn't know me. I can't risk him holding me until he finds out who I am. I mean, with the way communications are now, there's no telling how long that might be."

"I'm sure you don't have anything to worry about, DJ. The sheriff is a real stand-up guy, and with you being a cop, too, we'll be in and out in no time."

"I'm sure you're right, Peter, but like I said, things are different now. The feds might be in charge, and they might not be stand-up guys. I think it's best if I go ahead and leave before you go."

"Well," Peter said, "I can see why you might be reluctant. I guess I owe you enough without making you go with me. Come on in and eat breakfast, and we can leave at the same time. It'll be at least a couple of hours before I get back. That should give you a good head start."

"Thanks," DJ said with a big smile. He took a deep breath. "Say, Peter, talking about owing me, do you think you could see your way to selling me a couple of gallons of gas? I was refiguring last night, and I don't have quite enough to make it like I thought I did."

"Sorry, DJ, but I just can't. All we have is what's in the car."

"I can pay you top dollar, and you can get more when you go to see the sheriff."

"Last time I was in town, I was able to buy five gallons, but they didn't know if they'd have any after that. That was about a week and a half ago. If you wanted to go to town, we could see if they still have any."

"No," DJ said, his teeth clenched, "I told you I can't take that chance."

"Well, if you want to wait for me to come back, I can try to get you some, but there are no guarantees," Peter stated flatly as the men approached the back door of the house.

"Look, Peter," DJ said as he placed himself between the farmer and the house, "I really must insist."

"No, you look. I'm trying to be civil here, but you're making it difficult. I'll help you with some food or anything else I can, but gasoline is out of the question. Just drop it, and let's eat."

Peter stepped to the side to walk around his guest, but DJ was younger and faster. He sidestepped in front of Peter and pulled the big black .45 out of the drop-leg holster and leveled it at the older man. "I didn't want it to come to this, but I have to have a couple of gallons of gas. Now give me the key to the cap on the Buick."

Peter's eyes had flames in them, but he slowly put his hand in his pocket and pulled out his keys. "You fucking bastard. I can't believe you'd do this. You're no better than those pieces of shit from last night. I shouldn't have listened to Margaret."

DJ smiled at the insults. He couldn't care less what this bumpkin thought of him. He was just happy he'd get his gas. Of course, he wouldn't just take two gallons now. He stepped forward and reached out for the keys. As his hand closed around them, the big pistol barked. A red spot appeared on Peter's shirt, and the man took a couple of unsteady steps backward and then fell to the ground.

DJ stared in shock. What had made his pistol fire? He walked forward and looked down at the injured man. His mouth was moving, but the sounds coming out were too weak to be distinguishable. His eyes smoldered with hate as he looked up at DJ, but DJ's mind was too busy searching for an answer to notice.

It took a second, but DJ figured out that it had been a sympathetic response. He inwardly chuckled at the irony of the term.

He would bet that Peter wouldn't think it was too sympathetic. DJ had read about sympathetic responses before. It happened most often when a cop was cuffing a suspect. When one hand squeezed the handcuffs closed, the other hand sympathetically squeezed, as well. If the cop had his firearm pointed at the suspect, well, this was what happened.

"Sorry, man," DJ said. "I didn't mean to shoot you."

Peter's mouth moved to form his two-word response. Little sound came out, but DJ had no problem reading his lips. It didn't anger DJ, though. He would have been pissed, too. He began to think about what would happen now. Would Margaret be able to get Peter to the hospital in time? He hoped so. What would this mean?

Suddenly something bit DJ in the side and in the leg and roared at him. For the second time in less than a minute, he was confused. It burned like a red-hot poker and sent his brain back into overdrive.

"You son of a bitch! You shot my husband!"

DJ turned and saw Margaret charging at him with the shotgun. He distinctly saw her pump the action, and the empty shell arced out of the receiver. As her left hand pushed the forearm up to return the gun to battery, DJ realized that the next "bites" might really be hazardous to his health. The pistol in his hand came up instinctively, and three shots were fired before he could contemplate the consequences of his reaction.

DJ didn't know if all three of his bullets had found their target or not, but at least one of them did. It struck Margaret above the left eye and stopped her kamikaze charge in an instant. The shotgun flew out of her hands as she crumpled into a heap on the ground. It hit the earth a split second after she did.

DJ walked up to her, his pistol still trained in her direction. It was obvious that she'd been dead before she hit the ground. He felt a little remorse at having to kill the woman who'd insisted her husband take him in, but he'd seen last night how deadly she could be with the scattergun. It was her or him, and DJ wanted to live.

He turned back toward Peter and saw the man trying unsuccessfully to get up. DJ was pretty sure he wouldn't make it without some urgent care within an hour or so. There was no sense in letting the man suffer. He limped up to Peter and pointed the pistol at the prone man's head. "I'm really sorry about this," he said sincerely as the hate raged in Peter's face.

The boom of the big pistol echoed between the house and the detached garage for a moment, and then all was quiet.

"And you want to do this next Saturday afternoon?" the preacher said.

Gabe and Jane both nodded.

The preacher broke into a big grin. "I think that's wonderful, and I'd be honored to perform the ceremony."

"Thank you so much, Reverend Washington," Gabe said as he extended his hand to the preacher.

"You are more than welcome, brother Horne and sister Walker." The old man shook Gabe's hand energetically.

"And thanks for the sermon this morning, Reverend," Gabe said.

"You don't have to thank me for that. I was only following my convictions."

"Well, I think you got through to a lot of people. We'll have to see what happens with the meeting this afternoon, but I expect there won't be nearly as much resistance to Paul's plan as there was."

"I hope and pray you're right, brother Horne," the preacher said.

CHAPTER 27

DJ went into the house and climbed the stairs. He entered the master bedroom and walked into the master bath. Laying his carbine on the vanity, he opened medicine chests and cabinets, strewing items across the small room until he found a first aid kit. He gingerly hiked up his pants and looked at his leg. The buckshot had passed through his calf muscle. He wiped the blood away and got a clear, quick look at the wounds before they overflowed with blood again. DJ knew from the little EMT training he had taken that as long as he could get the bleeding under control, infection was probably the biggest threat he would face from this injury.

He pulled out a bottle of peroxide and poured it over both sides of the wound. Once it quit bubbling, he placed a large piece of gauze over the holes and wrapped enough tape over them to hold them in place. Next, he turned his attention to his side. Removing his shirt, he could see that there was no exit wound. He got a closer look in the mirror, and saw that the pellet had entered his flank well to the side of anything vital. It wasn't bleeding badly, but he cleaned it up and dressed it just as he had done his calf.

The wounds hurt, but he needed to get the backyard cleaned up before he worried about that. He pulled the bedspread and blanket off the bed in the master suite and made his way out back. First he wrapped Margaret's body up and then Peter's. He dragged them to the garage where the raiders' bodies were and placed them at the end of the line.

He headed back to the master bath and started looking through the medicine he had scattered on the floor. Most of the names on the bottles he didn't recognize. Finally he found one he did: a bottle of Vicodin with eleven pills left. He took two. Then he found the liquor cabinet and grabbed an almost full bottle of bourbon. He took two big swigs out of the bottle and then re-placed it. *That should dull the pain.*

Gabe decided that he would run the meeting. He didn't expect any trouble, but after what had happened yesterday with Paul, he couldn't take any chances. The auditorium of the small church was packed with people standing around the back, along the sides of the pews, and even in the aisle. Reverend Washington had asked his wife to take the children into the fellowship hall and entertain them so that there would be more room for the adults, but it wasn't enough. When people were still arriving right before the meeting started, he invited some to sit in the choir loft. That helped a bit, but there were still a few standing outside when Gabe called the meeting to order. He was sure that after the sermon this morning, the defense plans would pass easily.

"I'll get right down to business," he said.

"We can't hear you!" someone in the entryway hollered.

"I said, I'll get right down to business. We need to vote on the defense plans that Captain Lozano suggested last night. All in favor—"

"Excuse me, Mr. Horne, but I would like to say something before we vote," a voice called out from the floor.

Crap, Gabe thought. "Of course," was all he said.

It was the man who had complained that taking out a bridge would force him to drive farther to get into town at the last meeting. He seemed nervous about talking in front of everyone.

"My name is Jake Solis and I live across Cotton Creek, about five miles from here. At the last meeting, I objected to removing the bridge that I and others have to take to get here. I talked with most of my neighbors today and they feel the same as I do." The man paused. The fact that no one said anything appeared to make him nervous. "Anyway, we do understand why you all want to do it, but it would cut us off from help and from the closest route we have to town. We discussed it and we think we might have a solution that would benefit everyone. What if we established a roadblock two miles north of the Cotton Creek Bridge? There's a big hill on the side of the road there and we should be able to push enough of it over to stop anybody in a vehicle. This would not cut us off from town and it would add eighteen families to your community. That should add enough manpower to really help with the checkpoint and other things."

The man makes a good argument, Gabe thought. "Paul, what do you think?" he asked.

"I think that is a great plan."

"Then all in favor?"

The positive response filled the auditorium.

"It looks like the 'Ayes' have it," Gabe said as he looked at the faces in the crowd. They were all smiling at him. He wondered how things could be going so well. He wasn't drinking anymore, he was in love and going to get married, his neighbors respected him and looked up to him. It had taken the world falling apart to put his world back together. He smiled back at the people in the church. Suddenly he realized he didn't know what to say next. His brain raced for a solution. "I'm going to turn the meeting over to Paul to discuss how we can get our plan implemented in the shortest amount of time. Paul?"

Paul stood and walked to the podium. The expression on his face told Gabe that he wasn't really ready for this, either. He gripped the sides of the lectern tightly and looked at all the expectant faces. He cleared his throat. "I think that maybe the best thing for us to do is to get together with anyone who would be willing to work on the roadblocks or man one of the checkpoints. If you want to help out, stick around after the meeting and we'll see who and what we have. Gabe?"

Gabe walked back up knowing that he deserved to have the tables turned on him the way Paul had done it. He wasn't happy it had happened, but he still had to smile about it. "Is there anything else we need to talk about?" he said when he reached the podium.

"Yeah," someone said, "when is school going to start?"

Gabe looked around the room. "Mr. Evans, are you here?"

"Right here." The man stood up in the back corner of the sanctuary. "We were hoping to get started on Wednesday, but we still have some things to work out. We are aiming for next Monday now and we're pretty sure we'll be ready by then."

No one answered, but almost everyone over the age of thirty was nodding.

"That's good," Gabe said. "Is there anything else?"

No one said anything. Gabe was about to dismiss everyone when a thought crossed his mind. He looked at Jane. "I have a personal announcement I'd like to make if you all don't mind." Jane gave him a nod. "Jane Walker and I are getting married next Saturday at two and we'd like to invite you all to the ceremony right here at the church."

It was quiet for a moment and then applause started in the back and swept through the whole room. Gabe was a little embarrassed. He looked at Jane and could see that she had not expected this reaction, either. He held his hands up to try to stop the clapping. It took a minute, but finally he thanked everyone for their support and adjourned the meeting.

He wanted to talk to Jane before the next meeting started, but he saw that several of the ladies had surrounded her and they were all moving toward the door.

Gabe sat in the front row while Paul spoke about what they should work on first. Gabe caught most of what was being said, but his mind kept drifting to Jane. Had he really just told everyone that they were getting married? How was that possible? He loved her, he knew. In fact, he hadn't been this happy since . . . well, for a long time. What baffled him was that she could love him. He vowed that he wouldn't let her down.

"So it looks like the hardest project is blocking the road north of Cotton Creek," Gabe heard Paul say. "Mr. Solis has volunteered his tractor, but we are still going to need several people to run shovels. Can I get some volunteers?"

Gabe raised his hand. From the look on Paul's face, his must not have been the only one. "That's great," Paul said. "Thank you all very much."

Paul began to talk about manning the checkpoints once they were built, but Gabe was having more and more trouble focusing on the conversation. He just wanted to go to Jane, look in her eyes, and kiss her.

Finally the meeting ended and Gabe made his way to Jane's house.

"So, how was the roadblock meeting?" Jane asked.

"It went pretty good. We have one major problem, though," Gabe said.

"What is that?"

"Ammunition. Nobody has much ammo. Several guys have military-type weapons, but only one of them has over a couple of hundred rounds. Some of the guys don't have more than a few rounds for their deer rifles. I'm just lucky I found a few boxes for mine when we went to town."

"What are you going to do?" Jane said.

"I really don't know. I guess all we can do is be careful. Hopefully, we won't need much ammo. If we get the checkpoints put together right, Paul thinks that just the show of force should prevent most problems."

"What about blocking the roads off? Isn't that going to be hard?"

"A little. The bridge over York Creek is wooden, so that will be easy to take apart. Pushing enough dirt over Cotton Creek Road would be easy if we had a bulldozer, the guys told me. But all we have are some tractors with front-end loaders on them. They'll make it easier than using shovels and wheelbarrows, but it is still going to require quite a few man-hours. And Paul said that without some security at the sites, there's no way to guarantee the barriers won't be breached. We just have to hope it creates a big enough obstacle to discourage people."

"I see. Do you think it will work?"

"I hope so," Gabe said. "All we can do is hope so."

The sky was pink and purple when DJ woke up. He wasn't sure if it was dawn or sunset at first, but he rolled out of bed and stumbled to the window. The most brilliant hues were to the west. He turned back toward the bed and saw the mostly empty liquor bottle lying on the floor. Surprisingly, his side didn't hurt much at all unless he touched it, but his calf was still quite sore. At least the drugs and alcohol had worked on one of the wounds, although they seemed to have moved the pain from his side to his head.

DJ grabbed his stuff and cautiously went down the stairs one step at a time. In the kitchen he saw the uneaten breakfast Margaret had cooked still sitting on the table. He put his bag on the floor and started opening the cabinets. He was surprised to see how full they were. There was no way he could carry this much on his quad. Not without the trailer. It was too bad he'd never be able to come back and get it all. He limped out to the barn and unlocked the door. There was just the hint of a smell from the bodies. DJ removed his last good jerry can and his siphon hose from his machine. He unlocked the gas cap on the Buick and began to drain the fuel. When the can was full, he topped off the quad and refilled the fuel container. Then he pulled the quad out and locked up the building. He should be long gone by the time anyone found the bodies, he figured.

It didn't take long to load his gear and as much of the food as he could onto his big vehicle. It was stacked a little higher than he would have preferred, but there wasn't much farther to go. After sweeping through the house once more, DJ was back on the road.

The air was cool on his face and he smiled at the feel of the big engine growling softly beneath him. He would finally be at his old retreat by tomorrow night. Life had thrown obstacles his way, but he had overcome them. Others would not have been able to make the difficult choices he had made. They would pay for their weakness, maybe even with their lives. It was a new world and it would take hard men, men like him, to survive . . . no, to *thrive* in it.

DJ began to think about what he would do when he got to his destination. The first order of business would be to find a trailer to pull with his quad, or if that failed, a pickup truck. Then enough fuel to get back to his broken trailer. Between what he had buried from the trailer and what was in his cache, he could easily live for several months.

Suddenly his entire field of view in the night vision flashed white. DJ instinctively hit the brakes and turned to miss what-ever had magically appeared in his path. The big bike plowed into the large blob and DJ felt his momentum begin to lift him from the padded seat. Just as he thought he would sail over the handlebars, someone hit him with a giant pillow and he flew off the back of the quad instead. It felt as if he hung in the air for hours, wondering what had happened. The ground rose to meet him and he felt the mass that had knocked him off the four-wheeler, now not nearly so pillowlike, land on top of him.

It went dark as he felt his night-vision goggles fall off. He lay on the ground, under something warm and quivering, and attempted to breathe. Try as he might, he could not get his lungs to pull in a fresh breath of air. Finally he felt oxygen rush through his system. A split second later, he felt a searing pain in his lower back that almost took his breath away again. He tried to hold as still as possible, as if the pain would succumb to his playing possum. When it ratcheted down to a deep ache, DJ began to move his arms to see if he could determine what had hit him.

He felt short, soft hair on the blob and warm, sticky goo that could only be blood. He placed both hands on the body and pushed to try to exorcise his legs from underneath. A blinding, white-hot flash of agony traveled up his back. He heard himself moan out a sound that reminded him of a dying animal. He lay still for several minutes as the pain slowly subsided. When it was down to a tolerable level, DJ made himself think before he took any more action.

His lungs worked, as did his arms and hands, with little increase in pain. He turned his head fully to one side and then back to the other. That motion was painless, too. When he raised his head so that his chin touched his chest, there was a little discomfort in his back, but his neck seemed fine, thank goodness. He wiggled his toes and then his feet at the ankles. The left ankle was slightly sore, but nothing that he couldn't tolerate easily. Trying to bend his knees was difficult because of the weight of whatever was on him, and slightly painful, although nowhere near what he'd felt a few moments ago.

All right, let's try this again, DJ thought. This time he slowly pushed on the dead animal. It hurt some, but he moved it about two inches. He took a deep breath and repeated the procedure. After a few more tries, he was free. He tried to stand, but the shooting pain kept him from succeeding. He rolled over onto his stomach, climbed up onto his hands and knees, then slowly rose to his feet. His back hurt, and any twisting was excruciating, but it seemed as if he wasn't too injured. He walked a few steps, and as long as he kept them short, the pain stayed in the tolerable range.

DJ fished a flashlight out of his pocket and turned it on. He saw that the animal he'd hit was a deer, which was now lying in a tangled mess. Its legs and its neck were revoltingly twisted, each pointing in a different direction. DJ shined the light on his quad. It was turned on its side. He walked over and inspected it. The cargo had broken loose and was scattered, but other than that, it looked okay. He carefully bent his knees to get down so that he could flip it upright. As he lifted with all his might, the searing hot pain returned. He felt the quad tip back onto its wheels and found himself draped over the seat, struggling to regain his breath. Finally he composed himself enough to stand. He turned the key and the starter whirred for several seconds before the quad started. It ran for a short time and then stalled. DJ hit the switch again and this time the machine coughed to life. A few seconds later, the idle returned to normal.

DJ walked over to look for his night-vision goggles. As soon as he saw them, he knew they were broken. He immediately let loose with a string of obscenities that would have made the most hardened sailor take notice. He fussed and fumed under his breath for several minutes, then slowly realized he was accomplishing nothing. Calming himself, he rationalized that he didn't need the goggles nearly as much now as he did before. He was only a short distance from his destination, and there were few people out here who would cause problems. It would be all right to finish the trip using his headlights. He carried the night vision back over to the quad. Perhaps he could find someone to repair them. Now that he had calmed down, he got back to business.

Moving deliberately, so as not to aggravate his back, he began picking up his scattered belongings and stacking them back onto the monster quad. When he was done tying them in place, he carefully climbed back onto the machine. DJ pushed on the throttle and it began to move. He had gone only a few feet when it felt as if someone had applied the brakes. He checked the brake lever and it seemed fine. He mashed the throttle lever again, but something was holding the four-wheeler. He gave it more gas, and it began to move, but there was something wrong that DJ could feel in the handlebars. He pulled the flashlight back out of his pocket and shined it down onto the front tires. They were pointing different directions, not at all unlike the dead deer's legs.

CHAPTER 28

DJ's anger instantly returned, hotter than it had burned at the broken goggles. What the fuck was he supposed to do now? The night vision could be done without, but not the quad. He wanted to push the broken piece of shit back over, but pain shot up his spine when he tried to dismount. Sitting back down, he didn't even dare to take a breath until the pain began to subside. He realized he wasn't doing himself any good by losing his head.

All right, if it's broken, I'll just have to fix it. He carefully dismounted this time and found his tool bag. It was small, but well thought out, containing a wrench, screwdriver, or socket to fit everything on the quad. Cautiously lowering himself to the ground, he pulled out his flashlight to examine the front of the quad. Looking at the steering assembly, he saw immediately what the problem was. The tie-rod to the right wheel was broken. Nothing short of a welder could repair it, and DJ doubted even that would hold for long. A new emotion washed over him. It didn't warm him as the anger had done. It was despair, and it turned him cold.

*   *   *

First light found Gabe driving over the Cotton Creek Bridge. When he got to the hill where the road was cut through the side, he stopped and got out. A few minutes later, Jake Solis drove up on a medium-sized tractor, complete with a front-end loader. He parked it on the side of the road and climbed down.

"Good morning, Mr. Horne," he said as he extended his hand.

"Good morning to you, and please, call me Gabe."

"I thought I'd be the first one here, Gabe. You must be an early riser."

"Yeah, I guess," Gabe said. "Mostly it's because I tossed and turned all night. I finally figured I might as well get up."

"Nervous about the wedding?"

Gabe's head snapped around as if a heavyweight's left hook had contacted his chin. "Ahh . . . yeah, I guess a little. How did you know?"

Jake smiled. "I was nervous for all three of mine," he said. "It's only natural. Everything will be fine."

Gabe wasn't sure if the man knew anything about his past or not, but it was nice to know that he wasn't crazy for being anxious. He nodded.

"It'll be over before you know it," Jake assured him. "Just do what the womenfolk tell you and everything will go off without a hitch. You think we ought to get started?" he asked as he tipped his head toward the hill.

Gabe was glad the man had changed the subject, but somehow he found it comforting that he could talk about the wedding. "I'm ready if you are. But I hope you know a lot more about this than I do. I've only moved dirt a wheelbarrow at a time."

"We'll figure it out," Jake said as he climbed onto the tractor.

He drove it up to the top of the hill and had already pushed two loads of dirt onto the road when Paul showed up with several other cars and trucks behind him. At first all the men could do was watch Jake push down bucket after bucket of dirt. Once enough dirt had been pushed onto the road, they started spreading it to the other side. It was backbreaking, sweaty work, but everyone worked as hard as they could. Gabe noticed that some of the office types had to take fairly frequent breaks. Five years ago, he had been just like them, unaccustomed to hard physical work. He had pushed himself to work like this almost every day since then.

But this was different. This wasn't like a punishment. Gabe was enjoying the labor and the good-natured joking with the other men. They treated him as an equal and spoke to him with respect, even when teasing him about being a soon-to-be newlywed. He was surprised that he enjoyed the lighthearted banter and the company of the other men. It had been a long time since he had felt this comfortable around others.

DJ had spent most of the remaining darkness carrying his few belongings across a pasture and into a small group of trees. Lifting everything over the fence had been very painful. He would have cut the fence, but that would have made it too easy for someone to find him. He had also pushed the quad down into the ditch and covered it with some grass, mud, and debris. Now he lay on his back, the only position that gave some relief, and watched the sky turn from black to blue. As soon as it was light enough, he surveyed his surroundings. It seemed as if it might be secluded enough that he could hole up here for a few days while he recovered and figured out his next move.

He tried to get some sleep, but the pain in his back would not allow him more than five or ten minutes at a time. He thought about his options. He could walk back to Peter and Margaret's house and get their Buick. The only problem with that was that taking the car would tie him to their deaths. No, returning to the scene of the crime, as it were, was a mistake that he wouldn't make. That left him with three choices. Fix the quad, walk, or acquire another vehicle.

Fixing the quad was probably out. The tie-rod couldn't be mended with duct tape and bailing wire, and that was all he had. Realistically, only a new part would guarantee a complete repair. Walking was a possibility. Looking at the maps, he saw he was only about twenty-five miles from his old retreat. Depending on how much he carried and how his back held up, he could make that in as little as two days. Still, he didn't relish the thought of walking that far in his condition. Finding another vehicle was his best bet. But he needed to be very discreet. He was getting too close to his destination to stir up trouble, at least if he hoped to stay there for any length of time. Maybe he could find something that he could hot-wire.

He tried to lie back down, but every time he dozed off, he started to roll onto his side and the pain woke him up. He didn't want to take any of the painkillers he'd found at the farm since it was still daytime and he wanted to be as alert as possible, but he finally relented and took a couple. *Hopefully, this will take the edge off,* he thought. It did and he was finally able to get some sleep.

DJ woke with a start, and bolted to a sitting position before he could stop himself. A knife jabbed itself into his lower back and he winced. As the pain slowly subsided, he could hear tires on the pavement and realized that was what had woken him. Sneaking a peak at his watch, he calculated that he had slept for almost seven hours. The sound of the vehicle approaching grew louder and louder by the moment. DJ hoped they would zoom on by, but he grabbed his rifle, just in case. He eased out to where he could see the road. Finally the truck came into view.

It was older and had been lifted to accommodate the huge mud tires that had allowed DJ to hear it from so far away. As it approached where he had pushed the quad into the ditch, the pitch of the whine deepened. DJ knew that meant the truck was slowing down. *Just keep on going, dipshit,* DJ thought. But a second later, the soprano squeal of neglected brakes was added to the bass of the mud tires. *Just what I need,* he thought sardonically as the truck came to a halt fifty yards past the broken four-wheeler.

A very large young man jumped down from the cab of the pickup. DJ figured that if the man had been driving a normal-sized truck, he probably wouldn't have seen the quad. He walked directly to the quad, squashing DJ's last hope that he just needed to take a piss. The youngster wrestled the quad back up to the road with considerably less effort than it had taken DJ to put it there. He walked around it, much as DJ had seen cowboys do to a horse in old movies. He wondered if the big boy would have looked at the quad's teeth if it had any. The truck driver noticed the nonparallel front tires and bent over to get a better look. A minute later he reerected himself to his full height, which DJ estimated to be about six feet four inches, and yelled at the truck.

"Hey, Zach, come look at this."

The passenger door opened and a second country boy jumped out. This one was not as tall, but probably outweighed the driver by at least a full sack of feed. He walked back to the driver and looked over the quad.

"It's broke," he drawled.

"Of course it's broke, butt-head. Why else would someone leave it? But all it needs is a new tie-rod. Other than that and a few scratches, it looks good as new."

"Yeah?" Zach said.

"Let's load it up in the truck and take it to my house."

"It belongs to somebody, Jason. We can't just take it. What if they come back for it?"

"Look, Zach, it's covered in mud. This has been here for a while," Jason said.

"I don't know. We pass this way all the time. Why haven't we seen it before?"

"I don't know. Maybe it was covered up better before, or maybe I just looked in the ditch at the right time. The fact is, I got lucky enough to see it and, well, finders keepers."

"I guess you're right," Zach said, grinning. "Back the truck up."

A moment later the big truck was reversing, weaving from one side of the road to the other. DJ was instantly furious. Who the fuck did they think they were, stealing his quad? He started going over what he should do in his head. Shouting at them might get them to leave the quad alone, but he didn't want to yell and give his position away. He might need to stay here another day or two while he mended. Shooting them would only bring people looking for them, so that wouldn't work. What other options did he have?

The truck stopped a few feet from the quad. Zach stretched up for the tailgate release. He could barely reach it and the tailgate almost hit him in the head as it fell. He began to look at the quad and then the bed of the truck. DJ almost laughed. There was no way the two of them, despite their size, could lift the quad that high. He relaxed and looked forward to what could have been a Three Stooges film, except of course, there were only two stooges.

DJ heard the driver's door slam. Then Jason appeared at the rear with some rope.

"There's no way we can get this thing up there, Jason."

Jason looked at the height of the bed. It came just below his shoulder. He put his hand on the underside of the tailgate and slammed it shut.

"Dumb-ass, of course we can't lift it that high. We're going to hook the front on the trailer hitch and leave the rear wheels on the ground. Now help me."

The two youths grabbed the handlebars and easily lifted the front of the bike and hooked it onto the trailer hitch. Then Jason started looping the rope around both so that it wouldn't bounce off.

DJ felt a wave of panic tie a knot in his intestines. They would be gone with his quad in a minute or two. He had to stop them. Or did he? The machine was useless to him, and if they drove off with it, there would be no reason for anyone else to stop here. He could easily hide out here for a while and recover. On the other hand, the quad did not belong to them. It didn't matter if it was broken or how long it had been left here. He clicked the safety off on his rifle and centered the reticule on Zach's big fat head. His finger tightened on the trigger.

No, he couldn't do it. Even if he buried the bodies, someone would find that ridiculous truck. DJ slapped his head when he realized the truck was just what he needed. *Maybe I'm the third stooge,* he thought, snickering at how shortsighted he had been. He reacquired his target, then decided that he would take Jason out first. He was partially obscured by the quad and the plumper Zach would make a much easier moving target. When Jason's head appeared in his line of sight again, DJ squeezed off the perfect shot. Zach stared at his friend in shock, no doubt trying to figure out what had happened.

The fat boy must have realized what kind of trouble he was in just when DJ decided to fire. The bullet missed Zach, but not by much. Zach was now in high gear for the cab of the truck, and DJ was impressed with how fast the big boy could move. He put the center of his electronic sight on the leading edge of the rotund target's legs and sent another shot on its way. It missed, but the next shot didn't. Zach stumbled, and then fell to the ground clutching his knee. He began to scream in a pitch resembling fingernails on a chalkboard. DJ rose to get a better angle on the downed man. He fired one more shot. Then all was silent.

CHAPTER 29

Suddenly the big truck's engine came to life and it started to peel out. DJ hadn't considered that there could be a third person in the truck. He didn't want to shoot up the truck, but he couldn't let whoever was in there get away. He centered his rifle's sight on the door and let off three quick rounds. At least one of them must have found its mark, as the truck slowed and turned toward the ditch. The front right tire went down the embankment, making it look like a bull lowering its head in preparation to charge. A second later, it began to climb up the other side as the left front went down. It seemed like slow motion, but the high center of gravity coupled with the uneven terrain caused the truck to roll onto its side like a dead elephant. Its baby, the four-wheeler, came off the hitch and just stood on the side of the road as if it were mourning its dead mother.

DJ just stared as the wheels in the air turned slower and slower. "Shit," he said aloud. He walked toward the road, keeping an eye on the truck lest someone should emerge from it. He got to the fence and gingerly climbed over. Moving around the truck, he could see a young woman behind the wheel. She was lying over on the driver's door, holding her neck as blood squirted out between her fingers. DJ tipped his head to one side as he looked at her. She was very pretty. He shook his head, almost imperceptibly, at the indignity and hopelessness of this tragedy. She wasn't quite as attractive as Crystal had been, but it was still a shame. As he watched, the squirts had less and less force until they became a drip. The girl's eyes closed.

DJ looked at the impotent beast the truck had become. "Fuck me," he whispered.

"All right, I'm off to guard duty. Then I'm going home to get some shut-eye," Gabe said.

"You be careful, Gabe. Remember, you've got a big day coming up and I don't want so much as a scratch on you," Jane said with a wink.

"I have no idea what day you could be talking about, Mrs. Walker," he said with a big smirk.

She grabbed the dish towel draped over her shoulder and swung it at him. He jumped back just before it made contact. "Whoa, there. Not a scratch, remember?"

Her eyes narrowed, showing the laugh lines he found so appealing. He quickly stepped back in, grabbed her around the waist, and kissed her. It seemed to last forever, until it was over. He wanted another, but knew he had to get going. He gave her a peck on her forehead.

"Thanks for dinner," he called out above the squeaking of the screen door spring.

*   *   *

DJ didn't know what to do. He wasn't in any shape to walk anywhere, but he couldn't stay here now. He really shouldn't leave the four-wheeler here, either. It could be tied to him, but there was no way to push it far enough away for someone not to suspect it was connected to the three dead teenagers. He saw the rope the big one was going to use to tie the quad to the truck, and he got an idea. Maybe he could tie the steering apparatus on the broken wheel so that it would stay straight. He wouldn't be able to make any sharp turns, but if he leaned over enough to get the weight onto the working side, maybe he could at least get far enough to divert any suspicion. He grabbed the rope and went to work.

It took about forty-five minutes of trial and error, but the result worked even better than he had expected. The only real down side was that it hurt his back to lean out far enough to get the quad to turn, but he still had plenty of Vicodin. He would have to be careful how much he loaded on the quad and where, but he might be able to make it all the way to his retreat like this. He cut the fence and drove over to his camp. As quickly as possible, he loaded only what he had to have onto the crippled machine, careful not to leave anything with a serial number or any other identifying marks, and hid the rest. Then he made a huge loop on the quad and headed back out to the road.

Gabe was on the hill, in the overwatch position at the roadblock with two other men. Paul and Jerry King were down on the road. Gabe was amazed at the simplicity of it. Six large round bales of hay and one truck was all it took to make the roadblock. The bales were placed in alternating lanes, about twenty feet apart so that any car had to zigzag between them. Next to the last bale, Jerry had parked his truck so that it blocked the other lane. The fact that the road was cut through a hill here made going around the roadblock impossible. Anyone coming through had to slow down to about five miles per hour to negotiate the hay. The truck could be moved if the person was to be allowed entrance to the area, or he'd be forced to back up and turn around.

One of the men on top of the hill with Gabe had a bolt-action rifle with a scope and the other had a shotgun. Neither man had brought more than a box of cartridges. Gabe hoped they didn't need to do any shooting. If they did, they'd probably run out of ammo first. He tried not to think about it.

"So, Gabe, how are the wedding plans coming?" the first man asked.

Gabe was thankful for the distraction. "Pretty good, I guess. Jane is taking care of pretty much everything."

"Yeah," the other man agreed, "I pretty much just had to make sure I showed up on time for my wedding. Where are you going to live?"

"We've gone back and forth on it, but we're leaning toward me moving in with her. It's easier for me to plant a new garden at her place than it is to move all the chicken coops, especially since Jake Solis is going to plow it up for me with his tractor. Until it starts producing, I'll just go to my old place and work the one there," Gabe said.

"What are you going to do with your old house?"

"I've been thinking about letting the preacher and his family move in there. It's close to the church and I'd feel better knowing they're not in town anymore." *Plus,* Gabe thought, *he'd live here then and I could get him to run the meetings.* "He's coming over tomorrow to loan me a Rototiller, and I'm going to talk to him about it then."

"That's a good idea," the second man said as the first nodded.

The three men made some small talk, but mostly remained quiet as the hours passed. Three cars had come through the roadblock and all had been allowed to enter. Just before their four-hour shift was over, a pickup came barreling up the road. It seemed as if the driver was going to crash into the first bale, but he locked up his brakes and stopped just in time. He carefully weaved his way through the obstacles and stopped when he got to Paul and Jerry. Gabe and the other two pulled their rifles close.

"Why are you stopping me?" the driver said.

"Access to this area is restricted to residents," Paul said.

Gabe could see that Jerry was on the passenger side of the truck, behind the cab, while Paul was standing next to the front tire on the driver's side. A right-handed person would have to climb halfway out the window to get a shot at either man. *Pretty smart,* Gabe thought.

"This is a public road. You can't block it off," the man yelled.

"Obviously we can and we have. Now, if you don't mind, I'm going to ask you to turn around and leave."

"Yeah, I do mind. I have to go through here to get where I'm going."

"I'm sure you can go back to the main highway and find another way to reach your destination. Please turn around," Paul said sternly.

"No! Move that truck and let me through or I'll just ram it out of the way."

Paul and Jerry simultaneously took a few steps back and raised their rifles to the low ready position. They weren't pointing at the driver, but could be in an instant if necessary. Gabe didn't know if the two men had talked about when they would take this defensive position, but it sure looked as if they were on the same page.

"We have asked you twice to please turn around in the nicest way possible. If we have to ask again, it won't be so nice," Paul said flatly.

"I'm going to tell the police about this," the man screamed as the truck began to back up. A few seconds later, its taillights disappeared in the distance.

The going had gotten slow. After he went a ways, the rope would loosen up and the front tire would wobble at any speed over about three miles per hour. DJ had tried to tighten up the knots in the rope, but nothing seemed to help. At least he didn't have to walk, though, even if this pace was maddening compared to what he was used to.

He stopped for a break and pulled out his map. Maybe three more hours at this pace. He climbed back on and started the monotonous drive.

About an hour later, he had to stop. The road was covered in dirt where it went through the side of a large hill. At first he thought it might be a landslide, but on closer inspection, he realized someone had pushed the dirt off the hillside to block the road. He was annoyed at first, but then he laughed under his breath. This was exactly what he would have done. He began to wonder if his old retreat group was responsible. It was a little far from them, so probably not, but the thought could not be dismissed. Maybe they were still there. How would that go over? Probably not well. In hindsight, it had been unwise to sleep with his best friend's wife. Well, even if they didn't want him to stay, they might help him fix his quad and he could dig up his cache.

DJ walked back down to the road. He could ride over the dirt, but it was steeper than he would like, especially with the broken wheel. There was room for the quad to go up the side of the hill. That seemed like a better solution. He eased up the incline, careful not to tangle in the fence. It was very rocky and steering the hobbled mount was hard. When he was almost to the top, the front of the quad dropped. Concerned, DJ stopped the motor and went around to see what had happened. The front wheels had extended themselves as if someone had tried to make a chopper out of the four-wheeler. DJ bent down and saw where the frame had broken. It had probably cracked when he hit the deer, or more likely when the quad had torn off the trailer hitch of the big truck. DJ was too mad to curse. He simply shook his fist at the broken machine.

Gabe walked home looking at the stars. He didn't really see them, though. His mind kept wondering what would have happened if the guy had crashed through the roadblock and hurt Paul or Jerry. How could they handle a medical emergency like that? Daniel Easton was a navy corpsman. Gabe would talk to him about setting up a makeshift trauma center and ask at the next meeting if they had any other medical professionals in the neighborhood. Soon Gabe was home and not long after that, he was asleep.

CHAPTER 30

DJ hurriedly packed the old army green backpack, straining his eyes in the low light. He mumbled under his breath as he worked. "Fucking Murphy throws me another curveball and now I gotta fucking walk the rest of the way with my back still fucked up." He had thought about camping here for a couple of days, but there were two big problems with that plan. First, he was inside some perimeter that people had taken the trouble to keep others out of. If he was in charge, he would have patrols checking the perimeter on a regular basis. These people might not be doing that, but he couldn't take the chance. The second and bigger problem was that he hadn't brought any extra food or his camping stuff. He would just as well get on to his destination.

He lifted the pack up, feeling the weight. "Son of a bitch!" He disgustedly dumped all the contents on the ground in front of him. He began to sort out some of the items as he picked them up one at a time to judge their weight. Once he had gone through everything, he placed the remaining pile back into the rucksack. This time its weight seemed more manageable.

Next, he placed everything left in two large black plastic trash bags, wedged them into some brush that had plenty of spines and stickers, then covered them as best he could with fallen tree limbs and dead leaves. He stood back and looked at his work, carefully shining his flashlight all the way around the cache, and made some fine adjustments to his coverings. Satisfied that he had done the best job possible without taking the time to bury everything, he pulled on his pack and grabbed his rifle.

Before he had gone a hundred yards, he stopped to fish the painkillers out of his pack.

The knock on the door woke Gabe out of a deep slumber. He looked at his watch and, for a second, felt guilty for sleeping this late. Then he remembered that he hadn't gone to bed until after his watch. He rose, pulled on a pair of jeans and a T-shirt, and answered the door.

It was just getting light in the east, but as soon as he saw her, his world brightened as if the sun had sprinted to its noonday position. He grabbed her to give her a long, passionate kiss, but he saw Robby and decided a quick hug was better in this circumstance.

"Hey, sleepyhead," she said, noticing the lines the pillow case had left on his cheek. "Sorry to wake you, but Robby really wanted to go hunting this morning."

"Sure, I'll take him," Gabe said. "Let me go get some boots on."

"Actually," she said, "I was wondering if you think he's experienced enough to go by himself."

Gabe could see the twinkle in her eye. He played along, rubbing his chin. "I don't know. He's done well when we've gone together, but hunting by himself is a pretty big step."

"Please!" Robby said.

"I guess we could let him try. But, young man, you better not be shooting at everything that moves. Remember, if you can't take a head shot at a rabbit or a squirrel, then wait until you can. We can't be wasting any meat, or any ammo for that matter."

"Okay, Mr. Horne. I promise to be careful."

"Good deal. You run along and don't come back until you have enough for a couple of meals," Gabe said with a smile.

"You can count on me," Robby replied over his shoulder as he sprinted toward the door.

"And what can I do for you, Mrs. Walker?" Gabe said with a wink.

The sun was just rising as DJ crossed the wooden bridge. His back was still hurting and he was in a foul mood. He walked down to the creek, pulled out his water filter, and filled the water bladder in his pack. While it was open, he took a couple more painkillers. After resting for a few minutes, he resumed his trek.

The knock on the door made both of them jump like busted teenagers. They smiled at each other over the silliness of their reaction, and Gabe answered the door.

"Hello, Reverend Washington. How are you?" Gabe extended his hand.

"I'm wonderful, brother Gabriel! What a glorious day. Hello, sister Walker. So good to see you."

"And you, too, Reverend," Jane said.

"I brought the tiller, and I was wondering if, after we unload it, you could help me with a plumbing problem at the church," the old minister said.

"I'd be happy to, Reverend, but when it comes to plumbing, I'm a good hog caller," Gabe replied with a smile.

"Yes, we all have our God-given talents, don't we? I just need someone to hold the flashlight and hand me tools."

"Then I'm your man," Gabe said.

DJ dropped the pack as if it were an unwanted toy. He carefully sat down and slowly arched his back to stretch out the kinks. It helped a little, but not much. He grabbed a snack out of his pack and ate. Before he closed the rucksack back up, he took another Vicodin. He hoped the old group wasn't at the retreat. If it was unoccupied, he could stay there until he was better. He looked at his watch. He thought he would have been there by now. Surely it wouldn't be more than another thirty minutes or so. He hoisted the pack back on and trudged along.

Each step with his right foot caused him to flinch, so he tried to keep the weight more on his left side, but that was uncomfortable, too. He mumbled incoherently, not even really knowing what he was saying, just fuming at his bad luck. As he got closer, the sights became more familiar, but he also took mild note of things that had changed. Finally he made the last turn and set eyes on his property.

It was totally different from what he remembered. Just inside the gate were a number of old stakes and some surveyor's string where it looked as if someone had planned to pour a foundation for a house. Farther back was an older mobile home, with a storage shed behind it and a garden with varying hues of green. DJ saw that the front door was covered with a sheet of plywood. He cautiously made his way around to the back. A truck and a car were in the driveway, but it was quiet. He climbed the steps and knocked on the door. A trim and neatly dressed middle-aged woman answered.

"Yes, may I help you?" she said.

"Yes, ma'am," he answered in a friendly voice, "I was looking for Thomas Akers. Does he still live here?"

"No, I'm afraid he doesn't," Jane replied.

"Oh," DJ said as he turned to look around. His cache was under the edge of the garden. It was a good thing he had buried it so deep, or it would have been found. It would be a bitch to dig up with his injured back. He turned back toward the woman, trying to see if anyone else was in the house. "Do you think there's anyone here that might know where he went?"

"No, sorry. There's no one here but me. . . ." Her last word seemed to trail off as if she realized the mistake she'd made.

"I see," DJ said with a charming smile as he turned toward the steps. "Sorry to trouble you . . ."

The woman seemed to relax a bit.

DJ twisted back around and drew his pistol at the same time. ". . . but I'm going to need your help."

"Hand me a regular screwdriver please."

"Here you go, preacher. I'm glad you asked me to help you because I wanted to talk to you about my house."

"You need me to work on the plumbing for you?"

Gabe laughed. "No, sir, that's not what I meant. I am going to be moving in with Jane after the wedding and we wanted to offer you use of my house until things get back to normal."

The preacher took his eyes off the pipe for the first time since he had crawled down under it. "Are you sure, brother Gabriel?"

"Yes."

"Then I accept," he said as he rose to the tallest five feet five Gabe had ever seen and held his hand out to his helper. "Thank you."

"You're welcome, Reverend Washington," Gabe said as he shook the man's hand.

"I don't have all day, bitch. Dig!" DJ said almost jovially as he gestured at the ground with his pistol. He took another bite of the fresh-picked tomato from one of the plants she'd had to displace to dig up his cache. She had made it down about two feet, the distance the ground was soft from the tilling of the garden. Now it was hard and she was clumsily hacking at the ground with the shovel. *Well,* thought DJ, *better than doing it myself, even if my back doesn't hurt anymore.*

Gabe and the preacher turned up the driveway to Gabe's house. He saw Jane working in the garden. He would have wondered what she was doing if he had not been so enamored at the sight of her. She was one of the two most beautiful women he had ever beheld. But why was she hoeing an area that he had worked on yesterday? Surely the weeds had not grown up overnight. And that wasn't a hoe she was using; it was a shovel. Then Gabe saw him and the pistol he had trained in Jane's direction. Gabe drew his revolver from the leather holster and ran toward the garden.

DJ heard footsteps behind him and turned to see a scarecrow of a man running toward him. He almost laughed, wondering if the tin man and the lion were coming right behind him. He looked, but there was only an old black man trying to keep up with the scarecrow. Then DJ saw the revolver. That was no laughing matter. He came to his feet and planted them shoulder width, pointing directly at the charging man. DJ raised his pistol and found the front sight. It was the most focused point in his vision, covering the middle of the man whose revolver was now leveled in his direction. He felt his finger first touch the trigger, and then take the slack out of it as he had done thousands of times before in both dry and live practice. The black gun barked once, and when the front sight came back down to superimpose itself over the man, it fired again. The man fell face-first onto the ground. DJ was mildly aware that the man had fired his gun between his first and second shots, but he had missed.

Gabe could see nothing but the dirt underneath him. It was hard to breathe and a searing pain in his chest rivaled the one from when the state troopers had come to his house on the night Hannah and Michael had died. Suddenly Jane was there and he was looking up at her. She was still beautiful even with her face twisted up in fear and her eyes filled up with tears. He wanted to tell her that everything would be okay, but the only words that would come out were "I love you."

DJ was surprised that the woman could move that fast. He walked over to look at the scarecrow. The revolver was lying about five feet from him and DJ bent over to pick it up. The old black man was standing behind the woman, his eyes as big as baseballs, and his mouth was moving but hardly a sound came out. The two shots had found their mark and were merely inches apart. The ground underneath him was turning into a lake of blood. *Not bad shooting on a moving target,* DJ thought. He stuck the revolver into his waistband and had just opened his mouth to tell the woman to get back to digging when he heard the pop. It sounded like a firecracker and must have gone off close to his right eye, because it stung.

Devlin Frost didn't understand why he was looking at the sky. It was obvious he was lying down, but he couldn't get his arms or legs to do what he wanted. He felt something warm on his face. His mind both raced for an explanation and ordered his body to rise, but neither was happening. His vision was narrowing, perhaps from the sticky goo he felt in his right eye. Just before it went completely dark, he saw a young teenage boy looking down on him with hate in his eyes and a small rifle in his hands.

Gabe was freezing. "I'm cold," he whispered to Jane.

"Robby, run in the house and get some blankets," Jane said.

Robby didn't respond. He stared at the man he had shot for a moment longer. Other than the blood that filled his right eye and leaked off that side of his face, he looked all right. A second later Robby ran into the house and brought out a blanket. He knelt down on the opposite side from his mother. They worked together to cover the injured man. Robby noticed his breaths were becoming more and more shallow.

"So cold," Gabriel Horne said.

EPILOGUE

Gabe wasn't cold anymore. In fact, he was deliciously warm. He could hear her calling his name. But there was so much noise, it was hard to make out. He strained his ears to hear, and he could differentiate the sounds a little better. Yes, it was her. But what was the other sound? It sounded like waves on the beach. He was nowhere near the beach, though. Where was he? He couldn't quite remember. He opened his eyes and there she was, staring down at him.

"Wake up, sleepyhead," she said.

Somebody else had called him that recently, but he couldn't recall who.

"Hi, baby," he said as he propped himself up on his elbows. They were at the beach. In fact, they had been here before. Was this the day he had taken the picture?

Michael ran up and slid down on his knees, kicking a little of the warm sand onto his father. "Hey, Dad, we've been waiting for you."

"Yes," Hannah agreed, "we've been waiting for you."

Gabe smiled at both of them. "Well, I'm here now. Let's go home."

© Danny Crawford

David Crawford is also the author of the runaway Internet cult classic *Lights Out*. He is an avid outdoorsman and a fourth-degree black belt in karate. He lives with his wife and two children in San Antonio, Texas.